ALSO BY ELISA LORELLO

Fiction
Faking It
Ordinary World
She Has Your Eyes
Love, Wylie
Big Skye Littleton
The Second First Time
Pasta Wars
Adulation
Why I Love Singlehood (with Sarah Girrell)

Nonfiction
Friends of Mine: Thirty Years in the Life of a Duran Duran Fan
(a memoir)
*The Writer's Habit: Combining Knowledge, Skill, and Desire
to Write the Best Book You Can* (a sourcebook)

Join the mailing list at www.elisalorello.com
and receive a bonus gift

Published by Missouri Breaks Press, P.O. Box 50729, Billings MT 59105.

ISBN-10: 0-9986305-6-X
ISBN-13: 978-0-9986305-6-4

Faked Out

For *Faking It* fans everywhere

Chapter One

February

I knew it was going to be a hellish night the moment I saw all that gold lamé. Her dress. Her clutch. Her shoes. I wouldn't be surprised if her underwear was gold lamé too. And I hoped she wasn't planning on showing me.

Of course, I complimented her as if she were wearing something that didn't make me wish for cataracts.

Her makeup wasn't much better. She had fallen into the classic trap of trying to look ten years younger and coming out looking ten years older. Swap out the gold lamé for a classic black cocktail dress and perhaps a costume gold necklace, get rid of the eyebrow pencil and all that fuchsia and use a soft lip gloss, and she'd probably be stunning. I hoped an opening would come up tonight where I could tell her in a way that she wouldn't take offense. Some women were really accepting of suggestions; others took it as a judgment. Which, it probably was.

This was my first date with Laurel the Divorcée, who found me by way of her friend Carmella the Publicist, who was friends with Grace the Esthetician, I think. I tried to maintain my memory for such things—it was good for business—but in the last few years there were so many to keep track of.

Laurel the Divorcée needed a date for a charity dinner

for—wait for it—the cure for the common cold. The nonprofit organization, named something like Health Engineers, distributed tissue packets with their logo of what looked like a pair of pliers embedded in the sun. They gave out Sucrets in lieu of after-dinner mints. The cake was in the shape of a nose. A *nose*, dammit. With chocolate sprinkles in the nostrils. I didn't even want to know what the filling was. And they were as committed to and passionate about the cause as the National Cancer Society was to and about theirs. They debuted a PSA featuring the same kind of music used for starving kids in Africa or abused pets. People actually wept and had to break open their new tissue packets.

"Now remember, Devin," Laurel said before we'd entered the dining room. "We met under the Magritte at the MoMA."

"That's actually not a bad place to meet," I replied, seeing the famous painting of *The False Mirror* in my mind's eye. "Did you know that—"

I was about to offer up a factoid about Magritte, but Laurel was too focused on her ruse to indulge me. "You asked me out to coffee, and we've been seeing each other ever since."

"Right. And how long ago was that?"

"How long ago was what?"

"How long ago did we go out for coffee?" I asked.

"Oh," she said, and deliberated on a plausible answer. "Three weeks?" she guessed.

"Works for me. Anything else I should know about you? Favorites? Which Starbucks you prefer?"

"We'll play that by ear, I guess."

I extended my arm, elbow bent, as an invitation for her to link into it with her own, but she insisted we enter with my arm tightly wrapped around her waist. So we did. And she got the reaction she'd wanted. Heads turned in our direction. Women looked envious. Men looked defeated. I was used to it by now, but my clients loved it. Craved it.

By the main course of dinner not only did I not give a rat's ass about curing the common cold, but I was also hoping to drop dead on the spot from some random plague.

Thing is, the dates were increasingly resembling this one: Banal. Uninspiring. Ridiculous. My business partner Christian, long out of the field, had been progressively pestering me to resign as well and take on, as he called it, the more grown-up responsibilities of the business. At the very least, work part time. Or get out altogether, as he occasionally threatened to. Not long ago I'd thrived on the anticipation of meeting someone new or reconnecting with someone I'd been out with before, listening to their stories, learning about their occupations…I had come to know a little bit about a lot of things, and surmised that I'd make a killing on *Jeopardy*. And I loved the idea of bringing some color into a woman's gray life for one night. It saddened me how many women needed me to tell them they were pretty, were so starved for compliments that their self-esteem was emaciated. How many women needed to feel pretty, even for just a couple of hours, so much so that they were willing to pay for it. A lot. How many women simply needed to be *cuddled*.

And lately I was starting to feel guilty about it again.

Or maybe I was just tired. I hadn't been sleeping well. I stifled yawns all throughout dinner, and over-compensated by asking for a double-espresso.

Four hours later, even hopped up on espresso, I was ready to crawl into my own bed, and I was hoping Laurel would part company at goodnight. She asked me to take her home (not all are so trusting), and I obliged, as I always do. She lived in a four-story walkup just a few blocks away. When we reached her door, I cordially said goodnight and, without thinking, kissed her on the cheek. I've stopped initiating goodnight kisses; even cheek kisses. Now I wait for their cue. If they initiate it, fine. If they want more, then we'll negotiate that, although the contract clearly states where things end, no exceptions.

A lustful gleam appeared in Laurel's eye. *Uh-oh.*

She unlocked her door, thrust it open, yanked me inside, closed the door and pinned me to it, kissing me hard. I got a lungful of not only her perfume, but also her tongue. I guessed the PSA at the dinner didn't persuade her to think twice about kissing someone with thirty-gazillion bacteria in his mouth.

Wow. She was strong. And taller than I'd realized, her lips meeting the bottom of my chin. She didn't have far to reach, and for once I didn't need to slouch.

Then again, she was also wearing stilettos.

I unglued my face. "OK, hang on," I said, taking a breath. "Let's come up for air."

Damn, she was quick too. She forced my coat off my shoulders, followed by my jacket, and began to unbutton my shirt. Someone didn't read her contract.

I took hold of her hands. "Laurel, we discussed the rules. You can look, but you can't touch, remember?"

"You were serious? I thought that was pretense. You know, in case your client turned out to be undercover vice or something." She ran a lacquered gold fingernail along my exposed chest. Felt like a cold pencil.

"You might be, for all I know."

She laughed, and pressed her chest against mine. I resisted

and pushed back with as little force as possible.

"What are some other ways I can make you happy?" I asked. "We could make out a little. You know, first-base stuff. Or I could give you a foot rub or a hand massage or—"

Again with the dive-bomb kissing. Then she went for the jewels.

I was *not* enjoying this. I hadn't been enjoying it at all lately. *You just need a break*, I told myself. *Too overbooked. You're trying too hard to please too many people.* How ironic.

Once again I clutched her hands and unglued our mouths. "Laurel, if you don't respect the boundaries, I'm going to leave, and our business ends here and now, forever."

"What the hell kind of escort are you?" said Laurel, her frustration surpassing the sexual kind, I gathered.

"I thought I was pretty clear about that," I said. "And I thought Carmella filled you in. No drugs, no guns, no S and M, and *no penetration.*"

"I swear to God, I thought that was all pretense. Well, the last part, anyway. You mean to tell me you're not going to fuck me?"

"I am not going to fuck you," I said. "There are other sensual options on the table, but not that."

Most women held out for those other options and walked away satisfied. I didn't specify which ones, however, given that I wanted to go home.

"Now listen," she said, "We either get naked and you fuck me hard, or we're done. And I want my money back too."

"I'll give you a twenty-five percent refund," I said. That's how badly I wanted to go home.

She folded her arms like a petulant child, and then caved. "Fine."

I wished just one of them would be assertive enough. Some

would haggle with me up to fifty percent. But none ever went all the way, so to speak. Did *I* intimidate them, or did the contract? Or maybe they were taught not to be aggressive, that assertiveness equaled bitchiness. They were wrong.

Then again, I never gave them what they wanted.

I pulled the money she'd paid me earlier from the inner pocket of my suit jacket, unclasped the gold moneyclip, and counted out the bills for her. The room was still dark, lit only by the city outside her window.

"You know, you really shouldn't carry that cash around with you," she said. "In those clothes, you're just begging to be mugged."

"Hey, if someone really wants it, they can have it."

"It's what they'll do to you to get it that you should be worried about."

Great. I'm taking a cab home tonight.

"It was nice to meet you, Laurel," I said.

"Thanks for nothing, Devin. This was a waste of an evening."

"Not true," I said. "You got those designer wet wipes and a piece of nose cake."

And with that I found myself back on the other side of her apartment door as she slammed it on me.

As I stepped onto the Manhattan streets, I buttoned up my camel coat close to my neck. "Like stepping into a fucking meat freezer," I muttered. I hoped the muggers would be too cold as well.

Maybe it was time for another line of work. Or just retire early and see the world. I'd lost count of the number of times that thought ran through my mind. And that was just tonight.

Chapter Two

March

I met Allison the Textbook Rep at the National Arts Club in Gramercy Park for a cocktail party her company was hosting. At least half, if not more, of my clients were in some form of academia, which struck me as odd given that their salaries weren't conducive to such lavish spending on, well, a date with me... to say nothing of how expensive it is to live in New York City. I started seeing Allison about a year ago—she used to call me every few months, but lately it seemed to have moved up to once a month. I had a feeling she'd maxed out her credit card on cash advances, which bothered me—couldn't they derive the same sensual pleasure from, say, a trip to Italy? To me, that was the more practical investment. However, it didn't bother me enough to refuse their money, for I was also a fan of instant gratification. If they were being irresponsible with their finances in the process, well, that was *their* problem.

Alli (she liked when I called her that) greeted me outside and I gave her a quick peck on the lips—I was OK with kissing the regulars; they knew what to expect from me by now; or rather, what not to expect. When we entered the party, the familiar faces—all female—bombarded me, and the unfamiliar ones seemed to know me as well. The rules required that if and/or when my clients and I crossed paths outside of our contracted encounters, we were not to socialize, speak more than a cordial hello, or, in some cases, acknowledge each other at all. Thing is, despite the pretending and keeping up appearances, most of my clients knew each other. And they knew plenty. This was a word-of-mouth business, after all. It used to unnerve me to walk into such an environment and be able to secretly identify each client by her orgasm, not to mention which ones had guilty pleasures, phobias, or something like a shopping addiction.

Some—the men, mostly—looked at me with resentment, while others, men and women alike, looked with envy, or lust. As long as none of them made a move.

"You know the only reason why you're here is for me to show you off, right?" said Allison. Yes, I knew. These cocktail parties were spouse/date optional, according to her, and she wanted to be seen as "attached." She wore a sleek, black sheath dress with grey pinstriping—the perfect blend of classy and professional. She had specifically requested me to wear something Versace. I acquiesced and donned my taupe suit. It was finally springtime, after all, albeit still a little chilly.

I scanned the room—not only for current clients, but also potentials. Not that I was personally looking to take on anyone else. But it was always good to drum up business for our other escorts. My surveillance stopped at three women sitting on a high-legged table. The first looked a little like CJ Cregg on *The West Wing.* The second could pass for Naomi Campbell. The third woman, however, caught my eye, and I visually traced her features: cropped, dark hair that I guessed was naturally wavy but had been ironed straight; pale skin; and a black pantsuit that didn't fit her properly.

She seemed to have gone out of her way not to be noticeable. Precisely why she stood out to me. Or maybe she just didn't know any better.

I headed to the cash bar while Allison went to work mingling, our mutual acquaintances approaching her first. Before I was out of eye- or earshot I distinctly heard one of them say rather slyly under her breath, "You lucky bitch," and I turned to gauge Allison's response. She looked like a peacock flaunting its feathers. I cracked a grin of satisfaction. As I waited on line at the bar, I watched Pantsuit Woman leave her friends at the table, greet several attendees along her path, and eventually reach Carol, the other textbook rep. Also a client. I pretended not to notice them glance in my direction. Maybe that was a good sign; she had noticed me. And it occurred to me at that moment that I *wanted* her to notice me. I tried to inconspicuously observe her, playing a mental game of guessing her name while I waited on line. Larissa? No. She looked Italian, possibly Spanish. Mary? Mary Patricia? Mary Elizabeth? Mary Margaret?

Mary, Mother of God...

I re-joined Allison and one of her colleagues, handing her a glass of sauvignon blanc while I sipped my vodka cranberry. "Thanks, Love," she said.

"Sure thing," I replied, winking at her and putting my arm around her waist with my free hand.

Alli whispered in my ear in a rather sultry manner, "You're going to give me the usual after this, yes?"

The wink must've gotten to her. I put my lips directly to her ear and whispered back, equally sultry, "Have I ever let you down?"

She practically purred.

All in a day's work.

I accompanied Allison wherever she went, and even proudly held my own in several conversations with the professors—I'd been around them long enough to get the lingo. I liked this crowd, the majority of them English PhDs. Brought out the competitor in me—what I lacked in scholarship, I more than made up for in fashion. Plus I could talk anyone under the table when the subject was art. Allison introduced me to everyone simply as Devin—even the ones who already knew me, many of whom she had referred to me (or had they referred her?). I didn't encourage clients to call me their boyfriend, but I didn't forbid it either. I kept trying to steer Allison over to Mary Pantsuit (wouldn't it be awful if that really was her name?), but no luck. When I saw her go to the bar, however, I offered to fetch Allison and me a second round of drinks. I stood behind her, estimating her height (turned out she was vertically challenged, the top of her head just reaching my chest; then again, at six-foot-one, I was taller than most), close enough to get a whiff of her. Nice. Citrusy.

"Enjoying the party?" I asked her.

She whisked around, and finally we were face to face. Well, face to chest, anyway. Her eyes, the color of emeralds, flickered in response to my smile. She gave me a DeNiro *you-talkin'-to-me?* look. Not sociopathic; more like bewildered. I tilted my neck down to look at her. Her skin was olive-toned, yet she wore a foundation that was too beige. Her lips were soft, round, parted. Teeth small and straight. If only I'd had a camera.

"It's been a long time since I've been to one of these," she replied.

"Are you driving tonight?"

She looked at me, perplexed. "I'm sorry?"

"You've been nursing that ginger ale all night," I said,

pointing to her near-empty glass. "I was wondering if you were a designated driver."

I was also wondering if the question was too stalkerish. Because really, how many guys watch a woman's drink that closely? Plus, I looked at my watch. Six forty. *Evening, idiot. She's been nursing that ginger ale all* evening.

"No, I took the train in from the Island, but I'm staying with a colleague in Brooklyn tonight."

I extended my hand to her. "I'm Devin."

She gave me another perplexed look, but took my hand and shook it. "Andrea," she replied.

Andrea. I liked it. I liked it a lot. It suited her. Helluva lot better than Mary. Her shake was solid, her hand warm—delicate, but not dainty. I guessed she used her hands more for talking than manual labor. But she was also reluctant, I could tell. Guarded. Not client material.

"What university do you teach at?" I asked, so busy chiding myself for ending the question with a preposition—I was in a room of English professors, for chrissakes—that I didn't think to follow up with a request for her last name. Besides, I was used to enforcing a first-name-only policy.

"I came to Brooklyn U about six months ago," she replied.

I nodded in acknowledgement. "And you live on the Island?"

"Yeah, just moved back after ten years in New England."

I like a professor who says *Yeah.* Ten years in New England didn't soften her Long Island accent much.

"Wow," I said. "I'd like to see the foliage up there in the fall."

You'd like to see the foliage up there in the fall? That's your pickup line? Was I really trying to pick her up? Or was I doing my usual networking? The line between the two had blurred considerably.

"Yeah," she replied. "It's really beautiful." Props to her for indulging my dumbass small talk.

Suddenly I couldn't think of a single thing to say. *Holy shit, that's a first.*

"So," she filled the conversational lull, "I saw you with Allison? She's the rep who invited us here. My colleague and I are putting together a deal to write a textbook for her company—"

"Just a friend," I interrupted.

Whoa. I *never* got defensive. Especially in front of potential clients. Yet some part of me knew she wasn't client material. She knew things, though. I could see it in her eyes and her posture. The mystery, of course, was what she knew, and with every passing second I wanted to stealthily slip away with her, go to some coffeeshop, and converse until the sun came up. But why? Why her? Why now?

Andrea smirked. "Well, I didn't ask. But now that you mention it, I think your friend wants your attention."

No sooner than Andrea made the snarky comment did I feel the tractor beam behind me that was likely Allison. I turned and spotted her dismembering me with her eyes as she made a beeline for us. *Shit. I blew it.* I signaled to Allison that I was getting her a drink. Then I winked, hoping to pacify her.

Too late. Allison planted herself between Andrea and me. "Honey, I'd like to get going soon, OK?" she said. That was code for *We're at the Me-time portion of the date* and *Don't even think of talking to another woman when I'm paying you what could otherwise be a down payment on a condo.*

"Sure, Alli," I said, kissing her on the cheek and folding my arm around her waist not only to placate her but also assure her that Me-time was underway. She reciprocated by taking hold of my ass cheek with her talons and digging them in with a squeeze. Yikes. I probably deserved it.

"It was nice to meet you, Andrea," I said. "Welcome back to New York." I held out my hand one last time, and Andrea shook it.

I tried to freeze-frame her image (minus the smirk) in my memory—inexplicably saddened at the possibility of never seeing her again (and how had I never seen her before? I knew most of the women at Brooklyn U)—as I walked away with Allison when Andrea replied, "You too." Alli and I left our untouched drinks on a table and exited the venue.

As promised, I gave Allison her usual that night; it had become so rote that it didn't even arouse me anymore.

Chapter Three

May

My business partner, Christian, and I rented office space in a building in midtown Manhattan for our company, Strawberries and Champagne. We used the space solely for administrative work and screening calls. Interviewing potential escorts and/or clients took place in coffee shops, hotel lobbies, the steps of the New York Public Library, you name it.

Christian came to the office almost every day, keeping the books and ensuring everything we did was legal (he'd dropped out of law school eight credits short due to test anxiety—the Bar Exam terrified him), and we employed an assistant to handle the calls, schedule the dates, and communicate with the escorts. Christian and I met once or twice a week to keep each other in the loop.

"I can't believe we're still at this, man," said Christian at almost every meeting. Our most recent was no different. "I thought we were going to either fold or get shut down in six months."

"Just goes to show you how effective you can be when you play it straight."

"Aren't you even just a little bit tired of it?"

"Not since I weeded out all the crazies and clingies," I said.

"They're all a little clingy, aren't they?" said Christian. He looked a little bit like Ben Affleck with a hooked nose and jet-black hair.

"There are degrees of clingy. Anyway, I've got a following now, and I like them. I'm not taking on any new clients. At least not without doubling my fee, or a referral from a regular and a CV."

"CV?"

"Curriculum vitae," I said.

Christian rolled his eyes around. "What is it with you and the academics?"

"Beats the shit out of getting my own PhD, don't you think?"

"Speaking of which, Kate told me that one of your Brooklyn U clients called and can't make it to Heartland Brewery tonight for the end-of-semester party. And why are Brooklyn U faculty meeting at some bar in Manhattan?"

"Hell if I know," I said, secretly disappointed. I'd agreed to the date with Sadie the Twentieth-Century Lit Professor with the hopes that the woman I'd met at the National Arts Club a couple of months ago—Andrea—would be there.

I could just show up anyway...

I opted for a Versace suit again, this time in black, and paired it with a red graphic T-shirt I'd picked up in a thrift store. Years ago I'd read about a pop star who used to pair his most expensive suit with his cheapest T-shirt, and I've been doing such combinations ever since. Doing so either made me look stylishly eclectic or like a pretentious asshole that didn't know how to dress himself.

My luck panned out. I wasn't at the bar for more than fifteen minutes, Red Rooster Ale in hand, when Andrea entered Heartland Brewery with the CJ Cregg-lookalike. The very sight of Andrea in bootcut blue jeans, a black T-shirt hidden inside an oversized velvet blazer, and black leather boots piqued my curiosity as I tried to imagine her naked. I preferred fleshy to skinny; curves rather than carb-deprived. She was definitely the former rather than the latter, which pleased me. She wore more makeup than last time, but didn't look overly painted. And her earthy brown hair seemed even shorter, styled to perfection. Everything about her appearance suggested a subconscious battle between blending in and standing out. I wonder if she knew the latter was winning. If she wanted it to.

I caught her nudge CJ and mouth something to her while looking in my direction. Taking that as my cue, I flashed a grin and strode toward her, avoiding eye contact with other clients. I acted as if I fucking owned the place.

"Hey," I said. "Remember me? We met at a cocktail party a few months ago."

Andrea stood as if her boots were nailed to the floor. "Yeah, I remember you," she said. "It was back in February at the National Arts Club. I can't remember your name, though."

"Devin." I extended my hand as if meeting her for the first time. "You are…Andrea?"

Yeah, I didn't have to guess. I knew.

Her eyes widened as she shook my hand softer, more socially than our last encounter. "Wow, I'm surprised you remembered!"

I practically patted myself on the back. "I have a good memory for names. It's good for business. So, Andrea…" My clients loved when I used their names right off the bat.

"Most people call me Andi." *Oooh, I like that even better.*

"What brings you here this evening?" I asked. Like I didn't already know.

"End-of-semester party. And you?"

"I was meeting a client for drinks, but I think I've been stood up," I lied. "Can I get you a ginger ale while you're waiting for the rest of your party to come in?"

She turned and looked at CJ in such a manner that suggested my recalling her drink had crossed over from impressive to creepy. She then took me by the arm.

"Listen," she said, pulling me out of earshot from her colleagues. "I know what you do for a living. And if you're trying to recruit me as a client, well, I'm not interested. First of all, I couldn't afford you. And second of all, I don't do—I'm not that kind of...I'm not interested, OK?"

I couldn't take my eyes off her as she stammered her way through her rebuttal. Something about her I couldn't yet put my finger on... She was hiding something under that oversized blazer besides her bra size. And yet, she was bold enough to put me in my place. Which only intensified the challenge to win her over.

I grinned. "For the record, I don't recruit—I have more than enough business. You look like an interesting person to talk to, that's all."

"Isn't that a conflict of interest?"

Unable to contain myself, I burst out laughing as she turned a shade that matched the drink in my hand. She was downright sexy when she squirmed in self-consciousness.

"That's cute," I said, mischievously toying with her to make her do it some more. I'm such a bastard sometimes. "I'm sorry, I don't mean to embarrass you. Are you uncomfortable with me?"

"Well, yeah."

Mission accomplished.

"Look, Andi. I just wanted to say hello. Sorry if I made you uncomfortable. I'll let you get back to your colleagues."

Suddenly feeling rather cocky, I waved to all of them in a rare gesture of recognition. A gaggle of flirty smiles and heaving bosoms waved back.

"OK," said Andi.

Neither of us moved.

"It was nice to see you again," I said. "I like your hair like that, by the way."

"You too."

That is so cute. Holy shit, I was *smitten.*

And with that, I decided to put her out of her misery. "See ya."

I walked away, sans handshake this time, yet I couldn't help but turn for one last look at her as she headed to the ladies' room, her back to me. My conscience finally returned; she obviously didn't want her colleagues thinking she associated with me, and I didn't want to make trouble for her. I considered leaving my business card on the table for her, but instead I left Heartland Brewery, grateful for the bite to the fresh air that cooled me off.

Chapter Four

June

I am so fucking done with weddings.

Seriously. I can't take another Electric Slide, Macarena, Twist & Shout, Livin' on a Prayer, New York, New York kickline. And if I hear "Butterfly Kisses" one more time I'm going to punch the DJ in the throat.

I'd also like to whack whoever decided to make that Debra Messing-Dermot Mulrooney movie. With a cricket bat. Way to put the pressure on me.

And I am never getting married. Correction: I'm never having a wedding. Me and my hypothetical bride will elope in some Vegas chapel or a musty Justice of the Peace office. Just make it quick and painless. Maybe his-and-her knishes afterwards, just to mix things up.

These thoughts all rotated and rattled around my brain while I called in to the voicemail service, hoping for a much-needed break from Wedding Hell, when to my delight, I heard this:

Hi, uh, this message is for Devin? Uh, this is Doctor Andi Cutrone. From Brooklyn University? We, uh, met a few times? I was wondering if I could, uh, talk to you? Uh, please call me at this number...

I scribbled her number on my palm, hung up on the voicemail, and returned the call. Andi answered on the second ring.

"A colleague gave me your number," she said, her voice quavering. "I hope that's OK."

"Sure, it's fine," I replied. If only she could see how pleased I was. "What can I do for you?"

"Well, I'd like to meet with you, but not as a business meeting."

I padded across my apartment and stood at the arch-shaped window to take in the relentlessly breathtaking Manhattan view. "What do you mean?"

"I mean I just want a consultation."

Ten years I've been at this, and I don't think anyone ever asked for "a consultation."

A laugh escaped. Did she know I was laughing with her and not at her, even though she wasn't laughing?

"That's cute. OK. Why don't we meet at the W Hotel?"

"I live on the Island, remember? Is there something a little more in the middle? How about Junior's in Brooklyn?"

I would've booked a flight to Walla Walla, Washington, if she asked. "OK. When?"

"What's good for you?"

"Weekdays between one and four work for me," I said.

"Let's make it two o'clock on Tuesday."

"I'm entering you in my BlackBerry," I said, the landline pressed against my ear and the device in my hands, my thumbs patting away on its miniscule buttons. Although I wouldn't need to consult a calendar for this one. Hell, I was already counting down the minutes.

"Me too," she replied.

"Thanks," I said. "See you then."

"OK," she said, and hung up. When I resumed listening to the rest of the voicemails, I frowned. Another fucking wedding. The weekend was nothing more than a hurdle to Tuesday. Knowing that would hopefully make it less excruciating.

I took the subway to Brooklyn on Tuesday and when I reached Junior's, Andi was already inside, waiting to be seated. I recognized her from behind, dressed in capris and a chocolate-colored T-shirt. Every one of her wardrobe choices so far implied that she had a body she disapproved of, although she made the typical mistake of choosing clothing sizes and styles that made said body more than less noticeable, and not in a favorable way. And that wasn't to say she had an unattractive body, although I didn't have to tell her that to know she would disagree with me.

I, on the other hand, downplayed my wardrobe today, opting for jeans and a plain T-shirt. I figured she'd be more comfortable if I looked like a regular guy.

Rather than say hello, I playfully tapped her on the shoulder, which must have startled her because the swig of water she had just taken from the bottle she brought in with her got away from her, dripping onto her shirt.

"Hey," she said as if we were old friends, although the corners of her mouth twitched. Without dabbing the spilled water away, she capped the bottle and jammed it into the oversized tote bag weighing down her shoulder.

"Hi," I replied.

A server led us to a booth, and I barely settled in when Andi ordered a slice of classic cheesecake without even perusing the menu. Imitating her decisiveness, I requested coffee and Rugelach.

With the ordering out of the way, I dove right in. "So, how long have you been back to New York?" I asked.

"It'll be a year on August first," she replied. That explained why I'd never seen her until the cocktail party in February. "I grew up in Northport, though."

I grinned. "No kidding! I should've known you were a North Shore Girl. I'm from Massapequa."

"I should've known you were a South Shore Guy."

In the few conversations we'd had, several of her comments had come out either sarcastic or deadpan. I had yet to determine whether this was intentional.

"I'll bet we went to the same dance clubs in Hempstead back in the early nineties," I remarked. She wasn't amused by the thought. I pressed on. "What made you move back here? Certainly it wasn't for a better cost of living."

"No, but it was a better job offer. I got my PhD and needed full-time, and my good friend Maggie—"

I'll bet that's the CJ Cregg lookalike. "—the one you were hanging out with at the Club and the Heartland Brewery..." I interjected.

Andi didn't miss a beat. "Yeah, well, she's the director of the first-year writing program at Brooklyn U and needed an assistant, and managed to convince the dean to appoint me without doing a search, being that it was a non-tenure-track position."

Allison the Textbook Rep had explained the "first-year writing program" long before I took on any of its faculty as clients. Basically, it referred to the introductory English classes for freshman students, although the course titles and curricula varied among colleges.

"Do you like your job?" I asked.

"A lot."

"Are you good at what you do?"

"I think so," she replied before upgrading to a more affirmative stance. "Yes, I am." She seemed as satisfied with her response as I did. However, her confidence waned the moment she accidentally took a sip from my water glass. I pretended not to notice, although she blushed.

"So, how'd you get into the escort business?" she asked, avoiding direct eye contact with me as she spoke.

"Like you, I wanted to do something I was both good at and enjoyed. I enjoy being with women, pleasing women, and I'm good at it. Besides, the money is great."

"What do you do with them?" She seemed genuinely curious rather than asking for the sake of making conversation. Or interviewing me.

"Same thing other couples do. We go to parties, plays—I've seen just about every fucking musical on Broadway—the opera, gallery openings, even a movie once in a while. Then, sometimes I'll give them massages or shampoo their hair…"

Not sure why I tacked on that last bit.

"You *shampoo their hair*?" she asked.

I dialed up the escort charm when her self-conscious squirming resurfaced. "Have you ever had your hair shampooed?"

"Of course."

"At eleven o'clock at night in a bubble bath with candles?"

She was either trying to conjure the image or considering we go do it right now. "Are you in the bathtub with them?" she asked.

"Not usually. It's more about indulging their pleasure."

"I think they'd be pleased to have you in the tub with them."

I think I'd be pleased to have you in a tub with me.

I shook my head and continued. "Most women just want to be attended to without worrying about having to give something back. They feel like they're constantly giving so much of themselves, trying to please everyone under the sun." I leaned in a little and raised the stakes. "What's *your* pleasure, Andi?"

I watched every muscle in her body tense, and I could almost see an actual wall rise like an automatic car window as she barked, "Are you trying to come on to me?"

I leaned back against the cushioned backrest of the booth seat. *Game on.*

"Man, you are the most uptight person I've ever met, and I barely know you. I've never seen anyone so guarded. Were you raised in a religious household or something?"

"Yes."

"No kidding. What else happened to you?"

The server brought us our orders. Lousy fucking timing.

"Like you said, you barely know me," she said after the server left. "And by the way, I think I'm entitled to a little reservation."

She consumed a forkful of the cheesecake, and I swore she was going to have a Meg Ryan-esque orgasm right on the spot. I liked watching her eat.

"You're avoiding the question," I said.

She finished chewing. "Which question?"

"What's your pleasure?"

"Why do you want to know?"

Again with the defensiveness. "It's not something I plan to use against you, if that's what you're worried about. It's a valid question, right up there with what are your dreams in life and where do you see yourself living in five years."

"It may be a valid question, but it's also a personal question. Why should I share my sexual pleasures with you?"

Please do.

"Who said they had to be sexual? Reading a book can be pleasurable. Riding in a convertible with the top down, every bite of that cheesecake—and I can tell you're enjoying that cheesecake; that cheesecake is absolutely sensual to you, isn't it—is pleasurable."

She looked at me like she was envisioning stabbing me with her fork. Then asking for a new one so she could finish her cheesecake.

"So?" I teased. "What are your pleasures?"

She gawked at me, the fork lingering in her mouth, before she finally submitted.

"OK. You're right about the cheesecake," she confessed. (*Ha!*) "As far as my other pleasures go, well, I like chocolate; the sound of a really good acoustic guitar; a brisk walk on a warm, breezy day like today, and foot massages. How's that?"

I finished chewing my Rugelach, which was pretty damn tasty. "It's a start. Now, imagine someone feeding you that chocolate, playing your favorite song on that guitar, taking that walk with you—although the walk is a bit cliché, isn't it?—and giving you that foot massage."

She was contemplating all these things too, I could tell. If only I knew with whom.

"I can get that in a serious relationship—why should I have to pay for it?"

"For some women, it's worth paying for. For some women, it's the only way they'll get it. And when was the last time you got it? When was the last time you were in a serious relationship?"

A twinge of remorse tugged at me for going too far, especially when I could see the sting that had defied her deflector shield. Yet I sensed the infliction hadn't come from me. Nor would it stop me from poking further.

Andi didn't back down. "So, you're their savior. How nice of you. And all for a price."

She stung right back. I probably deserved it. Yet her refusal to cower provoked me to keep poking at her wall. "I'm providing a service using my talents; same as you."

"Yeah, but my service is legal."

"My service is completely legal. I'm a companion for the night. The contract states explicitly that I don't—how shall I say this?—go beyond certain boundaries."

She looked at me incredulously. "That's not what I heard. I heard you're pretty fucking amazing."

I tried to suppress a smile. *Don't look so damn pleased with yourself.*

Not to mention her dropping the f-bomb turned me on for some reason.

"And I've seen the looks on these women's faces. Don't tell me that's all from a kiss on the cheek at the end of the night."

She certainly didn't shy away from a fight. I admired that.

"I provide other sorts of pleasure, but you're assuming the rest," I said.

Her eyes remained fixed on me, yet she seemed tongue-tied. I decided to ease up a little. "So. Andi. You wanted to consult with me. Now that you've done that, what do you think?"

She paused for a second to deliberate. "I'm not interested."

Everything about her body language indicated the contrary.

"You sure?" I prodded.

She remained steadfast. "Sorry to waste your time."

I smiled amiably. "Not at all. I already knew you weren't going to be a client. But you are a very interesting person to talk to."

"What makes you say that?" she asked.

Was she referring to my knowing she wouldn't be a client, or that I found her conversationally interesting? I took a gamble. "You're not the type."

"What type is that?" she asked.

"You care too much about what other people think. You're too self-conscious."

My response sailed passed her as she became distracted by her own thoughts. "No—I mean, what makes you say I'm an interesting person to talk to?"

Did she genuinely not know? Had no one had ever paid her such a compliment?

"I don't know—there's something about you, Andi. I noticed you the minute I entered the room, and I just knew I had to talk to you."

The flicker in her eyes returned, and I finally felt satisfied, as if I hit a bulls-eye. But that flicker faded quickly, disappeared behind the invisible wall, and she glanced at her watch.

"I should go before traffic gets bad," she said.

I caught myself looking at her intensely, filled with a desire to know what had warranted the need to construct that wall in the first place, and to be the one to break it down for good.

I paid the check. When we stepped outside the restaurant, I thanked Andi and shook her hand yet again, although by now the gesture felt too formal. Empty, even. I didn't want to leave it at that, but I didn't know what else to do. She obviously wasn't going to let herself be a client—although I was certain she needed to be—and despite my taunting and tempting her, I didn't want her to be one. But what was the alternative? Friends? How would that work? Asking her out on a date was equally out of the question; past dating disasters put the kibosh on that, the most recent being a woman who, by the fifth date, casually suggested I wear a tracking device on my escort dates. Seriously. In short, being an escort and having a love life just didn't jive. How soon before Andi would "encourage" me to procure a new career, like all the others had tried?

Of course, procuring a new career was an option... Doing what, though? For what else was I qualified? What else would let me make my own hours and my own rules? What else would net me the material pleasures to which I'd grown so accustomed—prime real estate and pricy art and those fantastic Versace suits?

No. It wouldn't work. It couldn't work. I had to let her go. I headed for the subway as she walked in the opposite direction.

I was halfway down the block when I heard the sharp call of my name.

I whipped around and watched Andi break to a stop after catching up to me in a jog. We stood smack in the middle of the sidewalk while others apathetically maneuvered around us.

"Suppose I wanted you to teach me a few things," she said.

Oh, this is gonna be good. I peered at her, utterly amused. "Like what?"

She silently warred with herself over whether to spit it out.

"I'm kind of inexperienced," she finally blurted.

Well. I didn't expect her to say *that*.

"Huh?"

"I mean...I'd like to learn how to please a man, and how to be more relaxed, I guess, and I was wondering if you'd be willing to teach me."

Now we were getting somewhere.

"You want to be a better lover, is that it?"

"Yeah, I guess so," she said, fidgeting with her arms as if needing to cover up her nakedness.

"What makes you think you can't or don't please men already?" This I sincerely wanted to know. She didn't answer me, likely because she didn't want to delve into her sex life in front of a Laundromat. Can't say I blamed her.

A window of opportunity had just presented itself, and I wanted to jump through before it slammed shut on me.

Not only that, but the urge to toy with her self-consciousness returned. "Hmm," I said, scratching my head. "No one's ever made this kind of request to me before. You want me to teach you some things, is that it?"

"Yeah, whatever there is to teach. The problem is, I can't afford to pay you. I was thinking that maybe we could do some kind of barter system, and I don't mean sex."

"I didn't think you meant that. So, what have you got to trade?"

She looked down at the sidewalk. "Not much…" she trailed off before looking up across the street, and straightened up, as if she saw a sign giving her the answer. "I can teach you about writing. I'm very good at that."

I scratched my head again, hemming and hawing just to watch her squirm. "Why would I want to learn how to write? It's not something I use in my career."

I'd finally needled her enough to become agitated, which was exactly what I'd wanted to do. She was bold when her buttons were pushed, even if she bit back. "Look," she said, "I can stand here all day and lecture you on the benefits of being well versed. And it's not just writing I can teach. I know all about rhetoric, theories of writing and reading, nonfiction prose...by the time we finish, I'll be a better lover and you'll be fucking Aristotle—well, not literally, of course."

I pressed my lips together to suppress a laugh, especially since I was serious about and genuinely interested in her proposal.

She continued to sell me on the idea. "Look at it this way: You'll impress all your clients in academia. In fact, I'm surprised you don't know this stuff already."

"My clients don't really talk shop with me," I said.

"Maybe they'll want to after I get through with you."

I'd already made up my mind—she could've offered to teach me how to put nail polish on little dogs' paws and I would've agreed to it—but I kept right on poking just to see what she'd say next. "I'm not so sure that's a selling point. The last thing my clients want to do is talk or think about work."

It worked. "Look, Devin," she began again. "That's all I can offer you. If you're not interested, then we'll forget the whole thing. But if this is something you want to do, then this is all I know, all I'm good at."

Time to go in for the kill. I lowered myself to her eye level, leaned in, peered directly into those emerald gems, and winked.

"I find that hard to believe."

Mission accomplished. I had invaded her space so much she backed up a step. But it was too late—I was past the wall. I knew it. Better yet, *she* knew it.

I straightened up and said with a jaunty voice, "OK, you got a deal."

"Good," she said, as if we'd just negotiated a car sale. "And thanks."

"I'll call you next week and we'll iron out the details of the deal. But I'm going to tell you the one stipulation that I have with all my clients: You absolutely cannot fall in love with me."

Wait—what? Where the fuck did that come from?

And just like that, her smirk returned. "Don't flatter yourself."

With that, we parted ways once again.

Well, shit. I got exactly what I wanted.

I rode the subway back into Manhattan, wondering if Andi would take my call the following week. Would serve me right if she didn't. The thing about Devin the Escort was that he had a façade too. He just dressed it better.

Chapter Five

July, Week One of the Arrangement

It's a business arrangement, nothing more. I drilled that mantra in my head until I heard it in my sleep. To drive the point home, I drafted a new contract, something more specific, given that the standard Strawberries and Champagne contract didn't apply to Andi's and my unique situation.

We meet once a week at my place for seven weeks.

Each meeting lasts for two hours, allotting us an hour apiece of instruction.

Hour one: Andi provides an overview of writing and reading nonfiction prose. Includes weekly homework and "in-class" assignments/activities, plus a journal and portfolio to be submitted at the final meeting.

Hour two: I instruct Andi in foreplay, sexual positions, methods, and orgasms. She too will have weekly assignments, culminating in a climax (sorry, I couldn't resist) *at the final meeting, to be determined.*

From our standard contract, cutting out most of the legal jargon, I included: *If either party develops "inappropriate" feelings for the other (infatuation, falling in love, or obsession), or engages in behavior characterized as harassment, blackmail, or stalking, the contract will not only be nullified, but also a fine will be issued equivalent to the sum of total services rendered in either profession for that time period.*

Lastly, *both parties are prohibited from personally socializing with each other.* Also standard.

Despite my reluctance to tell him about the arrangement, I gave the signed contracts to Christian for notarizing and safekeeping. Andi didn't notice that my signature line was blank. Or she didn't comment on it.

"What the hell is this?" Christian asked.

Never had I experienced a moment with Christian, who was my friend as well as my partner, where he intimidated me. Until that one.

"What does it look like?" I said.

"I don't understand—you're giving instruction now? In your *apartment*? In exchange for lessons in...*nonfiction prose*? Were you drunk when you came up with this? Did you lose a bet?"

"Call this one a personal favor," I said.

His glare provided further evidence of his doubts about my sanity. "Since when do you do personal favors? *In your apartment*?"

Christian and I had always been adamant on hiding certain things from our clients, our residences and real names at the top of the list; so from his perspective, I understood the red flag it raised. However, to explain my motivations felt like a betrayal of Andi's confidence. Or maybe I just didn't want to reveal them at all, to Christian or myself. "Look, this is just a thing I'm doing— let's not make a federal case out of it, OK? It's a one-time-only deal, and I just wanted to cover my ass. And I'd appreciate it if you kept this between us only."

He dropped the contracts on the desk and pushed them to the side, shaking his head in disbelief. "Whatever, man. I'd keep it out of your apartment though. Either that or start looking for a new place to move, because this can't be good in the long run."

"Noted," I said.

The first meeting took place two weeks after Independence Day. I'd given a lot of thought about how to plan my tutorials—especially considering I've never even shown someone how to tie their shoe, much less how to perform a good blow job—and decided to go with the peeling-an-artichoke approach, beginning with the skin and working our way to the heart. (Too corny?) As the meeting drew closer, what began as some sort of gauntlet had evolved into an earnest intention for me not only to teach Andi to be a better lover, but also uncover what had made her so inhibited in the first place. For what purpose, though? To "fix" her? To somehow save her from herself? I probably could.

No. To provide a service, plain and simple. To meet her needs, same as with all my other clients. To do what she asked me to do.

Andi showed up dressed in denim cutoffs dominated by an oversized heather-gray T-shirt with "SCCC" in college lettering. (South Coast Community College, I found out. She'd taught there when she lived in Massachusetts.) While I went to the kitchen to get her a chilled bottle of water and me a microbrew, she circled the living room and viewed my art collection, which made me proud. I'd bought my first painting almost immediately after receiving my first payment as an escort—a two-hundred-dollar oil-on-canvas from a Parson's student (I've always believed in supporting students, especially the ones that showed promise—

it's paid off several times, too; that two-hundred-dollar piece is valued at about two thousand at the moment), and my collecting fervor had been like feeding an addiction ever since. The pinnacle of pride was the Warhol that I placed to neither stand out nor blend in. A client who didn't want to pay me in cash offered it in exchange for a year's worth of my services. For that Warhol I probably would've agreed to marry her. I still think she got the worse end of the deal, although her orgasms indicated that she wasn't dissatisfied.

"Is that a real Warhol?" asked Andi when I returned and handed her the water.

"Yep," I said, beaming. She was impressed. Or perhaps intimidated.

As much as I wanted to engage her in conversation about the paintings, I knew that if I started talking I wouldn't stop, and I was determined to keep things professional. *It's a business arrangement, nothing more. We're here to learn. Lessons in writing in exchange for lessons in sex.*

"This is quite an apartment," she remarked. Truth be told, I was pretty impressed with it myself. One of those high-end Soho lofts you see in interior design and architectural magazine spreads. Money certainly does buy you nice things, and I had grown to love those nice things. And although I could've equally afforded something in Midtown, and meeting clients often required a bit of schlepping, I liked the Bohemian aspect of the area, even though parts of it were a little sketchy.

I looked around the room, trying to see it from a newcomer's perspective. Neutral tones, yet warm. Hardwood floors. Mostly contemporary furniture and accessories. No tchatchkes. Floor-to-ceiling windows. Climate controlled. Tidy, but not so overbearingly neat that you were afraid to touch anything. Strategically placed artwork.

It also struck me for the first time that I displayed no family photos.

"I like it," I said. "I got a good deal on it, right before the market went through the roof."

"You own this place?"

"Yep."

"Do you get health insurance and retirement benefits with this job too?"

I laughed. "That's cute. Shall we get started?"

Andi kicked off her tutorial by assigning me to write a timed, on-the-spot narrative about my history of reading and writing. Not what I was expecting; although really, I didn't know what to expect. I sat on the sofa, my laptop in front of me, and poked at the keys with my index fingers—I hadn't typed much since college other than emails—while Andi continued to admire my art collection. From the corner of my eye I caught her gaping in front of the Warhol yet again. I barely finished one paragraph when she returned to the sofa, sat beside me, and read over my shoulder. My heart rate accelerated as beads of sweat appeared at my temples while she eavesdropped, my every breath filled with dread while my heart pounded in rhythm: *Am I doing it right?* Based on her pursed lips and the crease that appeared between her eyebrows as she read, I was convinced that I was not, which only made things worse. My fingers forgot how to move on the keyboard and just shook instead. My knowledge of the English language went AWOL. Any second I was going to break out in hives.

What was she thinking as she read? *Wow, I know fifth graders who write better than this.* Or, *Don't donate your brain to science;*

they'll use it as a paperweight. Or, *If I wanted to fall asleep, I would've napped on the train.*

When I finally finished—or rather, when she announced that time was up, she further turned the screws on me by instructing me to read the entire narrative out loud—all one hundred and fifty-four words of it—and I obeyed, fixing my typing errors along the way. Turned out I'd made several. This had to be some kind of karmic payback for some transgression I'd committed in my youth. Laughed at the nerds in school. Scorched ants with my magnifying glass. Bought that Falco record. My voice quavered as I read, and my stomach lurched as if I were singing the national anthem at Shea Stadium. I didn't remember feeling this inept in school.

When he was younger my father read all kinds of books about the history of World War I and II. He would tell me the stories when I was a kid but I wasn't interested. He also read the newspaper and liked to read the obituaries for some reason. My mother used to read to me at night before I went to bed. She read me the Cat in the Hat books and I memorized a few, like Green Eggs and Ham. I didn't take an interest in reading until I was older, between 13 and 18. I read book after book and didn't stop until I got out of high school. I liked who-done-its and museum capers. I also remember learning about the beat writers and liking them a lot. I don't know why I stopped.

The only writing I did was for school and occasionally I wrote a poem for my girlfriend.

"So how do you feel about what you've written?" she asked when I finished. Good God, she was going to make me say it too? She really was a sadist.

43

"Pretty much like a dolt," I replied. " 'Moron' probably works as well."

She neither affirmed nor denied my self-assessment, which probably didn't bode well for me.

"Do you know why I asked you to write it?" she asked.

I shook my head.

A literacy narrative tells the story of your relationship between reading and writing. When you understand that, you approach your present-day writing with a new understanding."

"I never even knew I was in a relationship with reading and writing," I said with a chuckle. She didn't laugh. Maybe she'd heard it before. Or maybe I sounded like an arrogant dick.

Andi proceeded to explain the theory of literacy narratives (who knew that stupid thing I'd just choked out had a *theory*?), quoting scholars and offering examples. The more she spoke, the more I paid attention and regretted being so flippant. And perhaps my joke wasn't a joke at all—perhaps that had been her point all along, that we take not only literacy for granted, but our connection to it, or rather, how our connection to literacy connects us to the world around us. Connects us to ourselves. As I shared these revelations with Andi, I grew increasingly stimulated not only by the discussion, but also with her authority on the subject. No longer the clutzy, blushing girl at Junior's, here she was completely in charge, confident and commanding. I guessed this was how she felt and behaved when she was in her comfort zone, and clearly the classroom—even when it was a living room in a Soho loft—was her comfort zone.

More than that, it revealed her real self. Except I don't think she saw it.

"What do you read today?" asked Andi.

"The Art and Leisure section of the *Times*, mostly," I replied. "I don't have time for much else."

"And what do you write?"

"Checks."

God. How sad.

Andi then handed me photocopy of a short essay called "Amid Onions and Oranges, a Boy Becomes a Man," and instructed me to read it silently, encouraging me to make notations along the way. I had no idea what I was supposed to take note of, however, and wound up reading straight through. The piece was nonfiction, in which the author recalls his own experiences of working in a grocery store after reading John Updike's short story "A & P." Something about it resonated with me—the *shame* the writer felt for his father. I understood that shame all too well. Except the roles between my father and me were reversed, and I was the target and the recipient of *his* shame.

Fuck.

When I finished reading, Andi and I talked about the style and use of sensory description by the writer, Donald Murray. Her own copy of the reading was crinkled and curled at the corners, the staple coming loose. In addition to circled words and underlined passages within the text, handwritten notes crammed just about every bit of white space, scripted in different colored pens from multiple readings. What's more, she discussed the content without even having to sneak a glance at the pages, the result of having read and dissected it many times over. She elaborated on the concept of writing our own story as we read someone else's, establishing the foundation for what was to come in the following weeks, I surmised.

After that, she instructed me to write a response to Murray's story. Not one of an analytical nature but something personal. I froze. I couldn't tell her *my* story, what had come to mind as I read the essay. I couldn't tell her how my father made me feel, how he'd berated and belittled me my entire life. Or could I?

I didn't want to write about that. Hell, I didn't want to *think* about it. No, instead I chose to write something that tied in to *my* lesson. Turn the tables. Reset the balance of power. Thus, I wrote about my first sexual encounter when I was fifteen years old. I should have known she was going to make me read that out loud too. Had I not heard the quiet purring of the central air conditioning unit, I would've thought the room temperature increased by ten degrees. I looked up at Andi midway through to find her dabbing sweat from her brow. *I'll bet her students never turned in an essay like this.* When I finished, she took a rather forceful swig of water, causing it to run from the side of her mouth and down her chin, just like when I'd tapped her on the shoulders at Junior's. It looked so cute, as if her mouth leaked. She was blushing, and I knew it wasn't from the water-dribbling incident.

"Sorry, didn't mean to embarrass you," I said.

"I can see you've already picked up on sensory description," she responded, speaking with a professorial tone. "That's an interesting word you chose to describe the encounter: *lascivious*. Where'd you get that word?"

"I read some sex books when I started the business."

"You didn't mention that in your literacy narrative."

"Didn't think that counted."

"Everything counts."

The timer on my athletic watch beeped, signaling the end of the hour. Already? Wow, that went quickly.

Oh, goody. My turn.

I stood up and took a swig of beer.

"OK, Andi. Take off your shirt." Might as well dive right in.

She transformed from poised to petrified in a nanosecond. "What?"

"You heard me." I clutched the remote control from the coffee table, aimed it at the stereo cabinet nestled catty corner across the room, and house music assaulted our ears after I pressed the Power button. "What kind of music do you like?" I asked as I surfed for the proper accompaniment. I knew what I was looking for.

"Beatles, Hendrix, Clapton, Nat King Cole, Diana Krall, Norah Jones, John Mayer…"

I shot a sideways glance in her direction.

"I like guitars and pianos," she explained.

"What kind of music makes you feel sexy?" I clarified.

She paused. "I'm not sure. I never thought about it."

"That's your first homework assignment: Listen to every CD you own and make a list of songs that make you feel sexy or put you in the mood."

Dissatisfied, I padded to the CD tower next to the stereo and perused the selection using my finger as a guide until I found the one I wanted and removed it. When I opened the jewel case, the disc slipped out and bounced to the floor, spinning like a pie plate until it rimmed out flat. I pried it up and popped it in the CD player carriage, the remote control still in my hands. I pressed Play and the fat brass introduction to Etta James's "I Just Wanna Make Love to You" filled the room. *Perfect.* I returned to Andi and led her to the full-length mirror that normally hung inside the bathroom door. I'd taken it out for the lesson.

"The first thing I want you to do is to get comfortable showing off your body in daylight," I said. "Nothing makes a guy more anxious than a woman who is constantly uptight about her body."

"Why?"

"It's like stepping into an alligator pit. If we try to say something to make the woman feel better, we ultimately say something stupid and make her feel worse. If we say nothing, then that's the kiss of death because then the woman wonders what we're thinking and fills in the answer for us, which, of course, is always the wrong one."

"What are you thinking?"

"Please don't fucking ask me if you look fat."

Wow. I'm enjoying this. I like being a teacher.

"What if she is, though?" she asked. "I mean, what if she's got layers of it and triple chins? Surely you must have clients who are both obese and insecure. What do you say to them?"

Good question. "I empower them by giving them the option to talk about it or not, or I simply start touching them and they forget about it. All they really want is to be touched, to be validated. And I've seen enough art depicting figures of every shape and size that all bodies are beautiful to me."

"You're really into art, huh," she said. Her cheeks flushed again. Did she know how cute she was when she said such things? How she made me want to keep teasing her just to see what she would do or say next?

"Don't change the subject," I playfully scolded. "Take off your shirt."

She didn't budge. I knew how she felt—like I was making her walk the plank—but I also knew I needed to get tough.

"Look, Andi. You agreed to trust me. I'm not going to harm you in any way, I promise. And if something is so uncomfortable that you have to stop, you can. I'll never force you to do anything you don't want to do. But if you can't even dip your feet into the water, then you might as well go home and we'll tear up the contract."

Her demeanor changed to one of determination. Like standing at the edge of the plank and deciding to jump rather than get pushed off. She removed her T-shirt and dropped it beside her, repositioning the bra straps that had slid off her shoulders. Wrong size. Geezus, how come so many women bought the wrong bra size? Did such a thing need to be taught to girls along with menstruation and hygiene? And why does a multi-billion-dollar industry let so many women walk out of their stores so ill-fitted and ill-informed?

Andi kept her focus on the floor rather than the mirror. She detached from the present moment.

"Nice bra," I said, trying to bring her back. "Body by Victoria. Are you wearing the matching panties?"

Ugh. "Panties" is such a vile word. So demeaning.

"No," she responded, sounding distant, still somewhere in her head. "They're blue cotton."

"Look at me," I said, deliberately assertive. She couldn't bring herself to do it.

Wow. It's worse than I thought.

"Tell me what you're thinking and feeling, Andi."

"I'm feeling massively uncomfortable, and thinking I've made a huge fucking mistake to do this since I hardly know you."

For someone who was so uptight, she used the word *fuck* with quite a bit of ease. Must be some sort of defense mechanism.

"Understandable," I said. "But you had enough fucking guts to ask me in the first place. And I commend you for that. Really,

I do. That's not something an inhibited woman does. Something in you wants to get past this fear and discomfort, otherwise you wouldn't be here."

She relaxed just a little bit, which affirmed I was on the right track. Moreover, I felt...*important*. Like I'd just made a breakthrough, regardless of how small. It propelled me to keep going.

"Just listen to the music," I said, this time more like a compassionate coach than a drill sergeant. "It's just you and me. No one else is in the room, no one can hurt you, and you can leave any time you want. But before you do, I want you to look in the mirror."

My words finally planted a seed of trust. She turned and stood before the full-length mirror, surveying the figure standing before her.

"What do you see?" I asked.

"Flab everywhere. What do you see?"

I've seen so many women in various stages of undress that I'd stopped looking. But I cleared my head, closed my eyes for a second, and opened them again, seeing Andi's body for the first time, as if I were in a drawing class and she was the model, or even a statue. She looked liked she'd been sculpted from clay, smooth in texture with rounded lines. Her breasts, although sagging due to their weight in the undersized bra, were probably round, slightly larger than softballs. *They'd conform perfectly to my cupped hands.* She had an hourglass figure, with short, muscular legs. Her feet were narrow at the heel and widened out, with dainty toes.

My God, she was a work of art, and she was completely blind to it.

"I'll bet if you stood here, completely naked and posed, you'd have a Rubenesque body. Really, Andi. You're voluptuous. You've got this fleshy belly, you're curvy, you've got ample breasts, your legs are great, and everything's in proportion."

She eyed my reflection in the mirror, her expression inferring that I'd just outright lied to her.

"*Oh, you're a smooth tawlkuh—you are, you are,*" she said in a spot-on imitation of Marisa Tomei's character from *My Cousin Vinny*. If I weren't so irked over her implying that I was full of shit, I would've laughed.

"Do I say what women want or need to hear? Yes. Is it bullshit? I don't think so. All women are beautiful, Andi. And I didn't get my reputation by bullshitting my clients. Women come back to me because I tell them the truth."

"*All* women? Oh, *come on!* Qualifier aside, you're a modern-day sophist! You tell them the truth, but it's a truth swaddled in words like 'voluptuous' and 'Rubenesque' and 'curvy.' Like putting Sweet'N Low in your ultra-caffeinated coffee after downing a greasy cheeseburger and fries—what difference does it make?"

Impressive. The force is strong in this one.

"First of all, I have no idea what a sophist is. Second of all, which would you rather hear, that you're curvy and voluptuous, or that you're not as fat but your breasts are bigger than some women I've met? Truth is relative, is it not? And you just told me in my first lesson that word choice goes a long way when persuading an audience to keep reading."

She stood there, agape. Me: One. Andi: Zero.

"It's perception," I continued. "Look…" I removed the top of the ottoman near the matching chair, pulled out a coffee table book, and opened it to Reubens's *The Judgment of Paris.* "Do you see a fat woman? I don't. These painters regarded the female body as the essence of human life. Her flesh was life giving, her curves life affirming. And painters captured that and all its beauty."

I handed the book to Andi and she turned the pages one by one, stopping on each to take in its contents, practically tracing them with her eyes and making a blueprint for herself.

"Go back to the mirror and look again, and tell me *one thing* you like about your body—any part," I said.

She closed the book and returned to the mirror. At first she stood there skeptically, as if waiting for something to happen. I tried to communicate with her telepathically: *Just look...*

Finally she said something. "I like my eyes."

Excellent choice.

"I do too," I said. "What else?" I came up behind her, and restrained myself from placing my hands on her shoulders or her hips—something told me she wasn't ready to be touched yet. "Look at your *body.*"

She was more focused and decisive this time. "I like that my body seems to be flabby in proportion. It's not as if I have these little boobs and an excessive belly, or a butt that is three times the width of my waist."

I nodded, thinking, *It's a start. Keep going.*

She continued as if she'd heard me. "I like my legs, too," she added. "They're muscular."

She took a step forward, immersing herself into her reflection. Wow—she was *getting* it! And at that moment, I knew: *now* it was time to touch her. However, she jumped and jerked away when I put my hands on her hips in order to move them in synch with the song, which I had set to Repeat.

"*Whoa*! I forgot to tell you that I am massively ticklish."

I backed off, amused by her admission, yet also relieved her recoil wasn't some kind of post-traumatic response. Although for some woman, tickling was akin to abuse. It's possible that Andi was one of them, but I decided to downplay it instead, turn it into a virtue rather than a fault or a bad memory. "That's cute. That's really cute. We'll make that work to your advantage. In the meantime, start dancing."

I directed her to dance in front of the mirror. "*Feel* the words. Don't just see yourself as half-dressed and dancing. See yourself as sumptuous."

I watched her physically morph from self-conscious to swept away, and was astounded. The sight of her—hips swaying, arms raised over her head, breasts bobbing—captivated me. As if her every line of defense had simply melted away, and she was revealing the *real* Andrea Cutrone—radiant and reckless and *free*.

I desired to run my fingertips along every curve of her arms and thighs at that moment, for our skin to blend like brushstrokes of paint. I practically ached for our bodies to come together and be one, to dance into eternity.

Dude. Snap out of it.

I aimed the remote at the stereo again and stopped the CD. Snapped her out of it as well.

"Good," I said, regaining self-control. "Your homework this week is to fall in love with your body. Actually be *attracted* to it. Also, practice dancing, because next week you're going to dance for *me*—not the mirror—and I'm going to have you strip further."

She seemed OK with that. I hoped I would be too.

"I also want you to make a list of sexy songs and dance naked in front of your mirror at home. If you don't have a full-length mirror, then buy one."

She seemed OK with that as well.

Andi gave me an assignment too: Write a first draft of a memoir about an event from my life, and read an essay (or was it an article?) she'd photocopied and stapled for me called "Memory and Imagination." I had to make a list too, mine consisting of twenty favorite words.

The moment she left, I flopped on the sofa, my head resting against the armrest, pen in hand, pages raised above my face, and delved into "Memory and Imagination."

I dozed off by the bottom of the second page. What a fucking bore.

Chapter Six

Week Two of the Arrangement

God, even the list of words kicked my ass.

It was bad enough trying to come up with twenty words that didn't make me sound like a dork, a child, or a gigolo. Not to mention that slogging through twenty pages of "Memory and Imagination" was like undergoing surgery with your eyes open. I'd started out OK, once I'd gotten past the first few pages. But the more I read, the more convoluted the content became. I didn't know if Patricia Hampl got paid by the word, if Andi was really testing my endurance, or if she actually liked this stuff. Every day the pages sat in view, waiting for me to pick them up again, and every day I did with a frown. If nothing else, I was determined to finish the goddamn thing. Understanding it would be icing.

Maybe my reading comprehension skills were rusty.

I'm sure I could've called Andi and asked for her help. I probably *should* have called her. But I wanted to figure it out for myself. I wanted to be better than a 19-year-old who despised reading, who fulfilled the assignment for the sole purpose of getting it done because he was supposed to.

I don't even want to talk about my memoir. Not yet.

I had to do all this while accompanying Joyce the Sociology Professor at a square dance (seriously? In Manhattan? On a

Friday night?) and Mariel the Anthropology Research Director to a screening of a documentary on Inca remains. Or was it Prussian remains. Or dinosaur. I was too busy trying to come up with ideas for my stupid memoir. On Sunday I went for a carriage ride in Central Park with Daphne the Mom. That's all I knew about her, because she started almost every sentence with, "Well, I'm a mom, so…" She'd always wanted to go for a horse and carriage ride in Central Park with her "dream man."

"My husband isn't so much a dream man as he is a convenience store item," she said just as our carriage driver snapped the reins.

"Oh, you're still married?" I asked.

She sighed. "If you could call it that. But I'm a mom, so…"

She asked the driver to go around once more and made out with me for almost the entire duration. Then she began to cry. "I probably shouldn't have done that. I'm a mom." *And married.* Which wasn't my problem.

"Moms need passion and romance in their lives too," I pointed out.

She sobbed. "You're perfection, Devin. I don't know if I'm in love with you or hate your guts right now. You've given me everything I ever wanted in this one carriage ride, and now I'm going to have to keep seeing you. I'll have to take it out of the fund for my son's karaoke lessons."

"Why don't you take this ride with your husband next time?"

She shook her head. "Can't. He has a horse phobia."

"OK."

Like the typical college student, I didn't start my memoir until late Monday night. Thankfully I had the night off. I typed while the baseball game droned in the background. I hadn't decided on what to write about until earlier that day, when I made an impromptu visit to the Museum of Natural History. There was a time in my mid-twenties when I'd gone at least once a month, like clockwork. The docents knew me by sight. Some even knew my name.

The memory rushed at me as I stood in the gallery. The class field trip. The painting. The awe, followed by the shame. Just like that. Maybe the Donald Murray piece had gotten to me, soaked through my skin. Maybe, as I was listening to my clients' stories, I was hearing my own. Or perhaps whatever story was hidden in the fresco hanging in front of me had unlocked the vault.

Regardless, I almost cried right in front of it.

Andi had said to just get the words onto the page and not worry about what she called "the small stuff." The hard part was coming up with the right words. I wanted to be as descriptive as Donald Murray in "Onions and Oranges," try my hand at the sensory description. But I also wanted to make sure I was getting the details right in terms of how it really happened. Although I think that's what Hampl was getting at—when writing something like a memoir, sometimes the line between memory and imagination was blurred. What was more important—telling the color of my shirt, or showing the color of my sadness?

A strange kind of dread and worry consumed me all week, shadowed me like a curtain, and it wasn't until I printed out the three pages of my memoir (she made me double-space it), that I identified what stood behind the curtain: I didn't want to disappoint Andi. It had been a long time since I'd feared letting anyone down. Mostly because I figured it was already a done deal.

The difference in Andi was instantly recognizable. She practically skipped into the apartment, she was so light on her feet. She wore a skirt. She acted taller.

"Wow!" I said. "You've been practicing."

"How can you tell?"

"Your walk. You entered upright, confident. As if you own this room."

She lit up, her cat eyes glistening. "It was incredible, Devin. I've never been so accepting of my body. It's such a good feeling to look in a mirror and like what I see, even if *Cosmo* is telling me I'm too many sizes too big."

I was just as elated—not only for her breakthrough, but also because I played a role in it. This must be what she experienced when a student had a writing breakthrough. The rush of adrenaline came from my having done something *meaningful*, performed a valuable service whose effects lasted more than an evening. I hadn't just appeased her appetite. I changed her *thinking*. And I wanted to do it again. And again.

"Fuck *Cosmo*," I said. "Those models are all airbrushed anyway. You're real. Besides, you look gorgeous." She did. Her hair curled from the humidity, the curve of her waves matching curves of her body, as if in approval. Her skin glowed, light as vanilla cream. Her lips were glossy.

Andi blushed and tried to suppress a smile before reverting to professor mode. "How did you make out this week?" she asked.

I forced myself to breathe as the curtain of dread smothered me, and I handed her the three pages. She began with the first page: the list of my twenty favorite words. I watched her in anticipation, ignoring the sick-to-my-stomach feeling as she attended to each word, gauging her reaction.

Was she reading the words, or was she reading *me*?

"What made you pick that word?" she asked, pointing to *tarantula*. She sounded repulsed.

"It's just a cool-sounding word," I said.

"And the others?"

"Mostly I either like what they are or the way they sound when they're said. The words that end in *s*, for example, can sound really sexy depending on what kind of voice you use." In a booming bass voice I belted out the word: *Lecherous.*

She laughed and imitated me. "*Carresssss.*"

Wow. That was hot.

I leered at her in a way that was… well, lascivious, and made a cooing sound to accompany my wink.

"What did you think about 'Memory and Imagination'?" she asked, ending our fleeting flirtation.

"It was…" I started, trying to come up with something respectful. "I think I'm out of practice when it comes to reading that kind of stuff."

"A little dry for you?"

"Like a fucking martini."

She laughed. It was the first time I heard her laugh, I realized. She was positively melodic.

"I'm not saying it was bad…" I backpedaled.

She stopped me. "You don't have to like everything I assign you," she started. I mentally exhaled. "But I want you to consider what you're not liking about it. Was it the style in which the essay was written, or the complexity of the subject?"

"Probably a little of both."

"Well, we'll discuss the role of style in writing in the coming weeks. For now, let's talk content."

She asked me a series of questions, and the next thing I knew, I was not only explaining concepts to her, but also finally understanding their context, as if it had been clear all along. And what I didn't grasp, I asked her to clarify or explain, no longer afraid of my intellectual limitation. Together we analyzed and desconstructed the text piece by piece, using examples and analogies. This must be how she keeps her students engaged— rather than lecturing and spelling out the text for them, she compels them to demystify it themselves by drawing it out through an exchange of questions and answers. And she somehow knows exactly where to lead them, even though they get there themselves. Brilliant.

She also commended me on my note-taking (or, as she called it, "annotation"). Following the discussion, she moved on to the draft of my memoir, and the dread returned. I hadn't even noticed it had lifted while we were talking. I watched her, my foot tapping rapidly while I wrung my hands, wishing for something to hold on to like one of those stress balls or squishy bean bags.

Or maybe it would've been better to just tranquilize me with a dart gun.

When she was on the final page, I shamefully confessed, "I didn't really know how to end it." She wasn't fazed. Or maybe she didn't hear me.

She then took out a pen (not red, I noticed; didn't all teachers use a red pen?), returned to the beginning of the draft, and re-read it. With the pen.

Oh God. It's like getting your teeth drilled. And then getting graded for it.

Like the Donald Murray article last week, she covered my

paper with scribblings in the margins, underlined phrases, and circled words. I didn't dare utter a sound, half expecting her to rap me on the wrist with the pen if I tried.

Andi finally broke the silence. "What do you like about this draft?" she asked.

What do I like about the draft? What the hell kind of question is that? I didn't write it to like it, lady.

She returned the ink-soaked pages back to me, and they looked like something I'd never seen before, much less written. As I began to re-read my words along with her notations, her initial question started to make sense. Something had made me want to write about that particular event in my life. Something had made me want to tell her *that* story, share a part of myself with her that I'd never shared with anyone else.

"Actually, what I like is what I didn't really write about," I said. "It wasn't just that I fell in love with those paintings, but that I also found them on my own. No tour guides, no teachers. It was the *solitude* of the moment—I was in my own world, and it could've lasted ten minutes or two hours, I really don't know. And maybe there was a little excitement at having escaped from the herd, so to speak."

"That's what I see," she responded. "A memoir is never about what you think it's about. There's so much to this story that's not on the page yet. So much you can do with it."

As we talked about the possibilities—directing my focus, organizing my thoughts and ideas, using figures of speech and adding sensory description to bring them to life, the "the moment of revelation" (to use Andi's words) went from being a blurred abstraction to a clear concept. My memoir was about the discovery of beauty, both in art and solitude, and the rejection of my father. I thought it was just about seeing a cool painting, and my father being a dick.

The more I saw Andi at work, the more in awe of her I became. She possessed a gift for peeling back the layers of people through their words on the page, getting them to reveal their authentic selves, and coming out of it better than they were before. How in the world was she not able to do that with herself? How did this intelligent, accomplished professor with emerald eyes and creamy skin cement herself inside her own body, buried alive? For all *she* had written, why had she remained that way?

"Wow. You're really good at this," I said. Geez, I sounded more like Butthead than someone trying to pay a genuine compliment.

"Thanks."

I tried again. "No, I mean it. You really know how to see what's going on while giving constructive criticism at the same time. I was expecting you to tell me it was crap. If I'd had a teacher like you the first time around, I might have remembered more about writing. Hell, I might even not have been so bad at it."

"Well, you're not a bad writer," she stated matter-of-factly. "Actually, I think this is quite good. You're inexperienced, that's all."

"Same as you."

She redirected her attention from the paper to me. "Excuse me?"

"There's a ravenous, sexy lover in you, and we're going to bring her out just like you're going to help me with my writing. You'll see."

She started to laugh and cough at the same time, prompting her to take a sip of water. What was so funny? I meant every word of it. And it was time to put the pedal to the metal.

I got to my feet. "OK. Your turn. Strip."

Her eyes widened to round circles, and she coughed again. Here we go.

"Geez, you could be a little more tactful. Whatever happened to foreplay?"

"First of all, foreplay is next week's lesson. Second of all, I don't want to be tactful. Tactful is: *now take off all your clothes, piece by piece, and don't worry, your body is beautiful*," I said in a mocking voice. "We did that last week. You're beyond that now. Let it out."

"How much am I letting out?"

"As much as you can."

She stood up. "Would you at least lower the blinds so I'm not giving the rest of the city a free show?"

I rolled my eyeballs and closed the blinds, blocking off the sun and potential stay-at-home peeping toms.

She removed her blouse first, followed by her denim skirt, revealing a matching Victoria's Secret solid pink bra and bikini. Still the wrong size bra, but I appreciated the effort and I liked the color. The moment I took a step towards her, she cowered.

"What are you going to do?" she asked. You'd think I was holding her at gunpoint, she looked so frightened and humiliated. What the hell? She was so radiant and confident an hour ago.

"Relax," I said, slightly impatient. "Geez, Andi. You have to trust me."

Her eyes went from scared to wistful to angry in an instant. And then she snapped.

"Fuck you, Devin. You take your clothes off. You think this is easy? I don't even *know* you."

I wanted to just come out and ask: *What happened to you?*

But I couldn't bear to think the worst. I'd met women who'd hired me to hold them while they shared every sick detail of what had been done to them as children or adolescents. With each one I'd given them their money back, and I finally vowed never to take on another client like that—I'd ended up crying myself to sleep every time, and they'd haunted me for days afterward. Too many women had been the object of unwanted advances, cat calls, leering, groping, and assault, for no other reason than they were female. Maybe I was going about this the wrong way, instructing Andi to strip so callously. My intention hadn't been to demean her, but to empower her.

No. Whoever or whatever had fucked with her wasn't going to get away with it anymore. I had to defuse this bomb, or minimize its impact to that of a dud. What better way than to lead by example?

Without batting an eye, I stripped to my boxers, dropping my T-shirt and jeans in a heap next to me. In the early days of my business, I'd volunteered as a model for figure drawing classes to prepare me for undressing in front of strangers and having them ogle me. Doing so had long since become second nature. I stood in front of Andi, whose arms were tightly folded across her chest, and stretched my arms out, the palms of my hands facing up.

"See how easy it can be?" I said.

It took her a few seconds to respond, as if she'd been stunned and needed to wait for it to wear off. "Of course it's easy for *you*— look at you! Who wouldn't want to show off a body like that?"

I had a good body, and I knew it. Let's face it—I was ripped. I'd worked hard for it, in fact. But Andi acknowledging it would have made me practically giddy had the moment not been so tense.

"Andi, you just got through telling me that you fell in love with your body."

"Well, that moment's over."

I refused to let her win this one. "Why?"

She wouldn't answer.

Whatever she was hiding, she was clinging to it for dear life—rather, it was clinging to her, and all I wanted to do was make her feel secure enough so she could release it like a dove into the sky and never take it back.

I closed the rest of the shades in the room. Next, I clicked on the stereo and scanned my CD collection like I'd done the previous week. "We've had enough of Etta James," I muttered. Once I found what I wanted, I popped it into the carriage and turned up the volume, flooding the room with syncopated bongos and bass and finger-picked acoustic guitar. I thumped across the hardwood floor until I was toe to toe with Andi, deliberately invading her space. I honed in to her gaze, locked it, and stayed there. *You are not less than*, I said silently, convinced the message was traveling pupils to pupils. *You are everything. You are here and now and you belong to you.* And my God, I was convinced the message was getting through. I could feel her muscles unclenching, and I wasn't even physically touching her.

I finally spoke out loud. "OK. It's just you and me and the music. No one can see us, and no one else is here. Pretend you're fully dressed. Do you like the music?"

She nodded slowly, mesmerized.

"Good," I said. "Let's dance."

I waited in position, but she didn't move. I goaded her, more patient and allowing than before. "You can't please a man until you please yourself. Men like women who like their bodies, who feel comfortable in their own skin."

"I never met such a man. I've only met men who like women with bodies that would make Barbie want to throw on a pair of sweats."

I practically bit my tongue to keep from laughing. "Then you've been meeting the wrong men. Close your eyes. Pretend you're in your bedroom." I leaned closer, tilted my head, and whispered directly in her ear, "No one can *judge* you, Andi, and no one *will*."

She closed her eyes, finally letting the words in, letting me in, and swaying to the music. After thirty seconds or so, she opened her eyes and craned her neck to look at me, and I broke into a bodacious smile—Real Andi had appeared, and I was thrilled to see her. She beamed back a bashful, yet trusting grin and moved into me, surrendering her inhibition, the heat between us charged like static electricity. I took her hand and together we immersed ourselves in the bossa nova beat, twirling and twisting and tapping, losing Andrea the College Professor and Devin the Escort and finding Andi and...I couldn't remember the last time I felt so much like...me.

The song ended and the next one came on. A ballad. We looked at the stereo, as if expecting to see a live Latin band in its place, and then turned our attention back to each other. She wore an expression of *Now what do we do?*

I offered my hand to her. "Shall we?" I asked.

She took both of my hands and drew close to me, her body tensing up again. God, she smelled delicious. Like chocolate-covered cherries. Her perspiration only intensified the sweet essence.

"I haven't done this in a while," she said softly. "I mean slow danced with a guy, not danced in my underwear in broad daylight. I've never done that."

Come to think of it, neither had I.

"You're going to be doing a lot of 'firsts' from now on," I said, followed by a silent *And all of them with me.* I wasn't sure what that meant, and I was glad I didn't give voice to it.

We circled twice out of step before finally falling into rhythm. I placed my hand on her back gingerly, as if she were made of silk. Her skin was hot to the touch. She was letting go; I could feel it. I could also feel my own skin tingling, my senses quickly overheating, like a pressure cooker whose lid was about to pop. The feel of her flesh, the sound of her breath, the scent of her hair, the curve of her breast... I'll bet she tasted like cherries too. We made eye contact and—

I could feel myself tilting, being lured in by her tractor beam, locked in an intense desire to kiss her. But I froze in terror.

Stop. Now. Before she sees you.

The music stopped, and whatever electromagnetic energy had switched on and pulled us together just as quickly turned off and released us. Our hands dropped, and I took a step back.

It's a business arrangement, nothing more. It's a business arrangement, nothing more. It's a business arrangement, nothing more.

I needed a moment to find my voice. "You're going to have to beat the men off with a stick," was all I could manage.

She didn't move, didn't speak, didn't blink.

"You can put your clothes back on now." I said.

I left her standing there while I went to the windows and lifted the shades one by one. By the time I finished, Andi was back in her clothes. I re-dressed as well.

"You know, you really do have a nice body," I said, bringing Devin the Escort back in charge. "You should show it off more."

I pointed to her blouse. "And you look really good in red."

She smiled in gratitude, yet remained speechless.

"In fact, that's your homework assignment: show off your body. What's mine?"

She returned to teacher mode. "Start keeping a journal, choose three paragraphs of your memoir to revise, and read this." She extracted another photocopied document from her tote bag—a scholarly article called "Closing My Eyes as I Speak: An Argument for Ignoring Audience" by a guy named Peter Elbow.

"Peter Elbow?" I said. "That's the guy's real name?"

"He's the Paul McCartney of rhetoric and composition," she replied sharply, yet with an air of levity, "so shut up and show some respect." I responded with a salute. In what was probably punishment for my irreverence, she also assigned two more memoirs for me to read: one by Annie Dillard, and the other an excerpt from Stephen King's *On Writing*. That one ought to be good.

The moment Andi left, I took a shower, leaning my head against the wet tiles as the cold spray hit my body like little ice pins. By the time I finished showering, I knew. I knew I didn't want to go on another date ever again. At least, not as an escort. I wanted to be with Andi. And I was willing to give up everything. *Everything.* Even the Warhol, if need be.

I would even tell her my name.

And pray she wanted to be with me.

But I wasn't ready to call to Christian just yet. I'd have to tell Andi how I felt first. I'd have to make sure it would work between us. And what about the arrangement? Should I call it off? Just pretend it never happened? Burn the contract?

I stepped out of the shower just in time to hear the phone ring. Hoping to hear Kate's voice telling me my client had canceled, I secured a towel around my waist and, still dripping, and raced to nab the call before voice mail did.

"Hello?" I said, catching my breath.

The caller paused for a beat.

"About goddamn time you picked up," I heard on the other end.

Fuck.

"What do you want, Dad?"

"Remember when you told me to drop dead? Well, it looks like you're going to get your wish."

Chapter Seven

The things we say that come back to bite us in the ass.

It's true—I told my father to drop dead once. We'd gotten into another one of our fights, about five years ago.

"You're a disgrace," my father had said.

"Why, because I don't have callouses on my hands?"

"Because you don't use your hands like a man is supposed to."

I had laughed. *"You know what I do for a living, don't you?"*

"That's not being a man. That's being a goddamn whore."

"Oh, really," I shot back. *"I take care of these women. I treat them like royalty and make them feel worthy of themselves. Not like you and your buddies giving them cat calls from your construction sites, harassing your female bricklayers, jerking off to your Playboy calendars in your trailers or at worksites. Yeah, that's real classy, manly behavior."*

In hindsight, I was most ashamed of having said all this in front of my mother, who covered her ears at one point and pleaded with me, *"Stop it, please!"*

He'd stood before me—we're the same height—aimed a thunderous stare, like the barrel of a gun to my forehead, and I thought for sure he was going to take a swing at me. Not that he'd ever hit me before, but there was a first time for everything. I refused to even flinch.

"You're a fucking child," he'd said. *"And you can go to hell for all I care."*

Without blinking an eye, I replied, *"Drop dead and I'll meet you there."*

I'd walked out and hadn't been back since. Occasionally I met my mother for lunch whenever I could, but I hated her being in the middle just as much as she did. Seeing what the animosity between my father and me did to her was the true pain of it all. I'd even once made the mistake of telling her how unfathomable it was to me that she could love a man like that, and that he could love anyone at all. She nearly took my head off, and called me an ingrate.

In the present moment, I stood frozen in place, beads of water dripping from the ends of my hair.

"You still there?" said Dad.

"What's going on?" I asked.

"Your mother didn't want me to tell you over the phone, but you've been blowing her off, so—"

I cut him off. "I work mostly late afternoons, nights, and weekends, which is the only time Mom is home. You both know that. I wasn't blowing her off; we were playing phone tag."

OK, so maybe I wasn't making much of an effort to call her back.

"Anyway, here's the deal. I've got cancer."

I nearly dropped the phone.

"Say that again?"

"Diagnosed a few months ago."

"A few months ago," I repeated, dumbfounded. "And you're just getting around to telling your son this now."

"Your compassion for me is overwhelming," he said.

"Do Jo and Ro know, or was I the only one in the dark?"

"Just you," he said. Like he was actually proud of it.

I pinched the bridge of my nose, right between my brows, trying to fight off being twelve years old again. My father was sick, and he didn't even care enough about me to let me know. He thought that little of me. To say nothing of my sisters not telling me either.

"That's just great," I snipped. When he didn't respond, I asked, "Is it bad?"

"It's fucking cancer," he said in a way that criticized me for missing the obvious.

"Some forms of cancer are treatable."

"It's in the pancreas, so no," said Dad. "I've got about a year if I'm lucky."

Well, fuck.

I closed my eyes and pinched the spot again.

"You should've told me, Dad."

"I wasn't in the mood for your gloating."

I wanted to throw the phone across the room. "You don't know a single thing about me," I said. "You've gone your entire life not wanting to know. Even now. To think…" The rest of the words choked in my throat.

He waited for me to finish, but I never did.

"Well, now you know. Your mother and sisters are going to need you to help them take care of a few things. You're better at handling financial matters than they are, got a better head for that stuff."

Right. They *need me. Not you.*

"Sure," I said. "I'll do whatever I can."

"I'm putting your mother on now," he said, and without

saying goodbye, handed the phone over to her.

"Hi, honey," said Mom. The strain in her voice was palpable. I wanted to scream at her, *WHY DIDN'T YOU TELL ME?* but knew my father had been the one behind the secret, not her; no doubt they'd had countless arguments about it, and no doubt she was adamant that the news had to come from him, not her, or my sisters, Joannie or Rosalyn. "I've been trying to get a hold of you, but..." she stopped.

"I know, I've been busy, Mom. I'm sorry. I should've called you back at work or something."

"I'd rather you had heard it from him in person, but getting the two of you in the same room..." she trailed off again.

"I know, Mom."

"Will you come home soon? There's so much to sort through—the taxes and the bills and the pension—"

"I'll come tomorrow, OK? Can you get the day off?"

"I'm trying to save all my sick days and vacation time," she said.

"Mom, take the day off. Don't worry about the money. I'll make up the day's pay, OK?"

I could almost hear the words behind her sigh: *Your father wouldn't like that at all.*

"OK," she said. "I'll take the day off. They know what's been going on. I just can't afford to lose this job, especially so close to retirement."

"I'm not going to let that happen. I promise."

She agreed to pick me up at the Long Island Rail Road station in Massapequa the following morning.

The moment I hung up with my mother, I dialed the S & C office, hoping to reach Kate directly. Luckily, she picked up.

"Kate, it's Devin. Cancel anyone I've got tonight and tomorrow, or delegate them to either Justin or Kyle if the client is agreeable."

"Are you OK?" she asked.

"Just a thing," I said. "And please tell Christian to call me as soon as possible."

"Will do," she said.

"Thank you."

I hung up the phone again, exhaled forcefully, and sat on the edge of the bed, overcome with exhaustion. The place was eerily quiet—I couldn't even hear the ever-present white noise of the city—and I stood up and paced around the apartment, still wrapped in the towel. Suddenly my magnificent loft space, full of art and affluence, was nothing but a cavern painted in pretty colors and things. It occurred to me that I was looking for someone to talk to, and none could be found.

For someone who had a date almost every single night, this sure was a lonely business.

Chapter Eight

"Even when we write, alone in a room to an absent audience, there are occasions when we are struggling to figure something out and need to push aside awareness of those absent readers."

I spent the hour on the train to Massapequa poring over the Elbow article, writing questions and comments in the margins:

What do we do when the audience of self is more critical than the outer, intended audience?

How have Piaget's and Vygotsky's opposing cognitive theories held up in modern times?

Chomsky? Really? You had to bring Chomsky into this?

I seem more aligned with the Piaget theory.

I am suddenly imagining you and Andi sitting in a living room with a fireplace, sipping brandy as you discuss this stuff. And dammit, I envy you.

I like this guy. He gets it.

I was beginning to understand what Andi meant by *talking to the text*. My notes felt like a conversation not only with Elbow, but also with Andi. I may have even had something meaningful to say. It was getting so that I was reading everything with some kind of writing implement in hand, and looking forward to discussing it with Andi the following week. At the very least, the reading took my mind off where I was headed, and why.

I can't believe I'm thirty-eight and doing homework. And liking it.

When the train pulled into the station, I stuffed the article into my laptop case and stepped onto the platform. My mother was waiting for me at the bottom of the steps, dressed in white linen pants and a nautical-style shirt. She'd lost weight since the last time I'd seen her, and was overdue for a hair appointment. "You're your mother's son," her friends used to tell me, ladies in the PTA and luncheon hostesses. I'd always wondered what they'd meant—in looks? Demeanor? Values? I knew they meant it as a compliment, but my father always said it with such disdain. "Such a handsome boy," they'd follow up with. "He's going to break plenty of hearts." Again, I knew they were complimenting me, but it always struck me as a premonition of doom, a curse I was fated to: *No, you're not going to build something of value. You're going to break hearts. You're not qualified for anything else.*

A lump of emotion congealed in my throat and barreled up the back of my head and into my tear ducts. I swallowed hard and mentally forced it back down as I greeted my mother with a hug and a kiss, and she did the crying for me.

"I'm so glad you're here," she said between sobs.

"Me too," I managed to choke out for her sake.

We walked to her blue Chevy, and I noticed the dent on the side. "What happened to the car?"

She waved it off with her hand. "Some teenager hit it in the parking lot at the A and P."

An image of an adolescent Donald Murray "stagger-carrying"

groceries came to mind, even though I had no clue what he looked like in real life.

"Were you in it?" I asked.

"No, it happened just as I'd finished up and was wheeling the cart to it. Poor kid was so sorry, she was crying and everything. I told her not to bother with the insurance; it's an old car."

"Mom, you're not doing her any favors by letting her off. You have to get that fixed."

She waved me off again. "It's an old car. I don't care about vanity."

I could feel the blood coursing through my veins as I grew increasingly agitated. "It's not about vanity."

She seemed equally agitated with me. "Your father and I have way bigger problems than a dent in a car."

With that I shut up and opened the car door. A sweater sat on the front seat. In this heat? The air conditioner wasn't working, so we rolled down the windows.

"So what's been going on?" I asked when we were on our way. At least she let me drive us to the house. A fifteen-minute ride, tops. "I mean, besides the obvious."

"Your father can't work anymore," she started.

"Oh, he must be loving that," I muttered, more to myself than her.

"You know he can count on one hand the number of days he's been out sick in his entire life." I think my mother failed to grasp my sarcasm.

"I know."

"So he tries to work around the house. Fixing things. We had to take him to the ER once already. Sliced his hand open with a screwdriver. When he's not doing that he's watching game shows and baseball all day."

"Maybe you should get him some books," I suggested. "He always liked that World War Two stuff, didn't he?"

"I guess."

We arrived at the house in no time, and my stomach lurched. The tan colonial I'd spent the first nineteen years of my life in looked the same on the outside—pristine lawn, rose bushes and azaleas, the old weeping willow in the backyard that we used to climb when we were kids. How had it changed on the inside?

Well, for starters, *he* was in there.

I backed into the long, narrow driveway with the car instead of pulling in frontways. After I killed the engine, I sat still for a second (Mom already opened the door and stepped out of the car), took a deep breath, retrieved my laptop case from the backseat, and headed up the walkway to the door. You'd think I was taking my final steps of freedom.

The sharp odor of disinfectant assaulted me the moment I stepped inside, followed by the arctic blast of the air conditioner wedged in the living room window, and its conspicuous hum. I took in the panorama of the living room and attached dining room. Like being in a time capsule, or one of those life-sized dioramas at the Museum of Natural History. Dark brown paneling on the walls. Popcorn ceilings. Stained hardwood floors. Minimal lighting. Furniture upholstered with floral patterns and matching curtains. I didn't remember the rooms being this dark. Or small. Or outdated. Mom closed the front door and draped the sweater around her shoulders. Now it made sense. She'd probably been living in that sweater for the last month.

"Sal?" she called. "We're home."

You're home. I'm just visiting.

"We had the place professionally cleaned," my mother pointed out. "They recommend you do that."

"*Who* recommends it?" I asked, suspicious.

"The cancer people. They've been so helpful."

Sounded like a bunch of charlatans to me.

"At least it doesn't reek of cigarette smoke," I said.

"Your father quit smoking years ago."

"He may have quit, but the smell doesn't," I said.

The words had just come out of my mouth when I heard a raspy voice say, "Well, look at you."

And there he was, standing in front of me: Pale. Gaunt. At least twenty pounds thinner since the last time I'd seen him. An old Mets cap covering up his now-bald head. Like he'd aged twenty years in two.

I became lightheaded and nauseated.

"Hi, Dad," I said. As if I'd just seen him yesterday. As if he wasn't dying.

He looked me up and down. "You're looking healthy."

"I work out."

He chortled. "I guess you have to. You don't oil yourself or anything, do you? Shave your chest?"

How long would it take me to walk back to the train station?

I clenched my teeth and bit my tongue. Literally. "How are you feeling?" I asked.

"I've got goddamn cancer," he retorted. "How do you think I'm feeling?"

A shiver shot up my back. "Why is the A.C. turned up so high?"

"Because I like it that way. Anything else you want to criticize? You've only been here, what, two minutes?"

"David, honey, do you want something to eat?" asked Mom as she headed for the kitchen. The name sounded unfamiliar to me, it had been so long since I'd last heard it. I almost said, *Who, me?*

I glared at my father with disgust. "Not right now," I called to her.

My father pointed to my laptop case. "What's in there?"

I tightened my grip on the handle of the case. "Just some stuff I'm working on."

He glared back at me as if I'd just made a stupid joke. "Almost makes you look like you've got a normal job. Well, don't just stand there. Come on in."

I was about to follow him into the kitchen when the dining room table caught my attention—or rather, the absence of—it was hidden under stacks of papers, envelopes, file folders, and metal boxes. My mother's words earlier words reverberated in my head: *Your father and I have way bigger problems than a dent in a car.* My stomach lurched again. Geezus.

Mom was in the kitchen making two BLTs. At the moment I couldn't even look at food, much less eat it, but no sense in telling her that and getting yelled at for being an ingrate.

Dad sat at the table, waiting for his sandwich, and I sat at the opposite end. *Make an effort.* "Mets seem to be holding on," I said.

He looked at me with surprise. "You've been watching the games?"

"When I can."

Did he remember the endless games of catch we used to play in the backyard when I was a kid? Did he remember the first and only Mets game he took me to? Did he know I'd saved the ticket stub? Did he remember how many hours I'd spent trying to learn how to properly pitch a ball and field a grounder, just to make him proud of me? Did he remember us sitting in front of the TV and me reciting all the Mets players' names by heart? Or was that all erased the moment I came home with a Picasso book? Did that automatically disqualify me from loving baseball?

"Hmm," he said. "Maybe there's hope for you yet."

I decided to take this as a compliment and an olive branch, and I extended one of my own. "I get to a game every now and then as well. If you want, I'll get you tickets."

His eyes turned angry. "I don't want none of your charity," he barked.

"Sal, it's not charity; he's offering to do something nice for you," said my mother. God, I hated when she got in the middle and tried to broker the peace.

"Any," I said. "You don't want *any* of my charity." I basked in my own smugness, and wondered if Donald Murray or Peter Elbow ever corrected their fathers' grammar for the sole purpose of being an asshole.

"You're a goddamn English teacher now?"

"I've been learning a few things lately, yes."

"You're never too old to learn something," said Mom, placing a plated sandwich in front of each of us. Dad picked up his plate and announced he was going to eat his sandwich in the den. When he was out of earshot, I mouthed to my mother, "Can he eat that stuff?"

"For now," she replied. "Doctors said he's in remission, but we don't know for how long."

I looked at the sandwich on the plate, and was nauseated again. I got up from the table and approached the counter, where my mother was wiping away crumbs. "Mom, thanks, but I'll eat a little later, OK?" I kissed her on the cheek. "I'm going to take a look at what's on the dining room table."

She turned to face me, and her eyes gleamed as she lovingly placed her hand on my cheek. "You'll make such a nice husband someday," she offered.

"Someday," I repeated, feeling warmed by her maternal affection.

"Don't wait too much longer. It's hard to find a woman at your age who doesn't already have children. You don't want to get mixed up in someone else's family. Being a parent to your own children is enough of a challenge. Even harder to have children at your age."

"Fortunately I'm not the one who has to have them," I said with a chuckle.

She sighed, saddened that I'd missed her point, which I hadn't. "Go into the dining room, honey," she said. "I need to make some calls for work. If you need anything, just holler."

Two hours later I re-emerged, shell-shocked. My parents were in debt. Overwhelming debt. Like, in-danger-of-losing-their-house debt. Because of my father's lifelong smoking habit (apparently he quit too late), the insurance company dropped most of his coverage. Thus, all of his cancer treatments had to be paid out of pocket. Unbeknownst to me, they'd taken out a second mortgage to pay for my younger sister's education, and she was only contributing half of that repayment. The property taxes were through the roof (which, by the way, needed repairing). Last year the furnace had needed to be repaired, they invested in a generator for blizzard or hurricane power outages, and the sump pump needed replacing. Their credit cards were maxed out, and they owed back taxes for last year.

My mother sat at the kitchen making a grocery list, the sweater still draped over her shoulders. I sat beside her and put my hand over hers. "Mom, why didn't you tell me things were so bad?"

She put the pen down, took off her reading glasses, and wearily rubbed her eyes. "It started before your father got sick. He was having difficulty getting work. You know how bad the economy's been."

"I thought it was good for construction." Actually, I never gave it any thought.

"Well, it's his age too. They weren't giving him the kind of jobs they used to."

I rubbed my eyes as well. "I organized things as best as I could in terms of priorities. It will take some back and forth with creditors, the bank, and the IRS, but I'll get it all straightened out."

"How?" she asked.

"I have a plan," I said. "Don't worry, I know what I'm doing. In fact, just leave it all to me, OK? Check it off your to-do list." I mustered a reassuring smile.

Truth be told, I didn't have a fucking clue what I was going to do.

Her eyes welled up. "Oh, thank you, David. I can't tell you how much your father and I appreciate it."

I looked at the clock on the wall. "I need to get back to the city," I said.

She was visibly disappointed. "Can't you stay for dinner? Or even stay over. Your room is still intact."

"I've got to work tonight," I lied. She pressed her lips together and didn't respond.

"I'll go say goodbye to Dad." I stood up and went to

the den, where my father was watching *Family Feud*.

"Well?" he said.

"Well, you certainly managed to fuck things up. Did you really think it was all going to go away if you ignored it?" I said.

Dad glowered at me as the TV blared away. He didn't even bother muting the sound.

I didn't wait for him to respond. "I may not be able to put a couple of two-by-fours together, but I can work a calculator. You should've called me. But I guess you didn't want none of my help."

He turned his attention back to the TV and the perky contestants clapping and cheering, *Good answer.*

"Are we going to lose the house?" he asked, still looking at the TV screen.

"I won't let that happen."

He narrowed his eyes at me suspiciously. "What are you going to do?"

"My job," I said. When his face soured, I amended, "My job as your son."

For a split second, I thought I saw sadness in his eyes. Maybe even remorse. Or maybe it was just the reflection coming from the TV.

"I'll take care of it, Dad." I paused for a beat. "Starting now."

He looked at the TV again. A full five seconds passed before he finally said, "OK."

That was as good as it was going to get.

"I'm going now," I said. "I'll be back soon, though."

"Call your sisters," he said. That was his goodbye.

At the train station, my mother took my hand before I got out of the car (I let her drive this time). She still looked as if she were balancing twenty-pound anvils on her shoulders. "Isn't there some other work you could do?" she asked.

I shook my head. "I know my work is nothing you can brag about to your friends, but I'm good at it. I really am. It's not about—" I censored myself from saying *sex*. "I care about them. I care about making a difference in their lives." I thought about Andi and me dancing in my apartment. Stripped down.

I knew that nothing I could say would ever persuade her to approve, much less be proud of me. She let out a sad, tired sigh. I knew the feeling.

I kissed her on the cheek and boarded the train. Rather than resume reading the Elbow article, I stared out the window in utter hopelessness. No way could I give up being an escort now, which meant no way could I be with Andi. I had to make as much money as I could in order fix everything. It was the only way, goddammit.

Chapter Nine

Week Three of the Arrangement

"So," Andi began, "tell me about your weekend."

If only you knew the half of it...

She was sitting on my sofa, her legs tucked underneath her like a cat. I was struck by how comfortable she'd become in such a short time, and how much she looked like she belonged there.

"You don't want to look at my memoir? I revised more than three paragraphs."

"We'll get to that. First tell me about your weekend. Rather, read to me."

I opened my laptop and read excerpts about my last two dates from my journal. No way I was going to tell her about what had happened at my parents. After all, *it's a business arrangement, nothing more.*

"OK. Now I want you to rewrite what you just read to me, only I want you to pretend you are writing a letter to your mother."

I froze. For a split second paranoia got the best of me and I thought perhaps she'd somehow found out about where I'd been this week and followed me. Wouldn't be the first time a client's done that. Once I'd dismissed that notion, however, a new one took its place: *What if the assignment is to actually send it to her?* I reluctantly began to type, repeatedly stopping and starting, constantly deleting what I'd just written. When I couldn't even get three coherent sentences out of it—the only words making sense being "Dear Mom," although even those felt awkward as hell—I gave up. Andi was reading my revised memoir paragraphs and making more notes when she noticed I'd stopped typing.

"What," she said, more like a statement than a question.

"Why am I writing my mother a letter about what I did over the weekend?"

"Because she lives across the country and you haven't written or spoken to her in a while. You want to give her an idea of how you're living your life."

Wow. Did she get that one wrong. I knew she wasn't being serious, but still.

"First of all, my mother lives in Massapequa. Second of all, she wants to know nothing of my life—at least not *this* part of my life. Third of all, for what purpose would I—"

Andi interrupted me with a victorious "*A-ha*! You said the magic word: *purpose*. Audience and purpose are inextricably linked. You write a cover letter with the purpose of getting an interview. You write a shopping list with the purpose of remembering what you need to buy, or giving the list to whoever's doing the shopping. You write a memoir for the purpose of recreating a memory or event to convey a new meaning for the reader, even if that reader is you. And each of these things takes place in a different context, be it the personal, daily life, the workplace....If you are uncertain about your purpose, then your audience is ambiguous. If you are uncertain about your audience, then your writing is ambiguous."

"Makes sense," I said.

"For example, what's the purpose of your journal?"

"I wrote it because you told me to."

"And the audience?"

The light switched on. "You know, I just realized, I knew you were going to read it, so I had you in mind most of the time." Ditto with the other journal, the secret one.

"How did that influence what you wrote?"

"Not so much what I wrote, but the way I wrote it. I thought a lot about the description and imagery. There were even times I felt like I was talking to you."

"And if you were writing for a magazine...say, a profile piece: 'A Day in the Life of an Escort'—how would you write that?"

I paused for a beat. "Depends on the magazine: *Reader's Digest*, or *Cosmo*?"

"You get the gist," she said with a pleasant smile.

I beamed with pride. Pleasing Andi was quickly becoming one of my favorite things to do. I decided to take another shot. "I liked what Peter Elbow said about the idea that sometimes you've got to ignore your audience, and doing so can lead to better writing." I flipped the pages of the article until I found the passage to support my statement—I was even starting to get the hang of annotation—and read it aloud: *"As writers, then, we need to learn when to think about audience and when to put readers out of mind."*

"Yes," she concurred.

"I had a hard time with the section in which he defended the claim that sometimes the audience is an audience of one: the self."

"Actually, I think he's responding to the claim that there's no such thing as private discourse, or no audience at all. And yet, I think both claims hold some truth. For example, in the film *Imagine*, John Lennon is trying to talk an obsessed fan back to reality. He basically tells the kid that the songs he wrote were for himself and no one else."

Another light bulb moment. "Wow. I never thought of that."

Andi continued, "The kid had a hard time with it too. When he asked Lennon what he meant by 'you're gonna carry that weight,' Lennon wryly answered, 'That was Paul's tune. You'll have to ask him.' "

This amused me, and I grinned, although perhaps I was more taken with how animated she was as she spoke. "The *Simpsons* writers, the writers for the classic Bugs Bunny cartoons, all confessed to writing for themselves. That's why they're so damn funny. In such cases, you can tell when a writer stops writing for him- or herself and starts trying to meet the expectations of an audience, especially when some executive asshole claims to know better. The show tanks as a result."

"So did McCartney," I pointed out.

I expected her to laugh (and was slightly disappointed when she didn't), but she continued, fully focused on the lesson. "But what if Lennon wrote songs that he didn't play for anyone or put on tape? What about the scripts that went into the fire without anyone's viewing? That's what Elbow means by private discourse. In those cases, you ignore all conventions of audience awareness, *including* the audience of self."

I wasn't sure how to respond to this, so I settled with, "Cool." I sounded like a surfer dude.

We then moved on to the other memoirs. "Why these two?" I wanted to know. "What do they have in common?"

She responded, "Annie Dillard and Stephen King couldn't be more far apart in terms of genre and style. In those aspects, it's as if they come from different worlds. And yet, they speak the same language—that is to say, they know language so well, and use it the way a good painter uses light and color and form."

Smart woman. She knew her audience.

As we analyzed each memoir's content and language, together we brainstormed ways I could use language to convey meaning in my memoir. "I could use words that keep a reader interested," I offered. "Not just for the sake of being smart or literary, but to make them feel like they're in that museum gallery with me."

"Very good," she said. Again I could feel myself beaming. "Make them feel what you want them to feel. You have absolute power, Devin. Other writers or teachers or readers can guide you, give you feedback, tell you what they like or don't like; but ultimately, it's your story and your truth."

It's your story and your truth. Something about those words resonated deep within me. In my mind's eye I could see a path that was mine and only mine to take. Which, or whose, road had I been on all this time?

"Wow," I said. "I had no idea."

"No idea about what?" she asked.

"That I could do such a thing. I mean, I know writing has power. I guess I never thought of myself having access to it."

"Why wouldn't you?" she asked.

"I don't know." I grinned. "But I'm glad that I do."

I was also frightened. Writing was an archeological excavation, uncovering the artifacts of my being that I'd buried for so long. Whether I wanted to dig through it or not.

My watch beeped, and I closed my laptop.

"So," I began, having adapted a professorial voice of my own, "tell me about your weekend. I see you went shopping. Nice espadrilles, by the way." I winked.

She stuck out her ankle and proudly showed off her shoe; I loved that she bought something with a wedge, and open-toed. She'd even painted her toenails a sexy red.

"Now it's *your* turn to do some freewriting," I said, wondering what kind of lesson Peter Elbow would teach.

Andi looked at me with mixed anticipation, kind of like, *I have no idea what's up your sleeve, but bring it on.*

"Make a list of what gets you in the mood," I instructed.

She tensed up, and the gesture was an immediate buzzkill. I rolled my eyeballs and muttered, "Here we go again."

"Didn't we already cover this?" she said.

"When?"

"That day at Junior's."

"Andi, if you can't talk about good sex, how can you have good sex?"

A flimsy argument for sure, but I was hoping she'd be too flustered to debate the point. She took out a notepad and with pen poised in hand, and looked at it blankly. *Espadrille's on the other foot, eh?*

About five minutes later, I made her read the list aloud. Payback. She gave me a look of *You're enjoying this, aren't you.* Which, of course, I was. She stood up and recited:

> *Having my neck (and pulse points) kissed.*
> *Having my feet rubbed.*
> *Nat King Cole ballads.*

Time to make her squirm.

"Cute," I said.

"*Cute?*" she retorted. If only she knew how much I enjoyed

needling her. If only she knew how it much brought out the fire in her every time I did.

"Yep. That's it?"

"Actually, Devin, I never gave it much thought," she said, sounding embarrassed by and ashamed of the admission, and/or the truth behind it. However, I appreciated that she was opening up.

"How come?"

"I don't know. I guess I was always so self-conscious about whether I was doing it right or wrong that I never considered what I liked or disliked."

I assumed the "it" in "doing it" referred to sex, or perhaps foreplay.

"OK. Then tell me what you do to get the guy in the mood," I said.

She paused, and after consideration, gave up with a defeated "I don't know."

How can you not know?

Without considering the consequences of my actions, I stood up and removed my T-shirt. "Pretend I'm your lover," I said.

No sooner had the words came out of my mouth and I saw the hungry—no, the *ravenous* look on her face did I second-guess my strategy. Maybe we should've stuck with the cerebral approach. Researched scholarly articles on seduction or something. However, it was too late; my shirt was off. Besides, I was curious to see what she would do. "Touch me the way you'd touch him. Come on to me the way you'd come on to him. Do everything but kiss me."

She looked like a puppy about to get crated. "But what if kissing is one of the things I do?"

"I just don't want you to get carried away." *Right. You don't want* her *to get carried away.*

She caved. "OK." She paused, and then piped up, "Don't you think you should teach me how to kiss?"

Had to give her credit for trying.

"You don't need to learn how to kiss," I replied.

"How do you know? You've never kissed me."

Her persistence was starting to piss me off. I knew what she was doing. She wanted me. I'd known since that day at Junior's that she wanted me. They all wanted me. Fine. I let my clients make out with me all the time. But Andi was different. I wanted her right back. If I kissed Andi, I'd enter the point of no return, and then what? Quit my job? Let down every single client? Go work at a WalMart?

Better to not let it happen at all. For her sake and mine.

"I don't need to kiss you to know that kissing's not your problem."

"What is my problem?"

"Your problem is that you *think* you're a bad kisser; you *think* you're a bad lover. You think too much. Just *do* it, Andi. Be a good kisser. Be a good lover."

She looked at me skeptically. "Ha. Easy for you to say."

"Easy to do too."

"Then what do I need you for?" she asked.

Her sarcasm poked at me like a sharp stick, only adding to my ire. "You're very good at avoidance," I said. "You're supposed to be showing me how you get your guy in the mood."

Intimidated, she stood up and approached me, attempting one deliberate, seductive step at a time and coming off as a bad actress trying to find her mark on stage and being far-sighted. I was embarrassed for her. She then stood on her toes, held out her right hand, and slid her my fingers through my hair, brushing over my left ear like a feather.

Holy shit. It felt good. I didn't expect it to feel good. How many women had run their fingers through my hair and I'd reacted as if it was nothing more than a hairstylist running a comb through it? How many had run their fingers through my hair while French-kissing me and pressing their thigh into my groin, and I'd let them? Those felt way better, right? I mean, I *expect* those to feel good—not some timid, awkward…

She took yet another step closer, stroked my hair again, and my own hand, almost on its own, touched her arm as if to guide it.

"I used to do this with Andrew," she said softly, in almost a whisper.

Wait—what? Who the fuck is that? So not what I was expecting to hear.

"Who's Andrew?" I asked, echoing her seductive tone, yet suppressing a growl.

"My ex-fiancé."

Son of a bitch! You'd think he'd just physically walked into the room. And yet one more piece of the puzzle in place.

"No kidding. I didn't know you had a fiancé," I said.

"Well, I did."

"And his name was Andrew?"

"Yep."

"Did people ever call you Andy and Andi?"

"You think you're the first jackass to think that's funny or original?"

Ouch.

"Well, did they?"

"He's always 'Andrew'."

"Not *Drew*?" She was going to pay for the jackass remark.

"Good God, no. I picture guys named Drew wearing argyle sweaters and Dockers and loafers."

"When'd you break up?"

"About a year and a half ago."

"Is that why you moved back to New York?"

She didn't answer. Instead, she slid her hand from my hand to my cheek before taking both hands and cupping my chin—I thought for sure she was going to kiss me, and I probably would have surrendered and let her had I not been so curious to see what she would do next; like watching some kind of suspense movie—but she chickened out. Instead she pulled her fingers along my neck and down my chest.

Mayday, mayday...

When she moved her hands back up to my shoulders and kneaded them like bread, her fingers like talons, I grabbed her by the wrists.

Shit. She aroused me. I hoped she wouldn't notice, but there it was.

"OK, that's good enough," I said, taking a step back so she wouldn't feel my erection. She looked at me, perplexed, as if she didn't have a clue as to what had just happened, or why I was stopping her. Not ignorant. More like naïve.

Get a grip, man. Take control. Turn the tables on her.

I took a deep breath. "Do you want to know what I think?"

"What?" she said, a taking deep breath as well. Apparently I wasn't the only one who'd gotten hot.

"I think you're doing what you want a man to do to you, and you don't even realize it. I think you'd like someone to, for instance, touch your hair..." I tucked a strand of her hair behind her left ear. "To run his fingers along your neck..." Next I turned my hand so that the back of it glided over her pulsing carotid, along the edge of her chin, and down the center of her neck, stopping at her heaving cleavage. *Holy hard-on, I'm going to explode right here.* "To just completely saturate you with touch..." I practically sang in her ear.

She closed her eyes and practically panted. I lazily, reluctantly removed my hand, grazing her breast as I did, and she let out a sigh that turned into a moan, and swooned against me. She caught herself just as I took hold of her again. God, I wanted to just have her—forget the fucking contract. Forget formalities and fine print and instead find a condom so we can both get it out of our system. I wanted to get back at her, awaken her passion, toy with her lust. I wanted to show her how good I was at my job.

A little *too* good. I didn't count on it messing with me too. That's what I got for messing with her.

I couldn't take my eyes off her; she was fascinating, invigorating, even—yet so shackled. Maybe I was making things worse by restraining her. Maybe I should've let her kiss me, feel my hard-on, do whatever she wanted. Maybe she needed that reckless abandon, to take leave of her senses and inner demons and ravish me. For her sake.

"Can I have some ice water?" she asked, gazing in my eyes yet sounding miles away.

"Sure," I said. "Sit on the sofa and ground yourself." I went to the kitchen and came back with a bottle of Dasani for Andi and a glass of wine for me. Perhaps I should've opted for something stronger; I could've downed it in one shot. I also wondered if I should offer her the wine as well, although I had yet to hear her even mention alcohol, much less see her drink it. Was she a recovering alcoholic? Or maybe the child of an alcoholic?

I wanted to go back to the kitchen and crawl into the freezer. Instead I joined Andi on the sofa and acted as if what had just happened was business as usual (wasn't it?). Andi the Client and Devin the Escort. Or, rather, Devin the Teacher. Devin the Escort got us into this mess, the jackass.

"It's all about communication," I said. "You want to let him know what you like, and find out what he likes. And like readers, each one is different. What one does well, another may suck at— forgive the pun. One guy may like when you run your fingers through his hair, while another may want you to put them someplace else. Lovers aren't mind readers, Andi. Never assume he knows what you want—you have to tell him. And trust me: he'll want to know. He'll feel good knowing he's making you feel good. Men feel a sense of satisfaction when they can make a woman come, because they don't know what the hell's going on in there. And he'll be more willing to tell you what he likes."

"But what if I don't like to do what he wants me to do, or what he likes? Or what if I don't like what he likes to do?" Her tone was riddled with worry.

"Well, then, he might not be the right man for you," I replied.

She went from worried to confused, as if she was hearing all of this for the first time. And maybe she was. "Just because we don't agree on foreplay?" she asked.

"Depends on how important it is to him, or to you."

She pondered this as she took sips of water from the bottle. I wondered if she was thinking about Andrew the Ex-fiancé.

"Isn't it true that most men would rather skip the foreplay?" she asked.

"Not if it's the best part of the sex," I replied.

"I thought the other part was supposed to be the best part. You know, the 'biggie.' "

Without warning, Devin the Escort took over. I leaned in to her and said, "Let me tell you a little secret, Andi."

"I was hoping you'd kiss me instead."

Oh God, forget cute. That was downright adorable.

I pretended not to hear her. Instead, I said in a clandestine voice, "Everything they told you about sex is wrong."

"Who is 'they'?" she lobbed back in a loud whisper.

"Whoever told you what you think you know." I then leaned back on the sofa as something else took over. "How *did* you learn about sex?" I wasn't sure which part of me was asking: the escort, the teacher, or the part that desperately longed to be her friend and more.

Andi propped herself on the sofa, tucked her legs underneath, and stared at one of the paintings on the opposite wall. She then began to fill me in on some of the details of her life: growing up in Northport in a household dominated by males. Two older, protective brothers: Joseph and Anthony—Joey and Tony— musicians that she clearly worships. Italian-American heritage (a.k.a. *strict Catholic*). Father died when she was thirteen. Shit. Normally I'd take the hand of a client who shared something like that with me, but I sat still and let Andi talk, not even breaking in with a nod of acknowledgment.

Next she rambled on about her brothers not only fighting off bullies but also chasing off potential boyfriends—I believe she used the term "off limits"—and a father who forbade her to, in her words, "watch soap operas, wear two-piece bathing suits, and swearing was absolutely forbidden in the house, dammit."

Ah, so that explained her fondness for the f-bomb: rebellion!

Her description further painted him as more interested in fostering her brothers' gifts than hers. And her mother wasn't much better—hypercritical, especially after her father's death. Explained her weight issues. Classic emotional eater.

"By the junior prom, I had gained thirty pounds and the boys reviled me and gawked at the Heather Locklear types instead." She seemed to be in a world of her own as she spoke, as if I wasn't even there.

I was riveted—one by one, the pieces of the puzzle fit together, and I was seeing a much clearer picture. No wonder she was so fucked up.

She kept right on going, condemning sex education, "as rote and sterile as the SATs," and her friends, "one of whom called me a prude after I refused to look at the *Playgirl* magazine she had managed to get her hands on."

She paused for a breath, and I thought she was done. I was about to say something when she concluded as an afterthought, "Judy Blume books, I guess."

I was exhausted from it all. Not to mention sad for her. No wonder she was so timid, so inhibited, so insecure. No wonder she felt defensive, rejected, abandoned. No wonder she doubted her worth, her sexual power—hell, she didn't even know she had it, and so much of it.

Worst of all, she recalled it all as if she'd deserved every single bit of it.

Finally, she snapped out of her trance and looked at me, as if the only thing she'd said was "Judy Blume books."

Momentarily overwhelmed, I responded as if that's all I'd heard. "Trust me, there are better sources."

She hung her head, as if to hide from me, and I recognized exactly what she was feeling.

"What are you so ashamed of?" I asked, my heart breaking for her.

Head still down, she mustered up the courage to confess: "My inexperience."

Oh, my dear Andrea. If you only knew how experienced you really are.

"I don't think that's anything to be ashamed of. At least you're learning something now. You're willing to own your experience. And besides, it's not like you had much encouragement growing up."

She cocked her head slightly to the side and directed her eyes toward me. "What do you mean?"

"I mean, you were told that you were off limits, and that sex was some big taboo, a secret, and you were not worthy to know about it."

I could see it behind those beautiful cat eyes: *the epiphany.* Like the entire picture was changing in front of her. *Run with it, baby.*

"And that's a bum rap," I continued. "It's bad enough that society teaches us that a woman's body is supposed to be a thing of service. You had a double-edged sword. Your brothers, although well meaning, sent a message that you were to serve no one. And both notions are dead wrong. They punished you for being you, for being attractive to and pursued by others. They probably thought you were too good for the average guy, but you took it to mean that you were the one who wasn't good enough. I'll bet you were vivacious and even sexy as a girl, and your family snuffed that right out of you."

I put my finger to her chin and gently lifted it, to find tears streaming down her cheek. I then smudged the tear away from her cheek, blending it into her smooth skin like a stroke of paint. Should I kiss her? I certainly wanted to.

"You're a very sexy woman, do you know that?"

She shook her head.

"Want to know something else?" I asked.

"What?" she said in the voice of that little girl being stifled by her father and brothers. I had to bring the woman back. I had to unlock that goddamn chastity belt that restrained her like a full-bodied straightjacket.

"You turned me on before," I confessed.

She sat up.

"Really?"

"Hell yeah."

"How? What did you like?" She was so eager to learn, I thought she was going to take notes.

"I liked the way you stroked my hair. It's been a while since a woman's done that." I didn't bother to clarify: it had been a while since a woman has stoked my hair and gotten a rise out of me, literally. I took her hand and held it, touching each finger. "I like the feel of your hands. You've got these delicate fingers. I'll bet men like your gentleness."

She took hold of my hand so that she was now holding it. "I like hair that I can run my fingers through," she said, looking at my head. "I like your hair."

A lustful gleam appeared in her green eyes as she added in a sultry voice, "And I loved the way your hands felt on my neck."

Uh-oh.

I smiled bashfully, trying to avert her gaze, but she moved

close enough so that our legs were touching, and leaned in to me. "Do you want more?" she asked.

I should have said, *Hell, yes.* I should have shown her how much. All she had to do was look at my lap. I should have set fire to the fucking contract, and then invited her to take a shower with me. I should have told her all about *my* childhood, *my* father, *my* broken dreams. I should have asked her out for a cup of coffee for the rest of our lives.

I should've told her I was a fraud.

But I didn't.

Instead I laughed nervously and slightly backed up, knowing I was one more person rejecting her, but unwilling to act on the alternative. I could tell she felt disappointed—no, worse: *foolish*—yet she feigned braveness, which made me feel like even more of a dick.

"So," she said, straightening her posture and resuming a scholarly voice, "is the purpose of foreplay to have better intercourse?"

I had no choice but to resume my role as well. "Depends on your audience," I said with a wink. "Actually, I think the purpose of foreplay should be pleasure, plain and simple. Stop worrying about it so much and the intercourse stuff will take care of itself."

"Again with the pleasure—you're a hedonist, you know that?"

"It's my job," I said.

She looked stung. Like we were in a switchblade fight, taking stabs at one another.

"Are you saying that your clients enjoy the foreplay more than the actual sex?"

"That *is* the sex," I said.

"What do you mean?"

"I don't go all the way with my clients, Andi."

Her jaw dropped. I wish I had a camera. *"You don't?"*

Hadn't I made it clear that day at Junior's? Guess not.

"Nope."

"But...you're *an escort*! What are they paying you all that money for?"

"To please them," I said.

"And you do that without actually..."

"Inserting my penis?" I knew it was blunt, but Andi needed blunt. Hell, she needed to be hit over the head with it. Well, not literally, of course. That's just gross.

She winced. Mission accomplished. Not to mention that it extinguished any trace of intimacy kindling between us, and other things.

"There are lots of ways to get laid, Andi. In fact, most female orgasms don't happen during intercourse."

"Actually, that I knew," she said.

"Have you ever had an orgasm?" I asked.

"Yes and no." Perhaps my bluntness was working, just a little. That is, until she realized I expected her to elaborate on her answer. "I never had one with a man. I mean—" She lost her nerve.

I refused to let her off the hook. "You mean, you did it yourself?"

"Yeah," she replied, her eyes darting around as if her brothers might be in earshot.

"That's pretty common," I said. "So, how did the men you were with react when you didn't have one with them?"

"Well, my first boyfriend took it personally that he couldn't get me to have one, so after that I started faking it."

I didn't bat an eye. "You faked all your orgasms?"

"Yes—that I've got experience in."

"How did you learn to do it?"

"Movies."

"Porn or regular?"

"Geez, are you kidding me? Regular."

I laughed and gave her a little something to ease her discomfort—"I know, I just wanted to mess with you."—before starting right back in on her: "So what kind of orgasm do you give yourself? I mean, how do you do it?"

She turned into a beet. "I can't."

"You can't what?"

"I can't tell you."

"OK. Last question on the subject: clitoral or vaginal?"

She buried her face in her hands, exasperated with me, then finally created an opening between her fingers to reveal one eye and squeaked out, "The first one."

Good to know.

"So then, what do *you* do?" she asked, finally taking charge—*about damn time.* A sign of empowerment.

She may have taken over, but I wasn't done teasing her. Bantering with Andi was fun. It was stimulating. It felt like... well, foreplay.

"I do lots of things with my clients, except, you know..." I made a fist and pumped it. She pulled a face/palm. "...and none have walked away dissatisfied. Well, few. I mean, they know ahead of time what they will or won't get from me, and they keep coming—forgive the pun—to see me, that is, so obviously it's enough for them. They love it, actually. For once, they don't have to work so hard, don't have to literally bend over backwards to please the guy, after which he rolls over and goes to sleep, leaving her feeling all alone. I told you: it's not about me; it's about them."

I felt very proud of myself. Dammit, I was good at my job.

"Are all the escorts you employ like that?"

"Not all. Christian used to be, but he stopped servicing his clients altogether. He manages the business now."

"How come? I mean, how come he stopped?"

"He wanted a serious relationship," I replied.

"And...?"

I knew what she was asking, *And... what about you? Don't you want a serious relationship? With me?*

Nope. Not fucking going there. I just couldn't.

"And women are much more tolerant when they find out you're not actually doing it," I replied. I continued, "James stopped, except with a few regular clients, and Simon still does even after we told him not to. Both of them charge extra and pocket the cash—that way, if they get arrested, Christian and I can say that we had no knowledge and can produce their contracts, which state that they're not supposed to." *Come to think of it, remind me to call Christian and tell him to fire Simon's ass.*

"Smart thinking," said Andi. "And you?"

Here we go.

"What about me?"

"You don't?"

"Nope."

"Never did?"

"I told you—in my experience, that's not what my clients need."

Yes, I lied. Or rather, I didn't answer her directly. The truth was that sometimes things got out of hand. If a client and I hit it off and we were both horny, then we made a *I-won't-tell-anyone-*

if-you-won't pact, and I dropped her as a client. Never charged extra for it, though. And I tried not to let it happen. For one thing, the pact didn't always stick, and I'd have client referrals asking why I gave one the "special" and not them. Or they'd mistake the gesture as something other than a one-night stand and would get massively attached.

I wasn't lying about their needs, however. The majority of them came to me precisely because of my policy. "I can get sex anywhere, from anyone," one of them had once told me. "I can't get what *you* give me, though," she said. "I can't get them to *look at me*. I can't get them to *listen*."

"It's what *I* need," Andi blurted.

"Oh, you definitely need to get laid," I said. I expected a reaction from her, but nothing. Maybe that was a good sign. "When was the last time you did?"

She looked up at the ceiling as she searched her memory bank.

"At least a year and a half ago, when Andrew and I were still together. Maybe longer," she replied.

"No kidding," I said. I wasn't surprised by the time lapse, but she seemed to be withholding something else, something I couldn't intuit. "So why'd you break up?"

"He decided to marry someone else."

"I'm sorry to hear that," I replied. And I was, but I was too distracted by what she wasn't telling me. I took a sip of wine. "That's it?"

Her eyes turned dark. "What do you mean, 'that's it'? Isn't that enough?"

"Didn't he give you a reason as to why he chose this other woman?"

"Are you implying that it was my fault?"

And just like that, Angry Andi was back. Angry Andi irked the shit out of me, especially when she showed up unannounced and uninvited.

I held up my hands as if to deflect a punch. "Whoa—*chill out!* I wasn't impl—I was just asking a question."

"Why?" she demanded.

"Look, I'm just trying to get to know you, that's all. You asked me to be your teacher. I need to find out what you need to learn. Don't you do the same thing with your students—assess their needs?"

She stood up and grabbed the water bottle.

"Maybe we should forget this whole deal," she said.

I rose as well. "I don't think we should. I think you really need it. And besides," I said, pointing to my laptop on the coffee table, "I'm liking this. I'm actually learning something."

She looked at the laptop as well, as if she were trying to think of a good comeback. I wasn't going to give her the chance, however. I was pissed off, sexually frustrated, and in no mood to let her win.

"Is this what you do?" I asked, invading her space. "Do you quit when it gets hard?"

"Do *you*?" she retorted, nodding toward my crotch and then back up at me, and then nodding in the direction of where we were standing during our contrived foreplay session. *Damn. She knew.* And she won.

All empathy I had for her went limp. I glared at her and said coldly, "Time's up."

Chapter Ten

Week Four of the Arrangement

"You're shitting me," said Christian as we finished the last of the dumbbell curls at the gym. "You want *more* clients? I thought for sure you were getting burnt out. In fact, I'm the one that told Kate to withhold all referrals and newbies to you and pass them on to the others."

"I am burnt out. But a situation has come up." I dropped the weights and wiped the sweat away from my face with a towel. "I need to make some extra dough."

"Like you don't make enough? Geezus, what did you do, piss it all away on art?"

I glared at him, and he chugged the rest of his Gatorade.

"It's a family matter," I said, lowering my voice. "My father racked up some medical bills, and I need to help pay them off so they don't lose their house."

Christian's tone and demeanor changed. "Shit, man, I'm really sorry. Is it serious?"

I nodded, but didn't elaborate.

"OK, I'll call Kate and rescind the orders."

"Already done," I said.

As we headed to the locker room, Christian changed the subject. "So how's that teaching thing going?"

I felt a pang in my gut—or maybe I pulled a muscle doing crunches. "Fine," I said. I felt pretty crappy about the way things had ended with Andi last week. She'd packed up her briefcase and left without even saying goodbye, didn't even give me a homework assignment. I had scrolled through my BlackBerry trying to find someone—a former client, a fuck buddy, hell, even an old ex-girlfriend from college would do—to release the frustration that had not only built up during our session, but throughout the week. Andi wasn't the only one who needed to get laid. I'd found no one, however, and rather than pick up someone at a bar (how fucking clichéd can you get?), I took matters into my own hands (literally) and de-stressed as best as I could.

Since she didn't give me an assignment, I didn't have much to do during the week other than write in my journal and keep working on my memoir, which remained untouched since we went over it together two weeks ago, save for the three paragraphs I revised. Instead I brainstormed ideas for our next session—if there was going to be a next session; I waited all week for her to cancel, or prepared for the notion that she wouldn't show up next week or ever again—and completely overhauled my finances, lining them up with my parents', in order to devise a plan to pay down the debt. As a contingency plan, I appraised and drew up a list of paintings to sell.

I paced around the apartment as I watched the time inch closer to two o'clock. I'd set everything out for Andi's lesson: an easel, a 19x24-inch pad of newsprint, a set of charcoal pencils, gummy eraser, and shading stick. I prayed she would at least show up before the models did.

She did, and I practically exhaled the sigh of relief in front of her.

Neither of us spoke about what had happened the previous week. Acted as if nothing out of the ordinary had happened. Just a business arrangement, nothing more.

For this week's instruction, I requested that we switch turns so that my lesson for her would come first, and when she saw the set-up in the living room, she obliged. I recruited two nude models—one male, one female—from Pratt to come to the loft so that Andi could do some figure drawings. The purpose was not to improve her drawing skills, but to make her look at those parts of the body she'd been programmed not to look at for so long. The moment the models disrobed, especially the male, she turned crimson and averted her eyes to her easel, trying to hide behind it.

"They've done this hundreds of times before," I said. "You're not embarrassing them. Just concentrate on the sketches."

She had no formal training other than one high school art class, and the quality of her sketches reflected that, which was expected. What concerned me more was her lack of trust and confidence and attention to detail—which, of course, was the real objective. That, and adjusting her comfort zone when it came to things like full-frontal nudity, especially *male* full-frontal nudity. Whereas she had attempted significant detail with facial features, she all but ignored the genital regions altogether, either blacking them out with shading, or stopping the sketch at the torso.

I stood over her shoulder and watched her, knowing my doing so would make her self-conscious. After her second drawing, I took hold of the pad and ripped out the pages, returning the pad to the easel with a clean sheet.

"Start again," I commanded, "only this time, no faces. I want you to draw the very areas you've been avoiding." I then approached the models and readjusted their poses to more fully expose their nether regions, and re-adjusted the lighting as well.

Andi looked mortified. The models looked bored.

By the fourth sketch, Andi had improved much to my satisfaction. I even showed her how to use the drawing tools to create contrast and value and intensity. She sustained longer intervals of observation of the models, even if just by seconds.

"Better," I finally commended her on her seventh drawing. "You're loosening up."

"Thanks," she replied without looking at me. Also a good sign.

"What do you think?" I asked.

"Of what?"

"Of your work?"

She pursed her lips. "I don't think I'm flattering them much."

"Ever seen a naked body this close up before?"

She didn't answer immediately. "Sort of."

I didn't ask her to elaborate, although I was curious. What did "sort of" mean? Had she only seen her lovers in the dark? Had she only seen pictures? I wanted to dig deeper, but the hour was just about up, and I was adamant about staying on schedule.

Not unlike the way I'd just pushed Andi to wrestle with line and shape and detail, she pushed me to wrestle with text and theory and critical analysis by introducing various opposing and complex rhetorical theories of composition: "Expressionism," "Social Constructionism," "Cognitivism…" "-isms" always made my brain itch.

"I don't often teach these explicitly to freshmen students," she explained, "but they all show up to their process in one form or another." One scholar in particular, Kenneth Burke, claimed all writing, even personal, is constructed from previous texts and writers and social influences. Thus, writing, reading, and even teaching are social acts, somewhat contradicting Elbow's stance on personal and private writing. Or, at least, as I understood it.

"Art follows this same logic," I offered. Or so it seemed. I'd never considered such a thing before, but suddenly it was a topic I'd wanted to explore and read about, wondering how I could access scholarly articles on the subject, both in art and rhetoric. Once again, Andi's magic was working on me—getting me to think beyond the confines of the lesson, understanding myself in connection to the bigger picture, seeing rhetoric as the subject that encompasses all other subjects. I was *learning*, absorbing like a sponge. I could actually feel myself changing, like a muscle stretching and strengthening.

She then invited me to freewrite (which was, far and away, my favorite writing activity every time, especially when Andi participated as well) about "social contexts"—lessons we learned in school (both in and out of the classroom), family mottoes, and regional dialects or word distinctions. "For example," she started, "people in Massachusetts call a water fountain a 'bubbla'." I especially enjoyed her demonstration of the dialectical pronunciations of "Fall River"—the gaudy New England pronunciation of "Foll Riv-ah" as opposed to the brusque Long Island "Fawl Rivuh."

"In other words, we're not just bringing our own interpretation to a text, but our upbringing, religious teaching, political persuasion. . . " I said, trailing off to let her finish the rest.

"You know, you would make a good composition teacher, Devin. You really get this stuff."

"Really?" Something about this touched me. Over the years I'd developed a knack for learning a little bit about a lot of things. It was the result of active listening, and engaging my clients in conversation. For some of them, their biggest turn-on was not only when I asked their opinion, but also heard them out and didn't shut them down. But for all my bits of acquired trivia and factoids, I wasn't proficient in any subject other than art and art history. When Christian and I had started our business, a career in either seemed nonexistent. I didn't have enough talent to make it on the creative end, and I didn't have the connections to make it on the business end. That left either art teacher in a public school (the first jobs to get cut, not to mention the idea of working with kids was about as appealing as working with power tools), or museum docent, which was a voluntary position only.

Even though I passed woodshop and automechanics in high school, I wasn't cut out for manual labor, much to my father's chagrin. Plus I loathed it. I had worked my way through high school and college in various "people positions," namely retail sales or as waitstaff. Every supervisor had advised me to pursue a career in sales, said I could sell a Macintosh to Bill Gates. Likewise, my academic advisors suggested I attain a Masters in Business Administration, try my hand in marketing or advertising.

I didn't want it. I didn't know what I wanted. The thing I truly loved and was passionate about—art—seemingly didn't want me. Plus I'd had enough of my father telling me art was for fags. And I wanted to make money, regardless of which career I chose. Not just enough to get by, but enough left over to play with. I wanted to go through life worry-free. I wanted to live a life of pleasure. Of beauty. I wanted to be the embodiment of the Italian aesthetic.

So that left sex. And dating. Both turned out to be a rather practical and profitable use of my skills. Just nothing I could put on a résumé. I was definitely good at both, and both sure as hell were pleasurable. From the time I was old enough to date, I approached it like a pastime or a hobby, like hiking or intramural soccer. My high school voted me Best Looking. My yearbook listed me as Most Likely to be a Centerfold. One of my guidance counselors had even asked me if I'd ever considered modeling. I hadn't. I knew I was good-looking, but I'd had no interest in being paraded down runways or posed for photoshoots. It took at least a year as an escort to get used to being ogled and watch women undress me with their eyes. A small price to pay in comparison the microscope women were put under on a daily basis.

Maybe being an escort really was the only career I was suited for. Sales and sociability. Conversation and copulation.

Andi's compliment went deeper, however. She was validating me as a good *thinker*. I could be a teacher. I could convey information. I could express myself. I could be someone who related to others by means of language, either written or spoken.

I could be more than a good thinker or teacher. I could be a good *person*.

Early the following morning, I took the train out to Massapequa. My mother had given me a key to the house the last time I visited, and this time I took a cab to and from the train station. I went to work sorting through my parents' financial mess, paying off the credit cards with smaller balances first, and calling to renegotiate the APR percentages. I also cashed out two certificates of deposit from my accounts, took out a loan against the others, and arranged a payment schedule for the back taxes.

My next conversation was with the bank that held the mortgage to the house. I used my increasingly proficient persuasive skills thanks to Andi's lessons in rhetoric—not to mention a little Devin charm—to keep them from foreclosing.

It worked. I bought more time.

My father stayed in the den and watched TV for the duration of my stay. The only thing I discussed with him was a list of everything in the house needing repair or replacement. The list alone was staggering.

That night I met a new client—Karen the Corporate-Something-Slash-Aspiring-Actress—who had just been dumped by her fiancé for another woman. She wanted to make him jealous by showing up with me at the restaurant she knew he'd be at with "the ho." I could never understand how women could be so deprecating to other women, even in the midst of betrayal. And yet, I was happy to oblige. I couldn't help but think of Andi and her ex-fiancé, Andrew, remembering her words: *He decided to marry someone else.* Had he dumped her first, and then met the new woman, or had he left Andi for her? Judging by the way she'd reacted, I assumed it was the latter. If only she'd had someone like me to make him eat his heart out. And really, what kind of idget would dump Andi in the first place? How could any man not see her for the intelligent, funny, beautiful, sexy woman she was? How could they not be moved by her insecurity and love her through her pain?

I was Devin to the max on this date—self-confident and

charming and flirtatious. The dumper did look like a bit of a tool, which, in turn, also made me wonder why women were attracted to such men in the first place and shed even one tear upon rejection, when they should be glad to get rid of them. Which was what I'd wound up telling her before the end of the night.

Turned out I may have gotten a little *too* carried away. A couple of Scotches later, I thought about going over to the table and punching him out. In fact, I got so caught up in the game that Karen and I had already made out once before dessert. And *I* initiated it, having also taken leave of my no-initiating-kisses rule.

The guy looked like he wanted to punch me. Bring it on, man.

When we left the restaurant, Karen and I were both on a high, the evening had gone so well. And neither of us were ready to end the role-playing. Or perhaps we had forgotten we were playing roles at all. Both of us drunk, we strolled down the sidewalk, my hand around her waist, her hand anchoring my back, loudly talking and cackling at her ex's expense. She was about my age, approximately five-foot-nine in heels, with wavy auburn hair that fell to her shoulders. Thin, but firm and muscular. Athletic as opposed to scrawny. She was smart and funny and her cherry lipstick was a red cape waving in front of me every time she broke into a snowy white-toothed smile.

Yeah. I knew what she was thinking. What *we* were thinking.

We entered the lobby of an office building and I pinned her against the wall, kissing her hard as she trapped my leg with her thigh, until a security guard yelled at us to take it back outside.

We exited the building and entered the hot, thick summer air, and I knew I should've put a stop to it right then and there, but I just couldn't bear to go back to my empty apartment. And

I didn't think it was fair to just leave Karen standing there when I was the one who not only initiated things, but also egged them on. I liked her and was sexually attracted to her.

Plus, I needed to get laid. Plain and simple. And it was about time a woman please me for a change. Sometimes the escort needed attention too.

"You know, I have very strict rules about sexual interaction with clients," I said to her, the words coming out slightly slurred. "I'm not a typical escort."

"Well, I've never met a 'typical escort,'" she said with a laugh, and kissed me again, mouths open, tongues co-mingling. "You're my first, so I'll take your word for it." She was wearing Chanel Number Five. If only she knew what Chanel Number Five did to me. I kissed her neck just to get another whiff of it.

"I'm serious," I said, moving down to her clavicle. "I swear I don't usually do this. The contract specifically states…holy god!"

She licked my earlobe.

"Do what?" she teased. "Take your clients to bed?"

"Exactly."

And that was exactly where we went—more specifically, we took a cab to the W Hotel in Times Square, undressed each other, and had pretty damn good sex. She was quite nimble. I was quite inebriated, but managed to sustain my erection long enough to satisfy both of us. Or at least I think I did.

Around one in the morning, I woke up after having dozed off. Karen lay naked, asleep and softly snoring. My head was already pounding.

Holy shit, I shouldn't have done that. It had been at least nine months since I'd crossed the line, having sworn the last time was indeed going to be the last time.

As quietly as possible, I slid out of bed and dressed. But I couldn't just leave her there. I wasn't going to be that asshole.

I tapped her on the shoulder; she flinched and opened her eyes. They focused in the dark and she cooed, "Hey, you." She then took hold of my arm to hoist herself up and felt my jacket sleeve. "You're leaving?"

"The room's paid for," I said. God, that came out awful. "Look, I meant what I said about having strict rules. I got carried away. I wouldn't have done it if I didn't want to, but—"

She put her finger to my lips. "It's OK," she said. "I got carried away too. I don't have any regrets, though. You made me feel incredible. No one has ever put me on a pedestal like that before. And you made me realize that I've got to keep myself there, not rely on some other man to do it. I can't thank you enough for that—it was worth every penny, and more."

"There's no tactful way to say this, but I didn't charge for the sex."

She smiled and gave me a peck on the lips. "I appreciate that."

"And I can't see you anymore. Ever. I hope you understand why, and I hope I didn't mislead you."

"No, I knew this was a one-night-stand. I think we'd both be disappointed if we tried to turn it into something else."

I breathed a sigh of relief. "I wish all women were like you. I mean—" Geezus, what happened to eloquence, and finding the right words?

She laughed, "I know what you mean, sweetie."

I pulled her into a hug. "Thank you."

"Thank *you*, Devin."

"Do you want to stay here, or do you want me to take you home?"

"I'll stay here and pamper myself. I don't live too far away."

I got back to my place sometime after two. I took a shower and went to bed, full of guilt and regret and finally facing what I couldn't come close to admitting all night: it should have been Andi.

Chapter Eleven

Sleep was futile. Despite showering, I could still smell Chanel Number Five on me. Or maybe it was just my guilt.

I was out of bed by eight o'clock. Still a bit hung over, I brewed a pot of coffee and ambled into the living room, staring out the window and ruminating on the possibilities of the day. I called in to S & C. No dates tonight. Thank God. I had been planning to see a gallery exhibit in the afternoon, but didn't feel like going. And yet, moping around and nursing a hangover wasn't my definition of a fun day either.

I knew what I really wanted to do.

Fuck it. Fuck the contract.

I looked through my Blackberry for her contact information. Then I dialed. The fourth ring cut off with a breathy "Hello?" from Andi, and my heart jumped like dog receiving a treat.

I opened my mouth, and for a split second, my mind drew a blank.

Play it cool. Better yet, play it comfortable. "Hey, it's me," I said.

She paused for a beat, and I second-guessed my strategy. "Hi," she said. *Well, she didn't say* Who is this? *That's a good sign.* "What's up?"

"Nothing much," I replied.

Nice to see that even when I was pushing forty years old,

awkward silence made me feel as much like a dumbass as it did when I was twenty.

"Did you have a question about this week's homework assignment?" she asked.

It was the first time I'd called her since scheduling the meeting at Junior's, I realized.

"Oh, uh, no." I paused. *Go for it, man.* The worst she could do was throw the contract back in my face and call me a hypocrite. Which she would be entitled to do. "I was just wondering, are you free this afternoon, like around three?"

I tapped my foot nervously and waited for her to say something.

"Yeah, I guess so. Why?"

Not gonna lie—I pumped my fist and mouthed a *Yes!*

"There's a gallery in Soho that's showing an exhibit of a new local artist. I thought you might like to see it."

"With you?"

That's cute.

"Yes."

Every pause was a cliffhanger.

"Um, sure. OK," she said.

Another fist-pump.

"Why don't we meet at my place," I suggested.

"OK." She sounded wary as opposed to willing.

"See you later," I said.

"OK."

"OK," I said aloud after ending the call. I tossed the phone onto the couch and then paced around the living room like a stir-crazy cat. Twice.

It's not a date replaced the *It's a business arrangement, nothing more* mantra. We're going to be friends, I decided. Sure, we were still in the middle of this business arrangement, and I didn't want to give that up. But seeing her only once a week wasn't going to cut it either. Since we couldn't be lovers, being friends was the only alternative. And maybe that would be the better alternative. Maybe that way we'd get to know each other without the complications of jumping into bed. Maybe it could be a way to find out if she really was the woman I wanted to be with. Maybe she would start seeing me as more than Devin the Escort. Maybe it was a way of *being* more than Devin the Escort.

Despite my regrets about having slept with a client, the sex really had done the trick, so to speak. Even with the hangover and lack of sleep, my body felt more at ease. Rather than do a workout at the gym, I went for a run in the park.

Andi showed up fifteen minutes early wearing a linen pencil skirt and a white cotton shirt, which pleased me. She was getting away from dark colors, which meant that she was beginning to accept her body. Plus, she had nice legs. I opted for my usual jeans and a T-shirt. I felt most like me when I wore jeans and a T-shirt. And not even the high-end designer jeans. Good ol' Levi's, washed and faded and broken in, and a faded maroon T-shirt. Not exactly gallery attire, but I assumed no one would be looking at me.

I couldn't contain my smile, and was warmed solely by the sight of her. Like someone turned on the sun in my apartment.

"You look nice," I said. The corners of her mouth twitched before finally giving way to a grin.

"Why do you do that?" I asked.

"Do what?"

"Force yourself not to smile when someone pays you a compliment."

"I wasn't doing that. I was just... I don't know what I was—do I do that a lot?"

Her flustered reaction delighted me even more. "You've got a great smile, Andi. Don't hide it."

She did it again, and I laughed, which prompted her to follow my lead, her emerald eyes twinkling.

It's not a date, it's not a date, it's not a date. We're just going to be friends.

I wanted to lick my friend's entire body like an ice cream cone.

I filled Andi in on the exhibit and the artist en route to the gallery. "You really know this stuff, huh," she said. I shrugged it off. "Why don't you pursue it? It's not too late, you know."

Oh, please. Not now. Not already. The wishful thinking. The if-you-weren't-an-escort-then-maybe-I-could-have-you-to-myself. Just a few short weeks ago I would've discouraged such false hopes for entirely different reasons. But I couldn't deal with it, especially not with what had happened the night before.

Before I could respond to her, she quickly added, "How old are you, anyway? If you don't mind my asking."

I cocked an eyebrow. About time she asked. "Thirty-eight. And nah, I already have a job. Besides, being in the art business is a lot more pressure than people realize. It's also extremely hard to get into, like music or acting."

"I'm sure with your contacts and networking abilities, you'd have no problem."

Nip it in the bud, man. "But I like being an escort." I don't know what felt worse—lying to her, or the reality that the statement was no longer the truth.

Once at the gallery, we viewed the exhibit rather quickly—the place was small, as was the showing. And I wasn't impressed with the silkscreens. Just being there with Andi, standing side by side while I explained how silkscreens are made, was far more valuable than the art.

When we exited the gallery, I stopped and turned to her. "Want to get something to eat?"

Her face contorted into that of someone who just got a whiff of an oppressive odor. Air seemed fine to me.

"OK," she said. Again with the wary.

We walked down the street and around the corner to a restaurant, about the same size space as the gallery, yet packed with patrons.

"So what did you think of the exhibit?" I asked Andi after we were seated.

She paused, as if deliberating what to say. "It was good."

She didn't sound convinced. "Just good?" I prodded.

"I mean, I obviously don't have the eye that you have," she said.

"You don't need one to enjoy it."

"Well, I did—enjoyed it, I mean. What did you think of it?"

"I think it shows promise. The silkscreen paintings looked a little muddy to me; other than that, though..." I trailed off.

"What do you mean by 'muddy'?" she asked, sounding like a student. Yes, a teacher moment!

"I like when silkscreened colors are vibrant. These just looked messy. The colors were..." —I paused to come up with the right word and drew a blank—"...I don't know, muddy. Like a kid mixing all his finger paints together, or dipping your Easter Eggs into every single dye."

She laughed, and the sound took me outside of myself, as if I was standing off to the side and watching the two of us together, observing and evaluating us. Did we look like a couple, or just friends? Certainly we weren't the pair who had sat at a booth in Junior's over one month ago, although at this moment it felt like another lifetime. We weren't dancing around each other, circling the wagons, wary of one another. We weren't behaving like two people in the midst of a business arrangement either. But we were still withholding from each other. And I didn't want that to be the case.

"I like your laugh, Andi," I said.

At that moment the server came to take our orders.

"Spaghetti and meatballs," said Andi. Something about her choice, and the way she ordered it, was perfectly appropriate for her.

"Primavera and roasted vegetables with a glass of Bera Dolcetto d'Alba for me, and a ginger ale in a wine glass for the professor," I said with a wink as I gestured towards Andi. The server politely acknowledged her with a smile before extracting our menus and taking them with her.

"Sorry, I didn't want to call you *lady*, and *her* just sounded rude."

She nodded in gratitude. "Word choice," she said. "It makes all the difference in the world."

"I've been really conscious of that lately," I said, hoping that would spark a conversation about writing; I loved watching her face light up when she discussed things about which she was so passionate.

"So, have you been to Long Island lately?" she asked.

Whoa—what? Definitely not what I was expecting to come out of her mouth. Like getting hit in the head with a pitch.

Two options flashed before me in one second:

Tell her. Tell her everything.

Change the subject. You're having a good time.

And then, a third option: *lie.*

I shook my head. "Not in a few weeks. I used to have a client in Manhasset, but she stopped calling. I think she finally met someone and started dating him." Well, at least that part was true. "The only other occasion I have is to see family, and I'm not much of a family guy." Also true.

"They know what you do for a living?"

I nodded in exaggeration. "Oh yeah."

"And they disapprove," she said, completing the thought.

"Yes." The server returned with our drinks and I downed almost half of mine in one gulp. Before I could dig myself into a deeper hole, I regained control of the conversation. Besides, I genuinely wanted to know more about *her.* "Tell me about your family, and growing up on the Island. Did you like it? You came back, obviously, so you must have."

"Yeah, I liked it, I guess. I didn't have anything else to compare it to until I left. I've always loved being near the ocean—not on it, mind you, but near it. On it makes me a little seasick."

I took mental notes. "What about *in* it?"

"Depends on how strong the undertow is. I almost got carried away by it when I was a kid. Thankfully, my older brother was close enough to pull me to safety."

"You really look up to your brothers, don't you."

She nodded. "They've always looked out for me. Even before my father died. They used to read to me and let me tag along with them and their girlfriends to Jones Beach, and they even used to let me help them record. We had a studio in our basement, and I used to come down and just listen to them for hours. I used to do things like adjust the microphone stands if I could reach them, or I used to press the Record, Stop, and Play buttons on the tape machine, that sort of thing."

I imagined Andi as a kid, gleaming emerald eyes, standing on her toes, eager to help.

"How come you never took up an instrument yourself?" I asked.

An expression of self-doubt clouded her smile. "I tried to play the drums when I was a kid. And they both tried to teach me guitar, of course. But I didn't have the patience to learn. They had all the talent. Not that I'm tone deaf or anything like that. I probably listen to music the way you look at a piece of art. I hear more than just the song; I hear all the little nuances of the composition."

"Well phrased," I said.

"I suppose I look at writing the same way. Writing was always my thing, from day one. And teaching, I guess. My brothers are lousy teachers," she joked.

"You're a very good teacher," I said, looking at her intently.

"So are you," she said. Her compliment tasted better than the wine did.

"What do you write?" I asked.

"Mostly memoirs, personal essays. The kinds of things I'm having you read and write," she replied.

"I'd love to read it some day."

"*My* stuff?" she asked, incredulous. *Again* with the self-doubt? Didn't she ever get tired from all that self-doubt? Didn't it suck the life force out of her? I could feel it drain from me every time she started in.

"Sure, why not?" I said.

"It's been a while since I showed it to anyone," she said.

"I'll bet it's good," I challenged.

"Maybe," she said. "Maybe you'll think it's muddy."

I guffawed. Well played. Like something a friend would say.

Our food arrived.

"So tell me something about *your* family and *your* experience of the Island," she said, picking up her spoon and twirling her spaghetti against it with her fork. "Do you have any siblings?"

"Two sisters," I said before taking in a forkful of pasta. Perhaps I was stalling, although the food was damn good. I finished chewing and continued, "I'm the middle child. They both still live on the Island. One's a soccer mom and the other is an administrative assistant for some company. I wouldn't call us a close family. My dad..."—I could feel my appetite fleeing the scene—"...my dad doesn't think too much of me."

Her eyes reflected sad recognition. "I'm sorry to hear that," she said. "If it makes you feel any better, I don't think my mom thinks too much of me."

I was even more saddened to hear this. "Then let's not waste a good meal on them." I held up my wine glass and waited for Andi to do the same. She followed suit. "Cheers," I said.

"To beautiful things," she said, locking her gaze with mine. The perfect toast from the perfect source.

"Hear, hear."

We clinked glasses and drank. If I could have, I would have bottled the moment.

"As for life on the Island, well, I was your average kid who biked everywhere with his buddies and got suspended for smoking in the boys' room once and bought records at Record World."

"And looked at art books and went to museums. Yep. Average kid."

"And you buried your nose in every other kind of book, I'll bet," I lobbed back, enjoying the volley.

"More or less. I went through phases."

"Please tell me you didn't have Boy George posters when you were a teenager."

"Simon LeBon," she replied.

I approved. "He was cool."

"And you?" she asked.

"Charlie's Angels."

She rolled her eyeballs around. I loved it.

"No Janet Jackson or Debbie Gibson?"

"Debbie Gibson was way too young for me," I said. "Janet wasn't my kind of music."

Next thing I knew, we were talking musical tastes and comparing our high schools and living in Manhattan as opposed to living on Long Island. As if all time and life ceased except our own, giving us the gift of viewing an exhibit of our hearts and minds, our memories; to explore each other beyond our bodies.

Although how I ached to go back to my place and explore each other's bodies.

It's not a date. We're going to be friends.

I took hold of the check the moment the server placed it on the table. Andi protested.

"Don't worry about it," I said.

"But, Devin…"

Goddammit, don't call me Devin.

"It's my treat," I said, with more bite to the words than I'd intended.

"Thanks," she said, her sincerity questionable.

Dusk had set in by the time we exited the restaurant and stepped outside.

"Want to catch a movie or something?" I wasn't ready to say goodbye to her.

She looked at me utterly perplexed, and that's when I realized my behavior was contradicting every rule I'd so strictly enforced prior to today. I should've just come out and told her right then and there: *Screw the contract. Let's be friends, because I like you, and I like hanging out with you.* Why couldn't I? Why couldn't I bring myself to come clean, to stop being a damn escort?

Because if I stopped being Devin, I'd be nobody.

No, the best thing to do was just carry on. If she brought up the contract, then OK, we'd deal with it. Otherwise, this was the only way for me to simultaneously get close to her and keep my distance.

Although didn't I recently yell at my father for ignoring things with the hope that they'd go away?

God forbid I was anything like my father.

Andi didn't say a word about the contract. However, she rejected my invitation. "It's getting kind of late. I really ought to get back to the Island. I have work to do tomorrow."

"You can always stay at my place—on the couch, I mean," I offered. *Wow. That was a massively dumbass thing to say.*

I was never so grateful to see someone look at me like I was nuts.

"Thanks anyway," she said. "This was nice. I haven't hung out in the city like this in a long time."

I rode the subway with her to Penn Station, and even offered to ride the LIRR with her in order to make sure she got home safely. *Get a grip before she gets a restraining order on you.*

"I'm fine," she said. "Really, thanks."

We stood facing each other on the platform in front of the train doors, impatient passengers impatiently scurrying around us, bumping shoulders.

"OK, Andi. See you," I said.

Well, fuck. Now what?

Kiss? *No.* Hug? *You'll never let go.* Handshake? *Are you fucking kidding me?*

Out of options, I could do nothing but wave and step back as she boarded the train. I lost sight of her as the doors closed, and I walked away, back to the subway.

Chapter Twelve

Week Five of the Arrangement

The next day I did a one-eighty. Being friends with Andi was a bad idea. It was leading her on. I didn't call her, and I was booked all weekend with clients—some corporate brunch thing, a wedding reception, somebody's nephew's bar mitzvah, and an oh-my-god-I-just-want-those-bitches-to-eat-their-hearts-out high school reunion. Meanwhile, I had been thinking about what to do for Andi's next tutorial, however, and kept drawing a blank. The lessons were was meant to escalate, to take her out of her comfort zone in order to make her more comfortable in the end, to remove every last line of defense. At some point that would mean escalating physical contact. I've allowed it with my clients, like Allison the Textbook Rep, and some of the other regulars. In fact, I had intended it with Andi all along. But could I really go through with it? Had the rules of intimacy changed on us because I changed the rules when I invited her to that exhibit? By becoming more intimate with her outside the bedroom, would I have to avoid all intimacy in it?

The morning of our fifth meeting, while in the shower, an idea came to me. It would definitely take Andi out of her comfort zone. It would also put me in a precarious situation. I had to ask myself, for whom was I really doing this?

I opted to go ahead with the idea. I called Kate and asked her not to schedule anything for me tonight. Then I called Andi. "Any chance we can move our meeting time to later tonight? Say, seven thirty?"

"What, no client?" she asked.

"I canceled."

"Why?"

"I thought I'd show you the finer pleasures of a bathtub date."

She paused for a beat before responding. "You're kidding me."

I smiled. "Dead serious."

"And you can't do this at two in the afternoon?" she asked.

"It's not the same when it's so bright outside. You need the proper atmosphere—candles and that sort of thing."

She agreed to switch the time, and I hung up the phone, feeling equal parts pleased and worried. Seconds later, Christian called.

"What the fuck is going on, man?"

I held the phone out and made a face at it, as if Christian could actually see me. "What's up your ass?" I said.

"First you're canceling clients left and right, then you tell me to double your client load, now you're asking Kate to clear your schedule tonight. Make up your mind, will you?"

"Relax. Nothing's changed. I'm just seeing Andi tonight, that's all. Part of the arrangement."

"Is she paying you?"

I huffed. "Did you hear me? I said it's part of the arrangement."

"I swear to God, I don't get this. What's in it for you?"

"An enlightened mind. And a chance to—" I stopped short. No. Christian would never let me hear the end of it if I said *a chance to heal someone.*

"A chance to what? Are you banging this woman under the table or something?"

Never have I ever wanted to beat the shit out of anyone as much as I wanted to beat the shit out of Christian at that moment.

"You can go fuck yourself, man," I said.

Christian gasped. "You *like* her!"

My cheeks turned hot.

"Holy shit, it finally happened!" said Christian. "What took you so long?"

I fumed. "Christian. It's a business arrangement, nothing more. She's a friend."

"You just said two totally contradictory things."

"Look, this is *my* business, OK? Andi is *my* client, and I'm telling you to back off."

"I'm just looking out for you, that's all. Look, seriously, man—are you OK? You seem to have a lot of shit going on right now. I'm worried about you as a friend."

I wearily rubbed my eyes. "I'm fine, man. I appreciate it, thanks."

Sometimes I wonder if Christian and I tottered on the same line as Andi and me—that one between business and social. We had begun as buddies—I can't even remember exactly how and when we met—someone's party, I think—and our partnership was always so effective because we got along so well and shared the same vision. But somewhere along the way Christian and I had stopped talking hanging out together, and stopped talking about the bigger picture. And I'd lost touch with most of my other friends since my schedule took up most of my nights, to say nothing of those who dropped me after finding out I was an escort. I assumed the guys were intimidated by me, if not outright jealous. Not only that, but by now they all were married with families and houses and domestic responsibilities. Mowing lawns and Little League coaching and fixing sump pumps on the weekend. They had lives I'd never wanted.

I had no friends, I'd just realized. City of eight million people, and I was a lone castaway on its island.

For some reason I had expected Andi to show up wearing something sexy, like a cocktail dress. Instead she appeared in jeans, a light blue tank top, and flip-flops. Her naturally wavy hair, growing longer every day, was pulled back in a headband. Then again, I hadn't dressed up for the occasion either, sporting my usual jeans and a U2 tour shirt, thus I don't know why I was expecting her to.

We started with the writing tutorial first. Andi had assigned me to read Plato's *Phaedrus*—a text so tedious it would've made a better form of execution than the hemlock. These were some of the classical texts and some of the earliest forms of argument and rhetoric, Andi explained. Furthermore, she explained *Phaedrus* to me as Plato's slam against the sophists and a philosophical foray into provisional vs. absolute truth. She lost me.

"The sophists were the talk show hosts, televangelists, and motivational speakers of their time," she explained. "The *Stephen Colberts*. Orators for hire—have quill, will travel. And they were regaled as rock stars with their grandiloquent ability to move the masses and make them swoon."

"Sounds like a good gig," I said.

"Plato didn't think so. He's saying that sophistry is nothing more than 'cookery,' a bunch of bells and whistles, and that rhetoric isn't so much a pursuit of truth as it is a means of persuasion."

"So, when you called me 'a modern-day sophist' that day, you weren't paying me a compliment?"

She opened her mouth, as if to say something, then closed it again. I winked. *See? I remember things.*

"But here's the cool thing," she pressed on. "If you really study the text, Plato is *teaching*, and he uses metaphor and tropes used in rhetoric to do so."

She was animated, clearly geeked out by this stuff, prompting me to tease her a little. "So?"

"*So?* Do you realize that this is the stuff that I'm still teaching to this day? Metaphor? Rhetoric as a means of communication and persuasion? Plato paved the way for guys like Aristotle who systematized the whole thing, modes of discourse and all."

Never let anyone tell you readers aren't sexy.

"And truth?" I asked.

"What about truth?" she countered.

"Is rhetoric a means to truth or not?"

"Plato didn't think so. He thought sophistic rhetoric actually got in the way of the search for absolute truth, which sort of contradicts what I teach today. I say language is a way to make meaning, to express truth in many forms. Plato sought to use rhetoric analytically and dialectically. Read the text again and you'll see it—look at the dialectic between Socrates and Phaedrus."

Read it again? I'd rather eat the paper on which it was printed.

"I'll pass," I said.

"It's an acquired taste," she replied, as if she'd heard my mental metaphor.

We moved on to her next lesson: describe the Warhol painting without using any words typically found in an art review—kind of like *Taboo* for art critics. After that, I had to write an impromptu speech—I even created a metaphor inspired by the Platonic "cookery," which impressed Andi. (Ha!)

When we finished, I left Andi in the living room to make the final preparations for the bath, having done most of it before her arrival.

"Ready," I called.

She tentatively stood at the doorway before entering. The bathroom glowed with lit votives I'd strategically placed around the jet-stream tub brimming with suds. Earlier I'd set white spa towels at the tub's edge. I clicked the stereo remote, and soft jazz music completed the ambiance.

"Wow," she said in a breathy voice.

Perfect.

"You like?" I asked, seeking extra validation.

She nodded like a woman entering Tiffany's for the first time. "Heaven."

I smiled with pride and satisfaction. "Well, get in."

She looked at me doubtfully. "Am I supposed to get naked?"

"It would kill the mood to wear your clothes, don't you think?"

"Do I have other options?"

"Did you bring a swimsuit?" I had been deliberately vague on my instructions this morning, curious to see what she would do.

Her face flushed. "No."

"Then no, you have no other options. If you were so concerned, why didn't you bring a swimsuit? It's not like you didn't know what was coming." I hoped she knew I was challenging her as opposed to scolding or shaming her.

"You didn't tell me to," she said. I thought about pushing

the envelope, confronting her on why she didn't ask for clearer instructions, but decided against it, thinking it was too far off tangent.

"That's because a swimsuit defeats the purpose," I said instead.

"Well geez, this tub is about the size of a pool."

I laughed and looked at it before turning back to her. "So, are you getting in or are you waiting for an engraved invitation?"

She looked like she was deliberating on whether to go through with it.

"OK. Don't look," she finally said.

I left the room and filled two Mikasa flutes—one with iced ginger ale, the other with champagne—and waited until she called me back in. I re-entered to find her submerged in the bath, leaning back comfortably against a terrycloth pillow, the suds up to her neck, her clothes—underwear included—loosely folded in a pile at the base of the tub. God, the vision of her in the votive glow was resplendent.

I set the glasses down on the corner of the tub. "How's the water?" I asked, my voice mellow and sonorous to match the mood.

"Divine," she said in a sigh. I kneeled next to her at the edge of the tub, and she closed her eyes, letting every care dissolve in the suds. I ached to kiss her.

"So, what do you want?" I asked softly, in Devin the Escort voice. "Want me to sponge your back, shampoo your hair, rub your feet…what?"

"You really do this with your clients?" she said, her eyes still closed. She must have recognized the routine.

"If that's what they ask for, yes."

"What else do they ask for?"

"To bathe other body parts."

She opened her eyes, sat up slightly, and the tension that had wafted away somehow zapped back inside her. I remained undeterred by it as I dipped my hand into the water, nonchalantly swishing it back and forth.

"Aw, Andi, you were beginning to let go—I could see it on your face. Now you're all tense again. How come?"

"In my house, we didn't talk about 'body parts.' GTO parts, yes. Guitar parts, absolutely. Not body parts."

Her family was starting to piss me off. I muttered, "Good God, it's a wonder you were even conceived. Where were your parents when Vatican Two came out?"

She seemed to genuinely contemplate this in order to provide a reasonable answer, but came up blank. "I don't know."

"It's just a body, after all," I said.

"A body is one thing," she said. "Body parts are completely different, though. Just saying the words 'body parts' makes you want to take a shower. At least in my family, it does."

"That's ridiculous. Why is a *body* sterile and scientific, or a work of art, but *body parts* are shameful and taboo? It makes no sense. How are body parts any less natural or aesthetic than the whole body?"

"A body is more than the sum of its gross parts?"

"I'm not kidding, Andi."

"Neither am I, Dev."

Dev?

In all the years I've been at this, no woman ever used a nickname to address me. *Dev.* It was endearing. Cozy. Intimate, even. I liked it.

Andi rolled on. "There are some body parts that I wouldn't

exactly want to photograph and frame. Take the nose, for example. An ugly protrusion with holes and hair in it. Eww. Did you ever meet anyone who said, 'Whoa, check out the nose on that girl!' Then there's..."

That's it.

I ignored her rambling as I stood up, stripped down to my boxers, and stepped into the opposite end of the tub. Andi's eyes widened to the size of apples when I sat, spreading my legs out with my knees poking out above the water.

"Relax," I said. "There's plenty of room for both of us, and I'm not going to look at or touch any part of you that you don't want me to see or touch. But for the record, I've seen and touched enough naked bodies to know—"

"—to know that all bodies are beautiful. Yeah, you used that line on me before."

I felt like snarling. "It's not a line," I said, putting Mean Andi in her place. "And I was going to say, to know how to make a woman forget her self-consciousness."

She looked at me as if to say, *Good luck, buddy.*

"Tell you what. We'll just talk—about anything you want. Music, the weather...you see the game last night?"

She started rattling off stats from the Yankees game, and in no time at all we were engaged in such casual conversation you'd think we were in a coffee shop rather than a candlelit bathtub. Next thing I knew, Andi went from trying to avoid physical contact with me to grazing her foot along my calf (and holy god, did *that* feel good), to turning around and allowing me to soak her neck and bare back with a lavender-scented puffy sponge. I ran it along her arms and shoulders while she regaled me with her opinions about the Brooklyn U writing curriculum, the practice of grading and why it should end, and why she loved working with her friend Maggie.

Who knew I could get so aroused over phrases like "current traditionalism" and "modes of discourse"?

This was how life should be. Sitting with someone who makes you forget where you are, and who you're trying to be.

It's a business arrangement, nothing more. Goddammit.

When our skin had shriveled and the suds reduced by more than half, I reached for one of the towels, stood up, and spread it wide open to hide my blaring erection.

"Here," I said. I closed my eyes and waited for her. "Say when."

She moved into the towel and I wrapped it around her, practically hugging her with it. She smelled like lavender and vanilla, and I fiercely envied the towel for getting so intimately acquainted with her body.

"My God, this feels good," she said. "Did you use the whole bottle of fabric softener?"

"That's cute," I said impatiently. "Can I open my eyes now?"

"Oh, yeah. Sorry. Thanks."

"You're welcome." I quickly stepped out of the tub and wrapped a towel around my waist before Andi could see anything. You'd think it would be something I wanted her to see—chalk it up to a teachable moment. But I just couldn't bring myself to cross that line. Fuck, who was I kidding? Look behind me and the line was back there, left in the dust.

I did my best to maintain a professional stance. "So? What did you think?"

"I think we should start doing *this* once a week from now on."

Fine by me.

I grinned. With that, she became my student again. I liked the notion of her as my student just as much as I did as my friend, if the first option as my lover wasn't on the table. "You did great. You relaxed and got comfortable with me. I'm proud of you."

She was glowing, completely blissed out. Yet she was also inquisitive.

"Why did you get into the tub with me?" she asked. "You said you don't usually do that."

"The situation warranted it—you needed the presence of a man's body, and to see that there's nothing sinful about it."

It wasn't a lie, I'd realized—in the spur of the moment, that's exactly what I'd been thinking when I undressed. Or was I just using this whole arrangement as an excuse to be close to her? Had I used it all along? That day at the National Arts Club, I knew Andi wasn't client material. Knew it right on the spot. Even at Junior's. I wanted to keep seeing her. Correction: I wanted her in my life. That was as far as I could bring myself to admit. That the arrangement had been so mutually beneficial in other ways was a bonus, wasn't it?

I could no longer trust my motives. Perhaps I'd been misconstruing the facts for the last ten years too. Perhaps all my justifications for being an escort were nothing more than thinly masked rationalizations.

"If that's the case, then why didn't you get completely naked?" she asked.

"I didn't want to overwhelm you. I mean…" *I didn't want to risk getting a boner.* I looked away and chuckled nervously. I don't recall ever blushing like a gawky teenager in front of a woman. Perhaps it was the rhetorical blunder of my word choice in front of my writing teacher.

"You're that good, huh," she said, in a mock flirtatious way.

I loved that we could be so casual in such a moment, especially since we'd been so incredibly intimate. And yet, it was the casualness—talking about baseball and basic writing—that made the intimacy so incredible.

I moved in close to her, pulling her towel tighter, encasing her in its safety like a cocoon.

"I think we're done for the day," I said softly, unable to take my eyes off her.

Kiss her. Kiss her, make love to her, and tell her everything. Right now.

She nodded, transfixed. "OK." She sounded spaced out. "What time is it?"

"A little after ten," I replied.

"Mmmmmmmm."

Kiss her, dammit.

"It's getting late," I said, trying to snap myself out of it as well.

"Yeah," she mumbled.

KISS HER! Drop the damn towels and have at it.

"Want to stay over?" I heard myself say.

"OK."

OK…

Wait—did she just say "OK"?

I'd expected her to rebuff me, to shut down or become defensive or give me an excuse. But she was too blissed out, I realized. Or maybe she was just as horny as I was.

I panicked. *What was I thinking?* I can't do this. I can't tell her I've been lying to her about who I really am, that I've been back to Long Island twice to get my parents out of debt, that the father I've spent most of my life hating is dying from cancer, and I have no idea how to feel about that. I can't tell her that I love her—my

God, it just hit me: *I have fallen completely in love with her*—and I want to spend the rest of my life with her, and then continue to caress the backs of other women with their puffy sponges for the next six months, or however long it takes to insure not only that my mother is financially taken care of for life, but that I am too.

I left the room and came back with a folded black T-shirt. "Here," I said, sounding cold and casual and, frankly, like a total asshole as I tossed it to her; it carelessly bounced off her towel-bound arm and fell to the floor in a silent thump. I followed it with "I'll take the sofa."

It killed me to see the expression on her face—bewilderment, disappointment, *what the fuck...*

"You sure?" she asked, as if trying to work through her confusion. As if she were thinking, *How did I misread the signs?*

"It's no problem," I said.

There was no way I could let her leave, but there was also no way I could go back on what I'd set in motion.

Andi dried off and swapped the towel for the T-shirt while I changed the linens on my bed. She then came into the room—the lights were out—and crept under the covers. I was about to close the door when I heard her call, "Devin?"

"Yes?"

"Why did you ask me to stay over?"

Crawl into bed with her, you moron. Kiss her neck and stroke her hair and tell her your name, for starters.

"You were too blissed out to take the train home at this time of night. I didn't want anything to happen to you."

"Oh."

At least she would know I cared. I hoped.

"Good night, Andi. Sleep well."

"Thanks. You too." After a few beats, she called out to me one more time. "Hey, Dev?"

Again with Dev. Maybe that's who I could be.

"Yes?" I said.

"Thank you for this. For canceling your client tonight, I mean. That must have cost you some money."

"Good night," I repeated.

Every part of my body, right down to the cellular level ached with the choking reins of muzzled desire.

Chapter Thirteen

I awoke around seven o'clock in the morning following a restless night, and not just because I'd relegated myself to the sofa. Tiptoeing across the living room, I peeked in the bedroom and found Andi sound asleep. *I could get used to seeing her in my bed. She belonged there.* Her clothes sat in a heap on the bathroom floor, right where she'd left them last night. I folded and set them on the chair beside the bed, went back to the bathroom, showered and dressed, set out everything she'd need—toothbrush, a travel-kit of soap and shampoo and deodorant, more towels—and went out to get something for us to eat for breakfast. I considered leaving a note for her, but figured I'd be back before she woke up.

Breakfast with Andi. I couldn't think of a better way to start a summer morning.

I entered my apartment juggling two tall coffee cups and a brown paper bag full of bagels and found Andi fully dressed, her purse over her shoulder as if she were heading for the door. She stopped in her tracks when she saw me. She was going to leave without saying goodbye? Had she thought I'd abandoned her? *I knew I should've left her a note...*

"Hey," I said, wondering how long she'd been awake. "You're leaving? I got bagels for us."

"Did you have a layover in Cleveland or something?"

She didn't sound like she was joking, but I laughed anyway. "There's a great place six blocks up with a line out the door. It's worth the wait, though, you'll see." I plopped the bag on the kitchen island and the cups more slowly. "I got you a chai latte and a half-dozen bagels—plain, pumpernickel, multigrain, an everything for me…"

She stood there, deadpan, motionless. What was wrong with her?

"You sleep OK?" I asked, trying to get her to talk, to *stay…*

"Yeah, it was fine." Finally, an answer.

"Good."

"How about you?" she asked.

"Fine," I replied, trying to smile past the tension that had wafted in with the bagels. I removed two plates from a shelf above the sink and put them on the island, then held the bag open, in her direction, inviting her to select one.

"Um, I have to go."

My heart sunk to my feet. "How come? There's no rush. I don't have to work until tonight."

Why, why, why *did you bring up work, you idiot?*

"I've got an orientation planning meeting that I'm going to be late for if I don't get a move-on," she said. She sucked at lying. "I still have to shower and change."

"You can shower here, you know. I left everything out for you."

"I saw that. Thanks, but I still need to change and get my briefcase."

"You don't even have time to sit and eat?" I asked, hearing the desperation in my voice.

She shook her head.

I looked down at the empty plate and knew how it felt.

"I guess I shouldn't have let you sleep late," I said, unable to conceal my hurt. "Well, at least take a bagel with you for the road."

"Thanks," she said, opting for a plain bagel and half of the pile of napkins that I had shoved into the bag.

"Cream cheese? Butter?" I asked. *The remains of my heart, smeared all over?*

"Plain is fine," she said.

This is what women must feel like when guys sleep with them and then run out first thing. It felt immeasurably shitty.

Utterly defeated, I pushed one of the cups toward her. "Don't forget your chai." I had been so proud of myself for remembering she preferred chai to coffee.

"Thanks."

We stood on opposite sides of the island, looking at each other as if trying to read each other's minds.

"Well," she said, "thanks again for last night, and for letting me stay over."

"You're welcome," I said, baffled. Just then I noticed my T-shirt that she'd worn to sleep, all balled up and spilling out of her purse. And for some reason, it pissed me off. *Anything else you want to take with you? The Warhol, perhaps?*

She caught me eyeballing her purse, and her face turned bright pink. "Oh, did you want your shirt back? I was going to wash it for you."

"No need," I said coldly.

She pulled the shirt out as it uncrumpled, and quickly scanned for a place to put it. I held out my hand. "I got it."

She seemed reluctant to hand it over.

"Well," she said, "I'm late."

"OK," I said, fully shut down. "Well, see you."

"Yeah, OK."

I walked her to the door, opened and held it for her. Just as she was about to cross the threshold, bagel and chai in tow, I leaned in and pecked her on the cheek; she seemed just as startled as I was by the gesture.

"See you," I said again, and closed the door behind her. I padded back to the kitchen, saw the bagels, and wanted to fling them out the window like frisbees.

"*Fuck*," I said.

Chapter Fourteen

I took the train to Massapequa and found my father asleep in the chair.

"I wasn't expecting you today," he said when I prodded him awake.

"Yeah, I wasn't expecting to come," I replied. "How are things?"

"Same is usual." He looked me up and down. "You look like shit. Where have you been?"

"Didn't sleep well last night," I said, pivoting my neck back and forth to work out the crick from dosing off on the train.

"Guy came to fix the electrical issue," said Dad.

"Good."

"And the roofers are coming next week." His eyes narrowed to a squint. "How is all of this getting done?"

"Legally," I said.

He chortled. High praise, indeed. "Where's the money coming from?"

"Sold a kidney," I said, deadpan. "Not mine, someone else's."

This time my father laughed outright. I can't remember the last time that happened, if ever.

"You're selling something though, aren't you."

For the first time, his words weren't filled with disgust. They were straightforward, honest. A plain and simple truth. My chest felt tight, and I pressed my lips together, swallowing hard.

"Yes, I am."

We said nothing more. And yet, we had communicated something genuine, and without judgment. For the first time, we *related* to one another.

I didn't do much. Updated the financial records (the surface area of the dining room table was becoming more visible with each visit), washed the dishes in the sink and cleaned off the kitchen counters for my mother, and re-filled the soap dispensers. My father came into the kitchen as I finished.

"Since when did you get so domestic?"

I knew what "domestic" was code for.

"You don't have a choice when you live alone," I said.

"I thought you were making enough to afford a maid."

"I am."

He cocked an eyebrow, as if to say *So?*

I cocked an eyebrow in return, like a monkey engaging in mirror behavior.

"Oh, I got you something," I said, reaching into my laptop case and grabbing hold of the hardcover. I pulled out and dropped Tom Brokaw's *The Greatest Generation* on the table. "Thought you might like this."

My father picked up the book, turned it over, and inspected it.

"Hope you don't mind, it's a used copy. I remember you liking hardcovers."

He didn't say anything.

"Unless you've already read it."

He shook his head.

I shrugged. "Anyway…" and trailed off.

My father placed the book back on the table.

"You leaving?" he asked. I could've sworn I heard disappointment. Man, I really was tired.

I nodded. "Short visit," I said, stifling a yawn.

He looked at the book on the table, and then at me.

"Get some sleep," he said.

"You too," I replied.

I spent the train ride back into the city with Plato and goddamn *Phaedrus*. He wasn't the only one searching for truth.

I called Andi when I returned.

"Just wanted to make sure you got to your meeting on time," I said, playing along with her lie. Maybe I thought she'd cop to it. Then again, maybe I should have given her the benefit of the doubt.

"Oh, yeah. It was fine." She paused for a beat. "I'm really sorry about rushing out the way I did this morning."

Well, that was some consolation. "No problem," I said, trying to be cool about it.

She paused for another beat. "So hey, do you want to come out here tonight to watch the game or a DVD or something?"

Wait—what? First she's all "get away, get away, get away," and now she's all "come here, come here, come here"?

I replied, "Can't. Got a client tonight. How about tomorrow afternoon? We can catch a matinee. Is the Shore Theatre in Huntington Village still around?"

"I think so," she said.

"Great, then let's do that. Geez, I haven't been there in ages," I said, sounding and feeling more optimistic than I'd wanted to.

"Me neither," she said.

"You know, I tried to read that Plato stuff again."

I could almost hear her smile. "And?"

"And I still don't get it."

"Then read it again."

"Can't I just get the Cliff Notes?"

She laughed. "Man, are you out of touch. These days the students use 'Spark Notes,' and they're all online. And I don't think they have them for *Phaedrus.*"

A grin escaped me. She was starting to sound like me when she spoke. Evidence that we were getting to know each other. That we were comfortable.

"Well, they should," I batted back.

We chatted for a few more minutes about getting through most of Shakespeare and Homer in high school thanks to Cliff Notes, and concluded with her agreeing to pick me up at the Hicksville station the next day.

Chapter Fifteen

Why we decided I would take the train to Hicksville rather than Huntington was lost on me; Andi lived closer to Hicksville, but the Huntington station was closer to the theater. Six of one, half a dozen of another, I suppose. At least this way I'd get to spend extra time in the car with her. As the train pulled in, I saw her waiting for me on the platform, and I didn't bother trying to conceal my happiness to see her, as if it had been months rather than days. I walked quickly to her, and caught myself just before I extended my elbow for her to link her arm into—something I've done so often with my clients that it had become habit.

Andi drove us in her five-year-old, blue Corolla to downtown Huntington. With street names like Wall Street, Main Street, and New York Avenue, and crammed with bars, pizza joints, coffee shops, law offices, and apparel boutiques, Andi called it "mini Manhattan." I remembered it as less dense and bustling. Although I used to occasionally go to the bars and dance clubs in Huntington in my late teens and early twenties, I'd never been to the Shore Theatre. I purchased two matinee tickets for us to see *The Bourne Supremacy*. We sat in two aisle seats towards the back. The only other people in the theater included a man by himself about five rows up from us, seated in the middle, and a woman and man behind us, in the last row, under the projector.

"Do you think they're playing hooky from work and are here to fuck each other?" I whispered to Andi in reference to the couple, while a screen sized, computer-animated hot dog asked the audience to please turn off their cellphones.

"Do you think they're actually married to other people?" she whispered back.

"Do you think they're wondering the same thing about us?"

"Not based on where we're sitting, no."

I loved how quick and witty she was, and so easy to talk to, to engage in playful banter.

Problem was, I couldn't shut up. Some kind of nervous energy had taken over. Maybe because once again I was trying to convince myself that this wasn't a date, that I was spending an afternoon with a friend—my only friend. Maybe because I'd last been to the movies with Wanda the Professor from Brooklyn U, and wondered if maybe she told Andi what we'd done afterwards. I chattered incessantly, speculating on plot turns, asking her if she thought the dialogue was any good, trying to get a little *Mystery Science Theater, 3000*-style commentary going. When Matt Damon crept down the corridor of a building, I leaned over and mentioned that it looked like a building in the city that one of my clients owned and made me play hide-and-seek with her in one night, while a voice in my head shouted, *Shut up, shut up, shut up, you fucking moron! Can't you see she's trying to watch the movie?*

From the corner of my eye, I caught Andi shiver and cross her arms tightly.

"You cold?" I asked.

"I can't feel my toes." she replied.

Next thing I knew, I was practically climbing over the armrest in an attempt to put my arms around her in order to warm her up. As I swished my hands up and down, Andi squirmed. "Dev, I can't see."

I stopped and leaned back in my seat. "Sorry," I said. Geezus. Had this been a first date, no doubt she would've been wondering how to ditch me the moment the credits rolled. It was a good possibility that even now, knowing me as well as she did, she was dreading the drive back to the train station. But it wasn't a date. Although if that was the case, then why was I behaving like such a bumbling fool and a blathering idiot?

Maybe I was trying too hard to be myself. I'd forgotten how to be me. Kind of like Cary Grant, whose greatest role was Cary Grant. He sucked at being Archibald Leach.

"I mean, thanks," Andi said, as if taking pity on me.

When the movie ended and the lights came on, Andi stood and stretched, looking around, while I remained seated.

"You like to stay for the credits too?" she asked.

"These people worked hard to get their names on the screen. We owe them that."

"My brother Joey's song got in a movie once."

"Really? What movie?"

"It was an indie film. Kind of a *Sopranos* meets *When Harry Met Sally*…. This man and woman from warring families become friends, yada yada yada. Joey's song was used while the mob father beat the shit out of the guy friend. Ironically, the song is called 'Peace in the Valley.' It's a jazz instrumental."

"That's really cool."

It was obvious how much Andi looked up to her brothers and admired their musical talent. Did she know, however, that people looked up to her as well? That her talents and accomplishments were equally admirable? She had a Ph.D., for chrissakes. She presented papers at academic conferences. She was in the midst of writing a textbook for publication. A *textbook*. Week after week, she introduced me to scholars in her field, and she was one of them. She was an expert in her field.

After the credits finished rolling, we exited the theater and squinted in the sunlight, lingering to let Andi warm up again. We simultaneously put on our sunglasses and looked left and right.

"God, I haven't been here in ages," said Andi. "Well over ten years. Fifteen, at least."

"Me too," I said. "Shall we walk around a little bit? See what's changed?"

"Sure," she replied. We walked across the village, naming which bars and dance clubs we had used fake IDs to get into; Andi pointed out two former dives where her brothers used to have steady gigs, and I wondered if maybe I'd seen them play somewhere during my high school years. Or had our social circles been too far apart, what with them being North Shore guys and me being South Shore? Musicians, however, seemed to know no geographical boundaries.

As we strolled up a side street to the public parking lot, neither of us having spoken in a few minutes, I became mindful of the present moment, and basked in it.

"This is nice," I blurted.

"Nice in what way?" she asked.

I hadn't expected her to ask that. How to answer without saying *Because I'm here with you. What other reason does one need?*

"Just...nice. You're fun to hang out with."

It occurred to me that I probably could've answered the question much better in writing.

"Thanks," she said, sounding indifferent.

"Want to get an early dinner?" I asked.

She didn't hesitate, much to my pleasure. "Sure. We'll go to Francesco's on Route One-ten for some pizza. I haven't been there in ages either."

She drove us there, and we shared half of a pepperoni pie and three garlic knots as well as more stories about growing up during the eighties. I kept forgetting I was four years older than she; most of the time she seemed to be the smarter, wiser, more mature one. Then I fired off questions about Massachusetts:

What's the seafood like?

How do the beaches compare to Long Island?

Which city do you like better, Boston or Manhattan?

Do they really say *paaahhk the caaaahh*?

And so on. As she answered each one, she grew increasingly wistful.

"You OK?" I asked.

"Yeah," she replied.

"You're a million miles away."

She shook her head slowly. "Just over the Braga Bridge."

With the ex-fiancé? I hoped not.

When we finished eating, Andi drove me to the Huntington train station rather than back to Hicksville, much to my disappointment. Given that we were in the thick of rush hour and commuters returning home, Andi pulled over near the cabs and kept the car running rather than park and walk with me to the platform.

I hesitated, reluctant to leave. "Well thanks, Andi."

"Yeah, it was nice," she replied.

Should I ask her what *she* meant by "nice"?

"I had a great time, really," I said.

"Me too."

We both sat there for a minute, helpless, in a game of chicken, the only sound being the Corolla's wheezing air-conditioner.

Kiss her.

I leaned in and pecked her on the cheek.

So the wrong kiss.

"See you next week," I said, and got out of the car, dodging and weaving through the crowd of oncoming commuters. I couldn't even look back at her.

On the train, when the conductor came to collect our tickets, I heard myself ask him if I could get off at Hicksville and change to the Ronkonkoma line. From there I went to Farmingdale, caught a cab, and ended up at my parents' house.

It was time to grow up. Strange that I'd start by wanting to go home.

Chapter Sixteen

I had called my mother from the train to let her know I was on my way. Told her I wanted to go to their bank and set up new accounts, write more checks, and do some minor work around the house. Not exactly a lie, but nothing that couldn't wait until the following week.

While Mom made up my room, Dad sat in the den and watched the Mets. I joined him, a bottle of Bud Light in hand. Ugh. Like drinking fermented water.

"So, Piazza," I said, trying to make conversation. "Best Mets catcher ever?"

My father looked at me as if I'd committed heresy. "Figures you'd pick the pretty boy. Gary Carter would leave Piazza in the dust."

"Of course," I said, thinking it was better to come out of it the fool. "I should have known that."

"Too bad you were too young for the Sixty-nine Mets. Tom Seaver, Nolan Ryan, Jerry Grote... the Miracle Mets."

"Damn straight," I said, and took another swig from the bottle.

We watched as Piazza fouled off, taking the count to two and three, and I could feel my father eyeing me suspiciously.

I turned to him. "What did I do now?"

"What are you doing here?"

"I told you what I'm doing here. I was on the Island visiting a friend, and decided not to go back into the city given that I'd had some things to do."

"You were just here yesterday. And you usually can't get out of here fast enough."

I took a swig of beer. "That's true."

"Who were you with?"

"Say it again?" I said.

"Who were you visiting today?"

"A woman I know."

"How much did you charge her?"

Was this his way of making conversation and trying to relate, or was he deliberately giving me a hard time? I honestly wasn't sure. I decided to treat it as the former rather than the latter, and answered without a hint of annoyance. "No charge. Just a friend."

"I didn't know you had friends."

"Shocking, isn't it."

And sad too.

"Does she know what you do?" asked Dad.

I took another swig of beer and stared straight ahead at the TV. "Yep."

"Must be a good friend."

"Yep."

"Maybe she can talk some sense into you one of these days."

I turned in my chair and faced my father. "Let's cut the bullshit, Dad, shall we?"

My father seemed unprepared for this line, despite his baiting me. "What now?"

"I really, *really* don't want my final words to you to be 'good riddance.' I want to make an effort. You don't like me. I get that. You've never liked me. I was a huge disappointment to you. But I…" I fought to keep from choking up. "I can do more."

"Of course you can do more," said Dad. "You could've always done more. You just never wanted to."

"Well, I want to now, OK? Are you happy? I want out of my job. It's run its course."

My father gave me a look of *ain't that a kick in the head.* "About damn time."

"I can't do it right away…" —my father's look of satisfaction morphed into righteous indignation in an instant, and I could feel myself not only losing my nerve, but feeling like the childish fool he always made me out to be as I finished my sentence—" …but I'm making plans."

"Sure you are," his tone was drenched in sarcastic condescension.

"I am, Dad. I just have to put things in order first."

"Like what?"

"Like, I'm pretty sure my business partner is ready to get out too. We have to find someone to buy us out. Then there's the whole mess, of—" I stopped short of telling him where my money has been going. Better to keep up with the story of my doing "creative accounting" with what they already had.

"And how long is all that going to take?"

"I don't know. A year, maybe."

My father looked at me incredulously.

He chortled. "Sounds like you're really dying to get out. Well, good luck with that."

I fumed. I was ten again, telling him about my signing up for baseball tryouts and him laughing; the next day I stayed home from school. I was seventeen, telling him about my indecisive college plans and him telling me I was wasting my time. I was twenty-two, telling him about a business idea involving mail-order custom T-shirts, way before the Internet and companies like Zazzle, and him calling it "more fag stuff."

Neither of us spoke. The Mets failed to score on bases loaded. I knew the feeling.

When the next inning came to an end, I stood up and spoke. "I want you to be proud of me before you die. That's my wish."

With that, I headed for my bedroom.

"I started reading the book," he called before I was out of earshot.

I stopped in my tracks for a nanosecond, then traipsed up the stairs.

In my room, without turning on the light, I kicked off my shoes, fell onto the bed, and stared at the ceiling, smelling dust and memories. My afternoon with Andi felt like days rather than hours ago. Tears fell, one by one, in silence until I surrendered to sleep.

He probably would've made fun of me for crying too.

Chapter Seventeen

August, Week Six of the Arrangement

Kill me now.

After spending the night in my old bed and waking up with an aching back, I went to work around the house changing washers, lightbulbs, and smoke detector batteries, disposing old paint cans and a broken vacuum cleaner, and shredding thirty-year-old papers. Then I showered and went to the bank and opened two new accounts, transferred money into them, and made a big enough payment on the loan to get the house out of foreclosure danger.

Then I took the train back into the city and had a date with Debra the Anthropology Professor.

I had dates all throughout the weekend: Cookie the Baker (seriously). Pamela the Social Worker. Jennifer the Market Analyst. Allison the Textbook Rep. And another once-more-around-the-park carriage ride with Daphne the Mom.

Then I spent most of Monday finishing my memoir.

Found and Lost

When I was eleven years old, my fifth grade class took a field trip to the Museum of Modern Art in New York City to see a Picasso exhibit. I would've preferred a trip to Shea Stadium during batting practice or Jones Beach for surfing lessons; looking at paintings, however, was not my idea of a good time. Prior to the day of the visit, we'd spent a week in class learning about Picasso, but all I remember getting out of it was that he was some weird Spanish guy who was supposed to be a genius.

Being a kid from the south shore of Long Island, Manhattan didn't impress me the way it might someone from somewhere else in the country, somewhere more idyllic and less crowded. It was always there, after all. In fact, on a very clear day, one could faintly see the very tops of the twin towers from a certain point on the Northern State Parkway. (Of course, you had to be looking for them.)

Although this was my first time going to the MoMA, I had no expectations of being impressed, but rather bored. Almost immediately, those expectations diffused when I entered. The place was a castle of marble— gigantic wall after gigantic wall of paintings, sculptures, drawings, and tapestries awaited my inspection, and I could not possibly take it all in. My preoccupation with the shiny floors (perfect for sliding on with socks, and I must say I was tempted) was replaced by the docent (a term I would soon learn on my own; but to my eleven-year-old incarnation, it stood for boring old guide) who announced that our tour of the exhibit was about to begin. He was a skinny man with white hair, and he explained each painting to us as if we were art scholars here by choice and not kids bummed because Shea Stadium had been ruled out. Many of my classmates, however, were either restless or bored and showed their appreciation by making fun of both the paintings and him, mimicking his mannerisms and voice.

By the time we reached the second room of the exhibit, my classmates had stopped listening to the docent altogether. Along the way, we passed another room that caught and held my attention. I crept away from Steven Marino, my dreaded "buddy" (in title only, assigned to us for the purpose of not getting lost on field trips) and when everyone was distracted by one of Picasso's cubist renditions, I escaped.

Time stood still in this new room. The first painting I saw spanned almost the entire wall. It seemed familiar, like a finger painting from my childhood. But when I moved closer, I could see just about every imaginable color in darting, tiny brushstrokes. It was as if my eyes had become blurry and I could neither make out shape nor image; but I could clearly see the movement of the artist, as if I knew exactly what he was thinking when he painted it. When I stepped back, the colors and brushstrokes dissolved together into the form of water lilies. I circled the room, again and again, leaning in as close as I dared to each painting. I practically walked on tiptoes, afraid I'd disturb them—they looked too alive and I was spying.

I must have been a curious sight: an eleven-year-old boy dressed in Levi's jeans, a Rolling Stones glitter T-shirt, and Adidas sneakers, so fascinated with these pictures on the wall. I didn't care. I was lost in the flurry of brushstrokes, thousands of them, all in one room. Furious and gentle, red and green, all tumbling over each other. All in one room.

The painting of a ballerina, seemingly tucked away in a corner, was the most breathtaking of all. She looked as if she would leap right out of the frame and dance just for me. She was fleeting, delicate, and sensual.

So, this was art. Picasso wasn't just a weird Spanish guy anymore, and these weren't just paintings—they were shapes, forms, and colors. Like the twin towers, you just had to know where to look. They took me to a place way beyond my childhood experience of paper mache and poster paints, to a world as much removed from time as I was from my classmates, until a mother chaperoning our trip found me (Steven must have squealed). She dragged me back to the bunch of school kids still staring at frame after frame of Picasso. I don't know if my teacher was angry at me for breaking away from the group or because I was unremorseful for my escape. I didn't even hear her scolding; instead, I saw her lips move in tiny, darting brushstrokes of red hues. Meanwhile, the docent droned at the children, the children dully eyed the Picassos, the chaperones watched me, and I saw nothing and everything: nothing that looked real, and everything in a world of brushstrokes. I wanted to make these kinds of paintings.

That night, still elated from my discovery, I announced to my parents that I was going to be an artist. I was sure of it.

My father grunted, while my mother looked up from the book she was staring at long enough to say, "That's nice."

I tried again. "Dad," I said persistently, "I'm going to be an artist—a painter."

"The only thing men paint is houses."

"But..."

"If you're so set on being an artist, then the first thing you oughtta paint is a pair of fairy wings for yourself."

It was final. I said nothing and turned away.

My heart broke that day. I found and lost passion in a manner as quick and fleeting as those brushstrokes. I discovered beauty, discovered a way of seeing, and I couldn't change it or make it leave me anymore than I could make my father see the harmony of chaos or the power of a single line. What's more, I saw my father not in shades of glory, but in washed tones of reality. He was not the man I wanted to be. He was everything I wouldn't become. In the coming years, my classes would take more field trips to more museums, but I would never match the elation of escape, or the joy of timelessness that found me in the fifth grade. But I would find solitude, and would never lose it.

It was far from my best work. I thought the writing in my journals and the freewriting were less stilted, more honest. Not to say that what I'd written wasn't the truth. It simply felt too much like someone who was desperately trying to impress his teacher. Someone who believed that if she liked his writing, she'd like *him*.

I didn't come up with any ideas for Andi's lessons and assignments until that morning.

We both seemed to be one-upping each other: She made me practice logical fallacies; I made her practice fellatio on ice pops.

She stretched my cranial muscles with "discourse communities";
I stretched her body's muscles to improve her flexibility and
endurance during sex. (I also told her to look up Kegal—rhymes
with "bagel"—exercises for a different kind of workout). She
assigned me to read Aristotle's *Rhetoric*; I assigned her a viewing
of *The Couple's Guide to Better Sex*.

Additionally, both had something to show for our hard work
these past weeks. Andi's confidence was improving. For one
thing, she could take off her top in front of me as if I wasn't in
the room. (If anyone was resistant, it was me; I didn't want her to
stop there.) She also seemed less embarrassed or ashamed to ask
me about things she didn't know.

I also saw a change in Andi on the outside. She lost weight
and increasingly made smarter wardrobe choices, was more
willing to show off her body without exploiting or flaunting it.

As for me, I was writing in my private journal more than the
assigned one. Plus, I had become more audience-conscious than
ever. Whereas my first few entries had been about my dates, now I
was writing about things I specifically wanted to tell Andi about—
going to museums (and every moment I wasn't at my parents or
with Andi or on a date, I was at a museum), people watching, you
name it. Moreover, I was making more of a conscious effort to
read for pleasure. I bought a copy of *The DaVinci Code* the same
day I bought my father *The Greatest Generation*.

I began calling Andi on a regular basis. What started as one
phone call a week gradually evolved to every day. The time we
spent together outside of our tutorials steadily increased as well.
If I planned to be at my parents' house, then I planned time

with Andi as well. We drove out to the East End and toured the vineyards one day, and hopped the ferries from Greenport to Shelter Island to Sag Harbor on another. I'd forgotten how beautiful the East End was, how it was like taking a vacation from Long Island without ever leaving it. We even went to a couple of baseball games—she was a Yankees fan (well, no one's perfect)—and I found myself wishing my father were with us. Somehow, I sensed my father would like Andi. And even though he'd give her a hard time about being a Yankees fan, she'd give him a hard time right back about being a Mets fan, and both would take it good-naturedly.

I loved being friends with Andi. Her companionship was the bright light in the dimness of my father's terminal illness, a refuge in the deluge of meaningless dates. Pleasuring women had once given me pleasure; now it just seemed to suck the life force from me. Not being sexually involved with Andi had its benefits and frustrations. Even something as simple as sitting on the couch and brushing up against each other felt so normal and familiar; and yet, I had to restrain myself, pull away from her, remain aloof. It would be so easy to seduce her, to have sex with her just to satisfy my own needs and relieve my stress. Not to mention hers as well. But Andi needed more than that. It had become clear to me that for Andi, sex was a major commitment. It was her way of going "all in," so to speak, of giving a man the ultimate gift of her love and trust. I wasn't about to take advantage of that just because our mutual lust was sometimes louder and more demanding.

My excursions to the museums now included Andi. I don't know which I liked better—teaching Andi about sex, or teaching her about art. One day at the Brooklyn Museum of Art during a Monet exhibit, she dreamily blurted out, "I absolutely adore the Impressionists," practically swooning.

I looked at her, incredulous. "You *what*? You *adore* the Impressionists? No. You can't *adore* them. No one *adores* the Impressionists."

"Why not?"

"You just don't. You—no one adores them. It can't be done."

"What are you talking about?" she asked, equal parts inquisitive and irked.

"The Impressionists are *not* 'adorable,' " I ranted. "Things that scamper are adorable. Fluffy bunnies hopping in meadows. Little dogs with knitted sweaters. Those little hats that newborns wear. Baby shoes are adorable. Not Impressionists."

"Wha—?"

"You don't 'adore' men who cut off their ears. You don't 'adore' men who eat lead-based paint. Men who refused to compromise themselves or their work, even when it meant depriving their families of food. Men who kept mistresses. Who died poor and alone and bitter. There's something bigger happening in these paintings, something way beyond adoration."

"Don't you think they're beautiful?" she asked, nudging towards the paintings.

"No, I don't. At least not the way *you* think they are. You see pretty things: lilies and bright colors and swirls. Monet was dark and serious."

She looked at me solemnly, focused, fully attentive.

I continued, "The Impressionists broke all the rules. People weren't supposed to paint like that. But they did what they wanted to do. They poured themselves into the pigment, onto the canvas. It takes great power to paint like that. They're not controlling; they're harnessing."

I took her by the wrist and led her to *Water-Lily Pond and Weeping Willow*, one of Monet's last paintings. "Look at this," I said, and began a deconstruction of color, light, texture, and composition—an artistic "rhetorical situation," if you will. "This is dark and intense—you'll never find *this* on a greeting card."

She stood before it, transfixed, and I could tell she was getting it. Even I succumbed to its marvel and lost myself in it, the way I've been losing myself in the Impressionists for almost twenty years. I wanted to live in those worlds, see with those lenses. A world where fathers didn't hate sons for what they loved, and weren't dying. Where mothers weren't caught in the middle, and sisters weren't apathetic. I wanted to live in that weeping willow with my best friend beside me. Where Devin didn't exist.

Andi only saw the six-pack abs and the coy little winks and the Versace suits. She didn't see the layers of color and texture and shadow, the darkness underneath the beauty. I wouldn't let her, or anyone else.

Devin was the forgery, not the original.

"Calendars with pictures of kittens hanging from trees that say 'hang in there, baby' are 'adorable,' " I muttered.

Andi and I looked at each other and broke into hushed giggling. We then moved to the next painting and stood before it in resumed silence together. One good thing about oil paint— you can scrape it off the canvas and start over again if you don't like what you see.

With Labor Day weekend fast approaching, my dating schedule

was rather hectic. Additionally, my father had a series of doctor's appointments, and I drove him to and from. We spent the time talking about *The Greatest Generation*—or rather, Dad talking about it while I listened, which I surprisingly enjoyed. He spoke about it in a voice that was animated rather than weary, one I don't think he's ever had in my presence, at least not since I was a child; a voice of *connection*. He even took the book with him to the appointments.

"I'd love to read it when you're finished with it," I said, adding after a beat, "I promise I'll give it back."

From the corner of my eye I caught him looking at me, wearing an expression of befuddlement, as if he recognized my face but couldn't place how he knew me. But it wasn't a look of disgust or even sadness.

"Can you get me tickets to the last Mets game of the season at Shea?" he asked.

The question threw me for a loop. "Sure," I said.

"I'd like to take your mother."

"I understand."

When I pulled back into the driveway and killed the engine, Dad opened the car door and, without looking at me, said, "What the hell, get three tickets."

I would've cried right on the spot had I not known he'd change his mind about the extra ticket if I did.

"No problem, Dad."

Because of my schedule, Andi and I had to postpone our final meeting. I had dates almost every night, one of them being drinks at the Heartland Brewery with Della the Adjunct from

Brooklyn U's English Department. One of Andi's colleagues. Della was a new client, referred by Sadie, I think. Or Wanda. I always mixed those two up.

Andi was going to be there. She'd told me so. It was a social thing following a faculty orientation for the new semester. However, I didn't tell her I'd be there as well. Seemed like a good idea at the time.

I saw her immediately: dressed in a floral-print dress, cut low in the back and scoop-necked in the front, accessorized with the espadrilles she'd bought several weeks prior and a clutch purse that matched the color of the print. Her legs—god, her legs! Smooth and lean and muscular. Because of her height, Andi usually had trouble with hems. She must have had this dress tailored, however, because the hem fell perfectly, and even made her look taller.

She was stunning. Even more so than the person I'd seen that day at the National Arts Club.

I almost forgot that I was there not specifically to see her, but because I'd been hired to be there. That I came with someone else. And that someone else was standing right next to me.

Andi was in mid-sentence, smiling as she gestured wildly with her hands ("Italian Power Point," she called it), surrounded by laughing colleagues, when she saw me enter with Della on my arm. I quickly turned my head and pretended not to see her, disgusted with myself for doing so.

Della said hello to a few people, and then headed straight in Andi's direction. I offered to get Della a drink and crossed over to the end of the bar, where Andi was standing.

I couldn't. I couldn't treat her the way I did my other clients. I couldn't pretend like I didn't see her, like I didn't *know* her. I couldn't negate her like that.

How could I have deluded myself for so long? I'd negated *all* of them, every single one I'd ever refused to acknowledge, in the past and at that very moment. I was *still* doing it. I had told my father that I cared about them. But I had stopped caring for them, and I didn't even realize it. And I was ashamed of myself for that.

I approached.

"Hey, Andi," I said.

She looked as if she were about to spit nails.

"Hey," she said, her tone cold.

"What's up?"

"You tell me."

So not the reaction I was expecting. We'd spent hours on the phone and hanging out together, were on the verge of finishing each other's sentences and reading each other's minds, but here I didn't have a clue why she was giving me the cold shoulder. Sure, I didn't tell her I was going to be here, but I *acknowledged* her, for chrissakes. I wasn't playing the game with her.

"I'm working. What are you doing?"

"I'm kicking back after a kick-ass orientation."

I took note of the repetition of the word "kick"—normally I would've teased her, for that was precisely the thing that she liked to snag me on with my writing—but I was afraid she'd throw her ginger ale in my face or something. No, better to suck up a little.

"So, it went well? That's great. I know you worked hard planning it."

My attempts to validate her resulted in her shooting an invisible laser beam from her pupils, aimed right at the center of my forehead. I swore I could actually feel the hole boring straight through, and coming out the back of my skull.

I tried again. "Hey, you free tomorrow? That new Woody Allen movie is out, and I thought you'd want to see it."

One of Andi's friends who'd been with her the day we met—the Naomi Campbell one, Jayce, I think was her name—conspicuously listened to every word. Meanwhile, I caught a glimpse of Della, her face a venomous expression of jealousy as she observed Andi move in close to me.

"Get away from me and don't talk to me for the rest of the night," she said.

"What is wrong with you?" I asked.

"I am with my *colleagues* here!"

"Half of whom are my clients, as you probably already know."

If there was a grand prize for Dumbass-Things-You-Don't-Say-to-the-Woman-You're-in-Love-With, not only would I have won, but I'd hold the record indefinitely.

"Not me—I am *not* going to be subject to this guilt-by-association," said Andi. "Just go back to your client—who has as much knowledge about rhetoric and composition theory as a rhesus monkey, by the way—and tell her how beautiful she is, because I think she needs to hear it."

This. This was exactly why I couldn't be with Andi. Not now. Not while I was still an escort. This was why I hadn't yet slept with her, fought so hard to maintain some semblance of boundaries.

I looked at her, furious, and stung by her rebuke. I thought her wall had come down. I thought her nasty and defensive outbursts were behind us. I thought I'd gotten through. Apparently I was wrong. Apparently the real Andi was nasty and defensive, and no amount of weight-loss or foreplay lessons was going to change that. I was a fucking lousy teacher. I hadn't gotten through to her at all.

Screw her.

"I'll call you tomorrow," I snapped.

I left her, crossed over to the other end of the bar and ordered two drinks. Seconds later Andi whisked past me, with Della shooting her a gloating smirk as she lit a cigarette.

"I don't think you can smoke in here," I said.

Della glued herself to me for the remainder of the night, and I let her, repulsed as I was by her cigarette-riddled breath. Turns out she really was pretty clueless about rhetoric and composition theory. For chrissakes, how could she not have read James Berlin?

At the end of the night, I took Della back to her apartment. She kissed me with her smelly breath.

"Go brush your teeth," I demanded, "or the date ends now."

Never, ever, had I ever treated a client so disrespectfully. She obeyed and returned, wearing a black, faux silk robe.

"I want what Andi gets," she said.

I was going to retch any second. No way Andi would've said anything to her. To anyone.

"Andi doesn't get anything," I said. "In fact, I don't know Andi at all. Perhaps you're confusing her with Allison the Textbook Rep."

She opened her robe and slid it off her shoulders, revealing a black teddy, likely purchased at Target.

"You sure look like you knew each other tonight."

Shit. It just hit me why Andi was so pissed off.

I pulled out the wad of cash Della had given me at the beginning of the date and gave it to her. Then I tacked on an extra one hundred dollar bill.

"Here's your money back, and a little something extra. We're not going to do anything tonight. We're not going to have any business together after this. You're more than welcome to sample one of Strawberries and Champagne's other escorts, on the house. And if you even whisper a hint of speculation about Andrea Cutrone to anyone, I will end your career. Understand?"

So. That didn't go well.

We never should've started hanging out together. We never should've become friends. Damn me for breaking the rules. For being so selfish. For trying to have my cake and eat it too. For blaming Andi when all along I was at fault. I was to blame for all of it.

Chapter Eighteen

I called Andi the next day, just as I'd said I would, certain she wasn't going to pick up the phone. The moment I heard her voice, I breathed a sigh of relief, followed by a moment of sheer panic that she was going to tell me we were done.

"I'm sorry about last night," I said.

"It's OK," she replied. She didn't sound OK. "It was the first time I saw you in mixed company since we started this arrangement. It took me by surprise."

A second wave of relief washed over me. "I shouldn't have approached you. It was completely unprofessional of me. I never acknowledge my clients unless they acknowledge me first."

Silence dominated the telephone space between us, and anxiety pushed its way to the surface again.

"So," I resumed, trying to stuff it back down, "do you want to see that movie? Got three-and-a-half stars in *Newsday*." I read off the movie times I'd jotted down when I'd called the theater prior to calling her.

She's giving up, I just know it. She's going to tell me to forget the movie, forget the final meeting, forget the arrangement, forget we ever met. She's going to tell me she's changing her identity and moving to Canada just to get away from me.

"Sure," she responded.

We finalized plans, and when I hung up the phone, I realized that I'd *wanted* her to tell me to fuck off. It would've simplified everything.

Chapter Nineteen
Final Week of the Arrangement

We divided our meeting into two days—my final writing instruction on our usual Tuesday, and Andi's final the following evening. I compiled and submitted a portfolio containing my memoir (all drafts), a commentary, the literacy narrative I'd written during our first meeting, five journal entries (not from the private one), and a reflective essay, something Andi assigns to all her students, in which I reflected on what I learned about writing throughout the course of our sessions.

> *I learned that my strength in writing is my patience. I let the process guide me rather than trying to force something to happen. And yet, I'm often surprised by what comes out. Oftentimes it takes a couple of drafts for me to uncover what I really want to say. I like being descriptive and using imagery. Language is not unlike art in that words contain values of lights and darks, hues and tonalities, texture and sensuality. Words can paint complex pictures.*
>
> *My weakness would have to be writing persuasively. Again, I think this has to do with taking time to uncover my meaning. By the time I find my claim and get to*

the point, I've distracted the reader with information not necessarily pertinent to the argument itself. I am certain that by studying more examples and with practice, I could improve. I also want to improve my critical reading of a text, much like I can do with a visual.

The pleasant surprise is how much I enjoyed myself and the process. I'm reading a lot more (although, I have to admit, the Greek Classics were not my taste—perhaps I'll try the Romans sometime), and I noticed I'm seeing things differently. That's something I never would've expected. Not only that, but I'm thinking about what I'm seeing. I also recalled a lot of memories—some pleasant, some not so pleasant, that offered a new perspective. I understand context so much more now. Overall, I think I did well, and I'm grateful to have had a teacher who was thoughtful, challenging, and talented.

I hoped she didn't think I was sucking up with that last line.

Andi, in turn, wrote an evaluation letter and delivered it to me the following night.

Devin,

This portfolio demonstrates that you've not only accomplished a variety of writing tasks, but that you are able to adapt your writing voice and style to accommodate your purpose and/or audience. I am particularly impressed by your use of metaphor and description. Your descriptions are detailed, your words energetic, your sentences rhythmic; each of these elements paint a panoramic view of meaning. You also have an excellent command of vocabulary. I like your voice.

I agree with your self-assessment regarding argument; however, you've shown me that you take time to think about your topic, and you have an ability to see multiple sides of an issue. Your journal pieces get better and better—you have a knack for recalling details and a critical eye, no doubt the result of your art training (the account of the Matisse exhibit read much like a review to me). Overall, you've embraced the concept of revision as a process that is constantly unfolding and nonlinear. You've been open to the process, willing to explore, and I derive so much pleasure from seeing the results of that willingness on the page. Indeed, you are a writer.

The last four words made me choke up. I planned to frame the letter. If only she knew how much journaling I'd been doing in private. Proficiency really did come with practice, I guessed.

Unbeknownst to her, I'd spent the day at my parents' house and borrowed their car to drive to Andi's apartment in East Meadow. My first time there. It was a typical residential apartment: a second-floor, one bedroom set-up with a living room large enough for her to designate part of it as an office. She decorated the place mostly with second-hand furniture (with the exception of her bedroom), books everywhere—crammed in bookcases, stacked in piles on tables and floors in just about every room—and photographs of herself with her brothers, her friends Maggie and Jayce, and one of herself in full academic regalia on the day of her doctoral graduation—she looked equal parts elated and sexy in that one. The apartment had an air of transience to it, however, almost like a layover.

My only instruction to her was to wear something sexy, and she didn't disappoint—she appeared and greeted me at the door dressed in a black cocktail dress and thigh-high sheers, three-inch sling-back heels, and emanated a scent of vanilla. Her body was a luscious, firm hourglass. My blood rushed the instant I saw her; I actually gasped and exclaimed, "*Bellisima!*" blowing a kiss with my fingers. She beamed, and sent off fireworks of her own as she took in my own attire; I wore Versace. I loved who I became when I wore Versace—like transforming from Clark Kent to Superman.

I came with props: chilled sparkling cider and strawberries in sterling silver buckets, and Mikasa crystal flutes. Chocolate fondue. The flavor combinations alone were bringing her close to an orgasm.

As she stole a sip of cider, I looked at her. "You know, I always meant to ask: how come you don't drink?"

"I can't stomach it," she replied. "Like the way some people are with dairy."

"Do you miss it?"

"Alcohol? Never."

"How come?" I asked.

"I never liked it. I've been in too many bars and clubs, watching my brothers perform, to see its effects, not to mention knowing some once-brilliant professors whose intellect have just withered away in the slosh of booze. It's sad, really."

I listened and let her words sink in.

The music of Diana Krall (on her list of music that gets her in the mood) filled the room. We danced to Krall's version of "The Look of Love," our gaze locked as Andi clasped her hands around my neck, her fingers weaving through the ends of my hair. She was stunning. Sensual. Soft. As her instructor, I couldn't be more proud of how much progress my pupil had made. As her friend, I was so admiring of her courage and commitment to see the last two months through, with all its complications and conflicts of interest and whatever demons it had dredged up. As for me...well, I was silently ordering myself not to unzip her dress just yet, opting instead to delicately place my hand on the small of her back, knowing all her ticklish places and taking care to avoid them.

After our dance, I took her by the hand and led her to her bedroom. The one lamp turned on in the room cast a soft pink glow, accented by lit votives on the dresser and nightstand. Her bed was turned down, ready and waiting in anticipation, with fluffed up pillows and pressed percale sheets.

"Nice," I said in approval.

It was time for me to be Devin the Escort—not that I hadn't been all night, but I had to follow through on the commitment we'd outlined in the contract. This was, in some ways, a simulation. I had to push that ahead of my personal feelings and desires. It was, ironically, the only way to maintain my integrity. *It's a business arrangement, nothing more.*

I seductively goaded her toward the bed, dipped and let her fall back onto it. She looked ready, willing, hungry. Better yet, she looked *fearless.*

"Close your eyes," I practically sang. She did so, and I pulled out the long, thin box from the inside pocket of my jacket. "OK, open them now."

She did, and they immediately found the white box bound in red ribbon. She tentatively took it from my hand, removed the ribbon, and opened the box.

She looked at the object, then at me. I wasn't sure if it was a *What is this thing?* look or a *Are you out of your skull?* look.

"Do you like it?" I asked.

She stammered, "I'm…a bit…surprised."

"Haven't you ever used a vibrator before?"

She didn't respond, and I wasn't sure how to read her silence. We'd come so far; surely she wasn't embarrassed or appalled, was she?

"Haven't you ever *seen* one?" I asked.

She raised her eyebrows. An equally vague response. Was she teasing me?

"Well, this one is for you. I thought you'd like the leopard skin print." I winked.

She removed it from the box and turned it on.

"The batteries are included," I remarked, obvious when the vibrator purred.

"What, no blinking lights? Does it also talk dirty to you?"

Ahhh, there's my Andi. "No, but it'll call you tomorrow," I lobbed back.

I turned out the lights and blew out all but two of the votives. I then left the room momentarily to switch the CD from Diana Krall to Tchaikovsky's *Swan Lake* (also on the list) and returned with the cider and strawberries to find Andi stretched out on the bed, resting on her elbow. *Oh my God, I'm actually nervous.* I sat on the bed next to her.

"Take off your shoes," I commanded.

She loosened each sling-back with her foot and flung them off, one by one. I loved it.

I ran my fingers along her thigh and pulled each of the sheers down, one by one. My hands were shaking. How many clients had I so casually undressed without a second thought? But who was I kidding—I didn't *want* her to be a client.

Next I unzipped her dress and peeled it away, revealing a satin slip and leopard skin bikinis underneath.

"Hey, they match!" I said, holding the vibrator against them. Levity was the only way I was going to keep myself from ravishing her. Andi tossed her head back and laughed flirtatiously.

I love you. I want you. I need you.

It's a business arrangement, nothing more. You're my client tonight. My client. My client, goddammit.

She hoisted herself up and wrapped her arms around my shoulders and neck, but I removed them—in the interest of self-preservation—and gently, mischievously pushed her so that she fell back, her head landing on the pillow. Next thing I knew, she sprang up again, pulled me toward her, and clumsily pressed her lips to mine.

My blood raced. My heart rate quickened. My body temperature shot up. And that's not all that shot up.

I pulled away and fed her a strawberry instead, followed by a wedge of cider-soaked ice to suck on, but she wasn't settling any more. She spat out the ice cube, shooting it against the wall, and kissed me again, harder, determined, *persuasive*. Unable to resist another second, I willingly surrendered and French-kissed her. To finally know her lips—soft and round and wet—to taste her strawberry-flavored tongue, to glide my fingers along her silky skin, feel her chest heaving, her hips thrusting as I pinned her to the bed…

I slowly, mindfully lowered her bikinis, careful not to tickle her, coaching her movements. "Think of dancing," I whispered. "Relax," I encouraged when she was overcompensating. She did, and my entire body throbbed as I pressed into her.

Forget the arrangement. Forget the vibrator. I wanted her. She wanted me. After tonight, she'd no longer be a client. Why not end that right here, right now? I'd brought condoms just in case. I always brought condoms just in case.

I began to kiss her neck.

I love you, Andrea. I love you…

Just as I was about to remove my own clothes, I kissed her lips again and tasted wet salt, to find tears spilling down her cheeks. "Devin, stop…"

I jerked away and froze in place, catching my breath. *What had I done?*

"I can't," she cried. "I just can't. Oh God."

"Why not?" I asked, still panting.

"I've never actually done it."

I sat up, startled, my wits returned to me.

"What?" I asked out of shock as opposed to incoherence.

"I mean, I've done stuff with guys. You know, hand jobs and that sort of thing." She winced at the phrase *hand jobs*. "But I never went all the way."

Her confession slowly sunk in. "Are you telling me you're a virgin?" I asked.

She didn't even give me a second for the truth to sink in. She cried as she spoke. "I decided a long time ago that I would wait until I got married—that that was the romantic thing to do. I didn't even date until I was twenty—between my father's death and my brothers' overprotection and the yo-yoing with my weight, there was no other chance. The first guy I was ever with told me I was a disappointment. He said he'd had better. He told me I was too 'Catholic schoolgirl' because I didn't know anything and because I wanted to wait."

The more she explained, the more my heart ached for her. "What an asshole," I said. "I'm so sorry you believed him." I pushed a strand of hair behind her ear and caressed her cheek. She didn't seem to notice.

"After that, I changed my mind and decided not to wait. I wanted to learn, but I was too embarrassed, too afraid someone would find out that I didn't know what I was doing."

Finally, it was all making sense, as if I'd been looking at the Monet painting way too close to the canvas all along, could only make out the individual brushstrokes, and had finally stepped back enough to clearly see the entire picture.

"So you didn't have intercourse with any of the guys you dated?"

"I wanted to, lots of times, especially with Andrew. God, I loved Andrew more than any of them. But every time I tried, something stopped me, and I couldn't go through with it. As a result, my relationships never lasted beyond a few months. Except for Andrew. When he came along, at first I changed my mind again and told him I wanted to wait until we were married, and he agreed to that. He loved me a lot, and I was certain he was 'the one.' But we were both getting restless. I thought I'd get comfortable in time. I thought my inexperience and the insecurity that came with it would go away. It never did though, and the more time that passed, the more afraid I became that I couldn't actually go through with it. Every time I tried, I froze. Eventually, Andrew started telling me that I didn't please him. He kept telling me that what I didn't know was a hindrance. I tried to please him, I really did. I just didn't know how. I mean, how was I supposed to know?"

Andrew should thank his lucky stars that I didn't know where he lived. I would've driven up to Massachusetts right then and there and taken a baseball bat to the fucker.

"It's OK," I assured her, moving my hand along her shoulder and arm. "Andi, it's OK."

"It's not OK!" she countered. "I'm thirty-four years old!"

"So? What's wrong with that?"

"Everything!"

"Says who? Andrew? And who is he—Professor Wonderstud?"

I'd hoped she'd laugh, but she was too consumed by shame. "Every guy I've ever been with eventually left me because they were either turned off or unsatisfied, even if I tried to fake it or say I didn't want to or wasn't ready."

"How many guys have there been?"

She stopped crying long enough to search her mental database. "Including Andrew? Five. Although one of them only lasted for two weeks."

"Did they specifically tell you that that was the reason why they broke up with you?"

"Not all of them."

"Then you can't make that claim. False logic. Polarization."

I couldn't help but feel proud of myself at that moment, applying something I'd learned during our lessons. Although I wasn't sure I named the correct logical fallacy...

Again she didn't take notice. "Devin—" she started.

I cut her off. "Andi!" I cupped her chin with my hands, and spoke more softly. "Andrea." I looked into her eyes, wet and glistening and innocent. *Look at me*, I wanted to say. Not Devin. Look at *me*. But the words were lost. Stuck. Perhaps they were just too inadequate.

Andi nestled herself in my arms as she continued with her confession, revealing past incidences from childhood, moments when she was shut down, programmed to think she was dirty, violated not in body, but spirit. *More pieces in place. The picture so crystal clear now.* With each memory she freed, I listened intently and patiently, my heart bursting with empathy and compassion and love as I caressed her cheek. I wanted to take it all away from her.

Finally I put my fingers to her lips.

"Listen to me: There is nothing wrong with you. Do you hear me?" I locked eyes with her again. "Look at me: There is *nothing wrong* with you. You think the fact that you never had intercourse has been the problem all this time? That was *never* the problem—the problem all these years was neither your inhibition nor your inexperience. It was your *shame*. And there was nothing to be ashamed of. For God's sake, your family guilted you into suppressing your sexuality, and for no good reason. No matter what choice you made, you couldn't win. If you expressed yourself, if you 'gave yourself' to someone you loved, you'd be degraded. And yet, you were also given the message that you weren't worth waiting for. Add that to all the times your brothers said hands off…I mean, geez, Andi. If anyone's to be ashamed, it's *them*. Fuck 'em all—how dare they do that to you! They were wrong. They misled you."

The more I spoke, the more she seemed to come back to

herself. She stopped crying, sat up, and I could almost see her pain and shame and hurt floating out of her, like exorcising a ghost. My own eyes began to mist, my love for her threatening to overtake me.

I cupped her face again. "My God, Andi. You're so beautiful. All of you. You are a vibrant, passionate woman with abounding creativity and wisdom and humor. You are enticing and delectable. You have a body that is a joy to explore, a rapture to the senses. You smell and taste and look and feel and sound good. And above all, you are sexual. Always were. You don't need sex to be sexual. Never did."

She looked at me, astounded, as if the picture had finally become clear to her too, and she began to cry again. Only this time I knew they were tears of a newfound self-love, of relief, of regret for believing the wrong messages for so long, and catharsis over finally releasing them into the ether. I took her in my arms again, cradling and rocking her while she wept, rubbing her back and stroking her hair. And when she eventually cried herself out, calmed and quieted, I dried her tears with my thumbs, careful not to smudge the remainder of her makeup. I kissed her forehead. I kissed her cheek. But it wasn't enough. I touched her lips softly with my own, and gave in yet again. My body surged as I kissed her passionately, our breaths loud and swooning. She took hold of me, leaned back, and pulled me on top of her again, kissing me even harder, wildly raking her hands through my hair, pressing her body into mine, her desire and exonerated sexuality unleashed.

What should I do now?

I paused to look at her, panting, shining in the darkness. "You're a good kisser," I said, hoping to encourage her. I could feel the corners of her mouth turn upwards, into a smile. I then whispered directly in her ear, "Andrew was a fool to let you go."

Maybe I should thank him after I beat the shit out of him.

Andi's glowing eyes turned cat-like, ready to pounce and purr. "I'm ready now," she said in a voice I'd never heard before, full of resolve and authority.

It would've been so easy to make love to her right then and there, and make love all night. To tell declare my love and hold her in my arms for the rest of our lives. But my future flashed before my eyes: my father's imminent decline and death, the stacks of bills and papers on the dining room table, the next three months of clients booked in advance, and I knew I just couldn't take advantage of her like that, especially now that I knew everything.

We would be together, I silently vowed. Just not yet. She was worth waiting for.

Do what you came here to do. Do your job.

I blew out the last two votives, picked up the vibrator, and turned it on.

With every moan, every cry of ecstasy, every sigh of pleasure— and not a single one faked, she said, and I believed her—she was all faked out, I surmised—she exorcised every last ghost and goblin and demon.

My work was done.

I kissed her when she fell asleep, left her apartment, and drove back to my parents' house, hearing *Swan Lake* in my head and taking care of myself until I finally succumbed to slumber as well, close to dawn.

She was worth waiting for.

Chapter Twenty

October

I couldn't stop thinking about her.

When I was with a client, I imagined being with Andi instead. When I was falling asleep at night, I closed my eyes and tried to re-live that night at her apartment, recalling the touch of my hand on her thigh, the hotness of her breath on my cheek, the sound of her pleasurable moans. I bought strawberries and cider just to smell and taste her mouth.

I was a hot mess.

Thing is, I knew she felt the same way about me. You'd think it was a perfect situation—two people, mutually in love, wanting to be together. But it seemed more cruel to say, "I love you, but I have to keep on dating these women," than to be her friend and leave my feelings docked somewhere, hide them as best as I could from her, and stave off her own.

I could've told her the reason why. Could've told her about my father. She would've understood. She probably would've waited too. Maybe it scared me too much to open up. If I told her about my father being sick, I'd have to also tell her about our history. Or maybe I was still afraid Andi wouldn't love the *real* me. If I stopped being an escort, wouldn't I also have to stop being Devin? I still liked that guy, for the most part.

I couldn't bring myself to stop seeing her platonically. And I figured as long as she didn't say anything, then neither would I. We continued to meet for coffee or go to museums or out to dinner. I even went to her apartment a few times to watch a movie or a baseball game, having already been on the Island at my parents' house, unbeknownst to Andi.

It killed me when she tried to hold my hand and I'd pull away, although I'd be a total hypocrite and occasionally kiss her goodbye on the cheek, catching myself after the fact. I even tried to restrain myself with any kind of playful flirting—it was too tempting to take it beyond that. We were so casual with one another and had gotten to know each other's rhythms so well. I kept willing it to be enough, to no avail.

But it wasn't.

One afternoon, as we took a walk through Central Park in the midst of its autumn splendor, Andi finally asked the question I'd been doing my damnedest to avoid:

"Of all the women you've serviced in the last five years, have you ever fallen in love with one of them?"

I answered simply: "No."

"How?" she asked. Interesting that she didn't ask *why*.

"I simply told myself not to," I replied. "It's a matter of ethics. Think of your students. How would you respond if I asked you if you ever fell in love with one of them?"

"That's different," she said.

"How? You offer them a service. They're part of your working environment."

"Yes, but I don't teach them to write while rubbing whipped cream on their nipples and licking it off."

I stifled a laugh.

"But you make them get naked every day. Come on, Andi. There is nothing more vulnerable to those kids than to put their thoughts on paper and have you evaluate them. You know that. They want you to like what they write. They want to walk away feeling better about themselves. So tell me how that's different. And you're just as professional about your work as I am about mine, and you're just as good at what you do as I am at what I do. You wouldn't compromise that."

She didn't reply. Just walked beside me, her cognitive wheels spinning, until she found another way around. "Are you ever sexually attracted to a client? Have you ever gotten aroused?"

I replied honestly. "Sure, lots of times."

"What do you do?" she asked.

"I take a cold shower or whack off like any other guy."

I hoped my bluntness would turn her off.

"You're so fucking poetic," she said. Mission accomplished; her f-bomb usage confirmed it. And yet, she persisted. "And you're telling me that you never once let them..." Rather then finish the sentence, she raised her eyebrows and let me fill in the rest mentally.

"Not if I can help it. It's not in the contract."

"So, you've not had sex all this time?"

Shit. The ice was quickly thinning. "I didn't say that. I get laid—maybe not as often as I'd like to, but I do. Just not with my clients, that's all." Karen the Corporate-Something-Slash-Aspiring-Actress appeared in my mind's eye, and I pushed her and my guilt out before Andi caught it, certain she could see it too.

She certainly was suspicious, if not incredulous. "You've *never* slept with any of your clients? Never went all the way, never got paid for it? Never did it with them for free?"

"I told you, *never.*"

One-way ticket to Hell on the Liar's Express, coming up…

"Then with whom?" she asked.

"Women I meet at clubs or galleries or parties when I'm not working." That, for the most part, was true.

Andi looked crushed. As if I told her I'd been cheating on her the entire time. As if I *was* cheating on her the entire time.

"Do you call these women the next day?" she asked.

"Not usually," I replied. "Sometimes."

"Do they call you?"

"We have an understanding that's it's not a long-term thing." There was a time when I was proud of this. Now I felt like an asshole.

"Do you tell them you're an escort?"

"Sometimes."

"What do they say?"

"It's a turn-on." That was true. I don't know why, but women I met always found my being an escort the sexiest thing ever.

She scoffed, "I'll bet."

I didn't ask her to elaborate, and I didn't appreciate the snarky tone attached to it.

Andi didn't say another word about it until we were at Borders. As I flipped through the pages of a book about Van Gogh, she sidled up to me and leaned in.

"Do you kiss your clients?" she asked just above a whisper.

Dammit. Couldn't she just let it go?

I remained focused on the open page in front of me. "I don't initiate it, if that's what you mean."

"But you let them kiss you. Totally make out with you."

"If that's what they want, yes."

They always want.

"How come you stop me?" she asked.

And…there it was.

"It's different with you," I said.

"How?"

For someone so inhibited, she could be incredibly tenacious.

"It just is."

"That's a stupid answer," she said.

"It's the only one you're going to get," I snapped back.

I closed Van Gogh and picked up Mondrian, and I heard her footfalls on the carpet as she left in a huff. If she only knew I felt exactly like the shit-heel she was probably calling me in her head.

Later, as we sat in Café Dante sipping mochaccinos, she cornered me yet again.

"So when was the last time you were in a serious love relationship?"

I had to think about this one. "A few years ago, I think. Before the business took off. I haven't had much time for a personal life."

"You make time for me," she said.

"That's different."

"How?" she asked, more emphatic and demanding than ever. Normally I'd applaud such determination, especially coming from her. But I had to kill this once and for all.

"We're not dating," I replied coldly. And yet again, mission accomplished. I thought she might actually cry in her mochaccino as she stared into the cup.

And just as I thought she was down for the count, she got back up. "What's the difference?"

"A love relationship is more work. It takes more time and energy. I love pleasing my clients, but sometimes it completely wears me out, both physically and mentally. Some of them are so needy. They've been so neglected, either by themselves or their husbands or whoever. To go through all of that night after night, listening to them and touching them, and then have to attend to my girlfriend? Besides, what girlfriend would be so accepting of my line of work? How does she introduce me to her family?"

So there—I said it without saying it. Hopefully she'd read between the lines, change the pronoun from *she* to *you*.

"Small business owner in the service industry?" she offered.

Unable to tell whether she was joking, I cocked my eyebrow.

"Well come on, Dev, it's not like you face the same stigma as I would if *I* were an escort," she said.

Now I was irked. "Are you kidding?"

"From whom?" she persisted.

"My family, for one. Most of them have stopped speaking to me because of my work. Hell, my father's convinced I'm nothing but a pimp and a drug dealer."

She pressed on. "But overall, you make out OK. I mean, I've seen you at work. You talk it up with everyone, whether they're in academia or advertising. I've seen you hand out your business cards with no shame. You represent yourself very well."

"I have a lot of confidence," I said.

"And social support," she muttered.

I frowned. "What's that supposed to mean?"

"It's not fair," she said.

"What's not fair?"

199

"Men are *escorts*, but women are *hookers*. Men are *studs*, but women are *sluts*. Men are exonerated if caught in adultery, but women are stoned to death. Men are procreators, while women are used goods. No matter what, society shames women when it comes to sex, married or single, motherhood or—God help her—childless, in love or not. And virginity is a double-edged sword too. A man is a champion if he loses his virginity; a woman is 'de-flowered.' Come on! We're pressured to lose it, but once we do, we're considered untouchable because we've 'given it up.' And then if we hold on to it, we're considered prudes, prisses, frigid, or simply freaks of nature. And still untouchable. Did you ever see the *Seinfeld* episode when Jerry dates the virgin? They made her timid as hell. And they labeled her: *Marla the Virgin*. How ostracizing can you get?"

What was this, displaced anger? Sexual frustration? Was she antagonizing me for the same reasons I was antagonizing her?

I glowered at her. "What do you want me to say?"

"I want you to admit that you've got it made, buddy. No one calls you a prostitute. You don't even have to worry about getting arrested."

"That's because I don't go all the way with these women." Such a juvenile phrase—*go all the way*. Then again, this was a juvenile conversation. More like a competition. And a rhetorical one at that. Go figure.

"Oh, *come on*, Dev! Just because you use a vibrator instead? They didn't buy Clinton's definition of sex either."

Wow. Look who's being blunt now. If I wasn't so annoyed, I'd be proud of her.

"And don't get me started with domination and abuse," she plowed on. "You don't have to worry about getting slapped around, berated, or being judged on every little speck of cellulite that shows or gray hair that appears on your head—"

"—But I do have to worry about women stalking or harassing me, or getting the shit kicked out of me by a husband or two," I interjected. "And all of the above has happened. Do you know you're the only person who's been to my apartment since I started working? I've moved twice and changed my phone number three times in the last two years. Hell, Devin's not even my real name..."

Whoaaaa...shit, how could I have let that slip out? Andi raised her eyebrows. "It's not?" she asked softly, almost to herself, looking bewildered.

I pretended to ignore my blunder and finished my rant. "So don't tell me about fair. We've all got a burden to carry."

"Then why don't you quit?"

Finally.

I rolled my eyes. "Here we go..."

"No, I mean it. If it's that bad, then why don't you quit?"

"Because I love my work."

Or rather, I used to. Then you came along, dammit.

"Oh, that's right," she said. "It's all about the women. You're Captain Orgasm, rescuing us from the villains of neglect and abandonment and lands of Uglisville and Bad Sex. And you get paid a shitload for this. You know, I'm starting to think that that's what you tell yourself to justify and hide the fact that you're afraid of a serious relationship."

I leaned back in my seat and crossed my arms in front of my chest. "You think so," I said as a statement rather than a question.

"As Devin the Escort, you get to go on exciting dates. You show up with your cheap smiles and your Versace suits. Then, you haul ass out of there just as they start to get attached. No commitments, no sending roses the next day, no follow-up phone calls. No getting to the real you. Minimal investment, minimal risk. Do you honestly think these women aren't falling in love with you just because you tell them not to, because you dictate it in writing? Trust me, they are—they're so hooked in and they're too afraid to either admit it or get out, because some desperate part of them is hoping you'll actually fall in love with them and leave the rest behind. You're naïve if you think otherwise."

Don't back down. Don't give in.

"I think they stay because they get something out of it. They get a payoff."

"And what about *your* payoff? Sure, you may dance around in your boxers, but have you ever told a woman how you really feel about art or your father or growing older or anything else? Have you ever let yourself be vulnerable to a woman, tell her, even show her you're scared or hurt or angry?"

Shit. She got in. And now I had to get her out.

"Oh, you're a fine one to talk. Look at *you*, Andi. You're one of those needy women! *You're my client.* 'Show me how to be a better lover, Devin.' 'Make me feel less self-conscious, Devin.' 'Men reject me, Devin.' 'I'm undesirable.' What, you think just because you didn't pay me money, just because our arrangement was more intellectual, that that makes you better than them? Maybe if you didn't act so goddamn smug and superior, you'd hold on to a man."

I should have stopped there. But she'd hit more than a nerve. She let the monster out of the cage.

"And speaking of which, when was the last time you got laid by something not requiring batteries? For all your increased confidence and your new clothes and your trimmer body, I don't see any men banging down your door, or banging you, either. Why is that? Maybe your problem wasn't sex, Andi. Maybe it had nothing to do with your body or your upbringing. Maybe Andrew just wasn't that into *you*. After all, he married someone else, didn't he? So don't sit there and preach to me about my relationships until you get one of your own that lasts."

Oh my god. Oh, what the fuck did I just do?

We both looked at each other, shell-shocked.

Andi's face lower lip trembled as her eyes began to water. She stood up and grabbed her jacket in one move, then bolted out of the cafe. Her purse dropped to the seat. I picked it up and ran after her, calling her by name. She reluctantly stopped and turned around, but refused to make eye contact with me as I extended the purse to her.

"I am so sorry," I said, my voice quavering.

"Just give me the bag," she demanded, and grabbed it from my hand. She then turned and disappeared into the Manhattan crowd despite my calling her by name one more time. I considered running after her, but making a scene on a city street ended way worse in real life than on TV or in the movies.

For the first time, I heard what my father and mother and sisters had been trying to tell me for the last ten years. And because of that, I'd refused to hear the other thing she was trying to tell me. That she was hooked. She'd fallen for *Devin*. The escort. She had deluded herself. She'd clung to false hope, and was completely let down.

Perhaps I'd gotten what I wished for. I despised myself thoroughly for driving the final dagger through her heart.

I canceled my client that night, and for the next two nights afterwards. The thought of being an escort for one minute longer turned my stomach. However, according to the projections I'd made, I'd have all my parent's financial problems resolved by the end of the year, and then I could make plans for myself to get out, and give myself enough of a cushion to figure out what I could do next. I had to find a way to recover so I could finish what I started. I had to summon the will to hold on just a little bit longer.

Chapter Twenty-One

The next morning, I sent Andi a bouquet of two dozen red roses, with a single white rose in the center, and a card:

> Andi—
> *I sank lower than whale shit at the bottom of the ocean yesterday, and today my sorrow expands to the edges of the universe. Forgive me, please.*
> —Devin

She'd like the metaphor, I surmised. Although I hoped it wouldn't minimize the depth or sincerity of my remorse.

Later that day, I received a text message from Andi: *All is forgiven.*

I breathed a sigh of relief, but it did nothing to quell the utter hopelessness. We were over.

Chapter Twenty-Two

I was near the end of viewing an exhibit at a gallery when I overhead a couple, standing in front of one of the paintings, deliberating on whether to buy it.

"I don't know," said the woman. "I'm trying to picture it in the living room. We should've brought a paint swatch of our wall," she said with a laugh.

I approached them. "Excuse me," I said. They both turned around, and the woman's eyes widened as she gave me the split-second once-over, then remembered who she was standing next to. "I couldn't help but overhear your deliberations, but what color is your living room wall?"

"It's in the cream family," she said. "But we're planning to paint it a spicy golden mustard color."

"In that case, this painting will be perfect for you. Your lighting is more crucial than the color of the wall. Get a professional to set that up for you. Trust me, it's worth it. And don't hang it too high. Many people make that mistake."

"Do you work here?" asked the man.

"I don't," I said. "I'm sorry for intruding."

"No intrusion," said the woman. "In fact, you were very helpful. Thank you." She turned to her husband. "What do you think, honey? Now I really want it."

"Sure," he said. "Anything for you."

Just as I was about to leave, the gallery proprietor, who knew me by face, motioned for me to stay. I lingered toward the back of the gallery, and when he completed the transaction with the couple, approached me.

He extended his hand. "I'm Travis."

"Devin," I replied, following through on the handshake.

"Shame we haven't introduced ourselves sooner."

Shit, was he hitting on me?

"You're right."

"So..." he started, and turned his head, nudging in the direction of the painting I had just helped sell to the couple. "Do you do that often?"

"Do what often?"

"Sell artwork to strangers."

I held up my hands as if to deflect a bullet. "Hey man, I didn't mean to step on your toes. I just—"

"Relax, honey, I'm grateful. They didn't even haggle over the price. In fact, I wanted to know if you were interested in a job."

Breaking into the art world on the commerce side was almost as difficult as breaking in on the creative side. It was all about connections.

"I might be," I said, "but I'm kind of swamped right now."

"What do you do?"

"Self-employed."

Travis reached into his pocket, pulled out a business card, and handed it to me. "When you're ready, let me know."

"Thanks," I said. I was about to leave a second time, when I turned around again. "Hey, I'm unloading some pieces from my collection. Not sure where to start."

"I might be able to help you with that. Can you come by next week? We'll talk business then."

"Sounds great," I said. "Thanks." I shook his hand again.

He paused for a beat. "You're straight, right?"

I nodded.

He shook his head in disappointment and clicked his teeth. "Well, no one's perfect."

Another part of the plan in place, I thought as I left the gallery. Hopefully I'd be able to sell the pieces I had in mind, and that money would pay the rest of my father's medical bills—he was getting weaker, and I knew it was time to prepare for the end with a special bed and equipment.

And, for the first time, a new option I'd not previously considered appeared. Working in a gallery probably didn't pay much, depending on the gallery and the caliber of artists they dealt with. Also, one probably worked off commissions.

But hey, I just sold a painting, didn't I? I could fucking sell anything. And I still had time to pad the nest egg.

Could I really do this?

As Andi and I stood poised in front of a Picasso in the MoMA, I was about to tell her about the previous day's encounter with Travis the Gallery Guy when she blurted, "Art is a lie that makes us realize the truth."

I turned to her. "Where did you hear that?"

"It's a Picasso quote, but I read it at the beginning of Chaim Potok's novel *My Name Is Asher Lev*."

"Yes, I know it's Picasso," I said, not meaning to sound impatient or condescending. "Do you agree with it?"

"Sure do," she replied.

"Why?"

"All art, be it writing, painting, film, dance, whatever, is a manipulation of time and space. It's an interpretation and a recreation of the facts, using various artifacts that point us in the direction of our personal truths."

"Not the artist's truth?" I asked.

"More so our own. For example: remember the Lad Tobin essay I told you about, the one about Pogo the clown scaring the crap out of him when he was five years old and his parents having to call off the rest of the birthday party? He couldn't actually remember the name of the clown, so he made one up. And remember Patricia Hampl's essay 'Memory and Imagination'? The Thompson piano book, Sister Olive who looked like an olive, Mary Katherine Reilly—all lies, all artifacts that point us to a more personal truth: in the first case, a child's trauma. In the second, envy and insecurity."

It was as if we were back in my living room for one of our tutorials, and I suddenly found myself missing them. "But that's Tobin's trauma, yes?" I challenged. "His truth. And Hampl's."

"OK, now think of Donald Murray's 'Onions and Oranges' essay. Murray says that as we read someone else's story, fiction or non, we read—and consequently, we write—our own. In other words, all writing is autobiographical. Tobin's trauma with Pogo the clown takes me back to me shrieking and begging my mother to take me out of Debbie Doherty's birthday party because there were balloons all over the place and the kids were kicking and popping them. That's *my* truth."

She had me beat. "But was her name really Debbie Doherty?" I asked coyly, bordering on flirtation.

She narrowed her eyes and cocked an eyebrow, just as coy and flirtatiously.

I grinned and winked at her. "You win this one."

It had felt like ages since we'd bantered like this. Even though we'd put the fight in Café Dante behind us, the scars were still tender.

We parked ourselves in front of a Jackson Pollock.

"How's the textbook coming along?" I asked, looking at the painting. We'd talked so little about it I'd almost forgotten she was writing one.

"Mags is filling in some of the missing research, and I'm doing revisions." I loved that she now referred to her friend Maggie so colloquially with me, as if she were my friend too. "We've also got to finish the introduction and the last two chapters."

"Hm.," I said.

We stood in silence, staring at the painting. Then I turned to her.

"What's the title?" I asked.

"*This Book Sucks.*"

I spat out a laugh, grateful I hadn't been drinking anything at that moment. It echoed and even drew looks from nearby patrons. I quickly covered my mouth in an act of failed suppression.

Andi seemed pleased by my reaction, but turned serious. "Actually, we can't decide on a title. We vacillate from too stuffy and academic to too cutesy."

"Hm," I said again.

We moved to the next Pollock. In the chaos of the colors, it came to me clear as glass. I turned to Andi again.

"How about 'Truth, Lies, and Artifacts'?"

An expression came across her as if she'd just found the

answer to the mystery of life. And then she looked like she wanted to hit me, mad that she didn't think of it herself.

"You rat-bastard," she said under my breath, teeth clenched, eyes on the painting. I could've kissed her right there. Especially given that she was wearing a v-neck top that gave me direct access to her cleavage from where I was standing.

"You're welcome," I gloated. We turned to face each other, exchanging grins of mutual admiration, and locked into a gaze of familiarity, of connection, of understanding.

A look of love.

We didn't dare look away. A smile covered her face, her green eyes dazzling. The painting had nothing on Andi.

"What's your real name?" she asked. There wasn't a trace of longing or desperation in her voice. More like looking at a stranger you've known all your life, if that makes sense. It was the most natural question, the obvious question, the only question to ask at that moment.

I knew the time had come to tell her. I wasn't even afraid to.

"David," I replied softly.

"David what?"

"David Santino."

You know that moment when Pinocchio turns into a real boy? It happened. Right there in front of that Jackson Pollock painting.

Did she see it? Did anyone take notice? Because wow, I sure could feel it.

"Hm," she said.

Maybe we weren't over. Maybe we were just beginning.

We moved on to the next painting.

Chapter Twenty-Three

December

I was crazy-busy throughout the holidays. Parties, parties, and more parties. Office parties. Faculty parties. Family parties. Charity parties. Dates to ballets and plays and film festivals and the tree-lighting ceremony at Rockefeller Plaza. All of our escorts were slamming busy. Christian and I decided to throw a party for them as well ("Who does an escort take to a party?" we joked), and handed out bonuses. We bought Kate a trip to Bermuda. Christian had recently begun collecting movie posters, and I managed to snag an original *Wall Street* poster, mint condition, as my gift for him. He gave me a gift card to Borders. "I'm sorry it's so informal, man, but I know you've been reading more lately and I don't know what you're into."

"I've been slowly figuring that out myself," I said, "But thanks, bud. It's perfect."

I saw very little of Andi. But I was making a shitload of money, and that had been the plan. I missed her, however. One late night during the week before Christmas, I called her, not realizing how late it was until I heard her groggy voice. Turned out it was two o'clock in the morning.

"If I have to see the fucking *Nutcracker* one more time, I swear I'm going to have a seizure," I said in response to her sleepy hello.

"Could be worse," she murmured. "Could be the *Magnificent Christmas Spectacular* at Radio City. Real-life camels taking a dump on stage, fortunately *after* the Rockettes do their wooden solider routine. Or maybe *un*fortunately, if you're not a fan of the Rockettes."

I cracked up, and was instantly filled with warmth, although I longed to touch her, stroke her hair, kiss her pulse points. "You always make me feel better," I said.

"Good. Now let me get some sleep."

When I wasn't on dates, I was at my parents' house. Taking the train out to Long Island (I "bought" my mother's old car, leased a brand new one for her, and kept the old one parked at the train station in Massapequa) to help out with keeping the books, cleaning the house, moving furniture, and slowly dismantling my dad's workshop in the basement and other possessions he was ready to part with had become routine. In a sad, twisted way, I'd come to like the stability of it.

I refused to work on Christmas Eve, especially this year, knowing it would be my father's last. Before I drove to Massapequa, I met Andi at her apartment. A small, decorated tree sat on a table in front of her living room window, providing the only light in the room. It reminded me of the bedroom glowing with votive candles.

I unwrapped her gift to me first: a journal from the MoMA gift store, with a leather spine and Matisse reproduction on the cover, as well as a matching Cross pen.

"I thought of you when I saw it," she said of the journal, her voice tentative, awaiting my response. It was stylish. Tasteful.

Thoughtful. She'd selected something that represented us, and the activities we'd engaged in together. Did she actually think I wouldn't like it? She could've given me soap-on-a-rope and I would have treasured it.

"I love it," I said as soon as the words unstuck from my throat. "Thank you." I kissed her rather unsatisfactorily on the cheek, wishing for a sprig of mistletoe. With mistletoe I'd at least have an excuse. Hell, a sprig of parsley would suffice. Andi opened my present: a mahogany sculpture of a woman sensually posed, exquisitely nude, smooth and curvy. "It's a one-of-a-kind piece," I said. "Made me think of you." *It's how I imagine your body.*

She drew in a breath, and was as visibly moved as I had been moments ago. "Thank you," she uttered softly. Her eyes were wistful, distant, disappointed.

Tell her! Tell her RIGHT NOW. Then kiss her. Kiss her and undress each other and dance in the dark and make love until the sun comes up. That's what you really want for Christmas, isn't it?

"Merry Christmas, Andi," I said, and took her into my arms. We embraced for what felt like the better part of an hour, although it couldn't have been longer than twenty seconds. But something happened when she let go. An eerie feeling came over me, as if she released me from more than an embrace. And rather than stay and undo it all, I cradled my gift and carried it with me to the car, then drove to my parents' house.

New Year's Eve, I decided. *I'll tell her everything.* My New Year's Eve date had been booked six months in advance, and went to the highest bidder. Screw it.

My father insisted on no gifts this year. "More shit to throw out when I'm gone," he said. Sucked that he was probably right. My father and I hadn't exchanged gifts in years. Usually my mother would buy something and sign both of their names to it, and I would do the same in reverse. So imagine my shock when my little niece Meredith handed me a present, and the tag read simply, "From Dad."

I unwrapped *The Greatest Generation*. The copy I'd given to him.

I looked up at my father, dumbfounded.

"I'm not being an ingrate by giving it back to you," my father explained.

"I didn't think so," I said, unable to say anything else lest I'd break into tears. "Thank you."

Well after midnight, when I was upstairs in my old room and about to turn out the light, I removed the book from beside my bed, and for some reason felt compelled to open it. My father wrote on the title page, in script: *I know what you did. Thanks, Son.*

How had he found out? Maybe he saw the bank statements. Or maybe he had figured out why I wasn't quitting. But it was the second part of the inscription that got me. *Son.* And *Thanks.* I bawled into my pillow like a little boy.

I had it all planned: Andi had told me she wasn't doing anything on New Year's Eve other than sitting at home by herself watching *The Twilight Zone* marathon. Parties weren't her thing; too much drinking. I'd call an hour or so before, just to make sure hadn't changed her mind, would show up at her place with a dozen roses and wearing something other than Versace—jeans and a fisherman's sweater, perhaps—and take it from there.

I was at the flower shop when my BlackBerry rang. I looked at the caller ID: my sister Joannie.

"Dad's just been taken to the ER," she said, panicked.

"I'm on my way," I said, abandoning the store, Andi's flowers, and my plan.

Chapter Twenty-Four

March

My father didn't stay in the hospital for long. But we all knew it signaled the beginning of the end. I spent half a day going over all the finances with him. The house was safe. Credit cards paid off. Dad's life insurance policy would take care of funeral expenses. I'd re-invested Mom's retirement savings to yield a bigger return when the time came.

He exhaled a heavy sigh that broke into a cough. "This is a tremendous relief."

"You're welcome," I said.

"You were right—I shouldn't have let things get so bad. I let my pride get in the way."

"We're a stubborn breed."

"I know now that you couldn't have done all this without your job. I wish you could've taken care of it some other way, but I give you credit for following through."

"I meant what I said about getting out, Dad. I need a little more of a net, but otherwise I'm ready to move on."

"Any idea what you want to do?"

I shook my head. "Not yet. Something in business, I guess." I didn't tell him that I'd been talking to Travis, who helped me sell half of my collection (Warhol not included), or about learning more about art sales while networking. Knowing my father, he'd think Travis and I were dating. With the holidays finished, I'd even started working in the gallery one day a week for two hours. Commission only. I simply wanted to learn my way around.

"You would be good at that," he said.

"That's the nicest thing you've ever said to me, Dad," I said.

He chortled. "Don't let it go to your head."

I chortled as well, and he sat back in his recliner and closed his eyes.

Things had been weird between Andi and me since Christmas. I never did shake that eery feeling that she'd pulled away from me, nor had I given our friendship any attention lately. Between my father, the clients, and now the new gallery, I was swamped. Not to mention snowed in following back-to-back blizzards in January and February. When Andi and I weren't playing phone tag, our calls were curt.

I needed to get away from everything—the city, the business, my parents' house—so I called Andi one Saturday afternoon, and our schedules finally meshed. We drove in separate cars out to Claudio's for dinner. Greenport, and the East End of Long Island in particular, was a great way of getting away from the rat race of New York without actually leaving it.

Something about her looked different—a brightness about her, like the way plants become in springtime.

"So what's up?" said Andi as we opened our menus. "I haven't seen you in ages. And what were you doing on the Island today?"

"I had a get-together with my family," I said as I perused my menu, emotional exhaustion pounding on my forehead yet again.

"Special occasion?" she asked.

"My mother's birthday."

"How was it?"

"It was fine," I said tersely. I couldn't help but feel like she was pestering me for information, even though I knew she was trying to find the rhythm that had once come so easily between us. But I didn't want to talk about it. Another *last* for my father. Ro broke down in tears when we presented my mother with the cake, my father unable to eat a bite of it, my mother rubbing her eyes every ten minutes, as if she hadn't slept in years, while trying so hard to put on a happy face.

I would've been happy to sit and eat in silence, comforted solely by Andi's presence. But no way I could tell her that either without her misinterpreting it as disinterest in her.

Andi ordered the shrimp scampi. I ordered the swordfish.

After the server left, Andi and I looked at each other, minds ablank.

"So..." she started. Geezus, you'd think we'd never met before. On a blind date or something.

"How's work?" I asked.

"You mean school? It's fine."

I liked her word choice; for her, work was something to be taught and learned rather than endured.

"Good classes?" I asked.

"The usual, I guess. Not bad. How about you?"

"The usual," I replied. I was done talking to Andi—or anyone else, for that matter—about my work. She didn't press me either, which made me think she was done feigning any interest in my work as well.

"I've got spring break next week," she said.

"Any plans?"

"Maggie and I are driving down to Florida for a few days. I know that's a bit clichéd, Florida and spring break. Then I'm going up to Massachusetts for the weekend."

She averted her eyes from mine the moment she said Massachusetts. Well, *that* got my attention.

"Really?" I asked.

"It's been awhile since I've been back. I'm looking forward to it, actually."

Still with the averted eyes. Clearly she was holding back a crucial piece of information.

"Are you going to visit anyone in particular?"

Like your rat-bastard ex-fiancé, perhaps?

"Just some friends," she said, suddenly rather interested in her flatware.

Right. Friends. Male friends. Or one male "friend" in particular.

I seethed with jealousy. "Well, have a good time, I guess," I said, not even trying to muster more encouragement.

"I will," she said with conviction.

Fuck.

We spent the duration of our meal, and our conversation, with that invisible wedge between us, the wedge of that missing piece of information. The mystery friend who awaited her visit in Massachusetts, for whom she had a gleam in her eye, a spring in her step. I had no right to be resentful—after all, I'd been holding back key information for months. Hell, almost a year.

I was convinced it was Andrew, and that she was going back to the cheating loser. Or maybe she was going to give him what she wanted, now that she learned how. He was going to get to touch her and hold her and kiss her .

No. She wasn't like that. She couldn't be. Not anymore. She'd come too far.

Please, let me be wrong.

At the end of the following week, I called Andi and got her voicemail instead. I left a message: *Hey, are you there? Did you get lost in the wilderness somewhere? Give me a call…*

Two days passed, and no phone call.

I called again, and again got her voicemail. *Hey Andi. It's Devin.* The name was beginning to sound downright foreign to me. Especially when I used it with her. It still didn't feel comfortable to call myself David with her at this point, especially since she hadn't volunteered it herself. *Um, I guess you're not back from your visit yet. I was hoping we could catch a movie or something. It's been a while since we've done that. Anyway, give me a call when you get this message.*

She didn't call back for another two days.

I felt like Harry Burns did in *When Harry Met Sally…*, after he and Sally had ruined their friendship by sleeping together and she tells him, "I am not your consolation prize." I suspected Andi and I had ruined our friendship because we *didn't* sleep together.

Chapter Twenty-Five

I slept with Allison the Textbook Rep. A going-away present, I told her, since I was leaving the business. She understood it was a one-time-only offer.

Christian and I sat in my office, the desk and walls bare, files of each of our escorts spread out between us. We pored through them, deliberating on who would be most suitable to take over Strawberries and Champagne. I'd finally filled him in on everything—my father's illness, my feelings for Andi—and he said simply, "I'm here for you, man." For the first in a long time, he felt like a friend. "We'll get you out of this," he said. "You'll get everything you want, don't worry."

After two weeks of phone tagging, Andi and I finally touched base and arranged to meet at Junior's one late Tuesday afternoon. We sat at the same booth as the first time—Christ, was it almost a year since we'd first met?—and didn't order anything more than tea and coffee.

Andi looked like she was about to tell me she ran over my dog.

"You're unusually quiet," I said, hoping it would give her the in she needed, although I wasn't sure I wanted to hear whatever it was she was dreading to tell me.

Her expression turned from dread to resolve. She took hold of my hand, sending tingles up my arm. Her fingers were warm.

Tears came to her eyes. "I think you're my best friend," she said, each word as delicate as a china cup.

I sat across from her, motionless except for my thumb gliding back and forth on top of her hand.

She took in a breath. "I love you, Dev. And I'm leaving."

And with that, every metaphorical china cup smashed to the ground.

I tried to open my mouth, form words, make a sound, and eventually spilled out, "What did you say?"

"I accepted a teaching position at Northampton University. I'm moving back to Massachusetts." She spoke with more authority this time.

Baffled didn't even begin to cover my state of mind. Flummoxed. Fractured. Shattered.

"When?" I asked.

"Next month, after the semester ends."

So these were the "friends" she had visited in Massachusetts? A hiring committee at a university?

"When did this happen?" I asked.

"I interviewed back in January."

Holy fuck, January?

"Why didn't you tell me?"

"I didn't tell anyone," she said. "Not even Maggie."

I didn't know whether to be angry or devastated or indifferent. My eyes drifted past the hustle and bustle of Junior's into some foggy nowhereland. And then suddenly, as if on a delayed reaction, my brain translated something else she'd said.

"Did you also say you love me?" I asked.

She nodded. "Yes."

"As in, you're in love with me?"

"Yes."

"Since when?" I'm not sure why I asked; I'd known the answer all along. Maybe I just wanted, no—*needed* to hear her say it.

"Since the day we met. I just didn't admit it to myself until that night of the final."

Me too. Since day one. It had been mutual love at first sight, and we spent a year dancing around each other, around the truth, faking each other out. What fools. And now she was leaving.

I stared into my coffee cup, trying to process it all. "I don't know what to say," I said, my voice sounding so faint and distant.

You don't know what to say?! Tell her you love her too, moron!

"I'm sorry," she said. "I didn't mean to drop both bombs like this. They just sort of fell out of my mouth at the same time."

"Why didn't you tell me sooner?" *Right. Blame* her *for this mess. Like it was her responsibility.*

"That I was in love with you? Because you forbade it, remember? We signed that fucking contract. And then, when the contract expired, I didn't think there was any chance of it working out. I mean, you were right, Dev. I could never fully approve of what you do for a living. And that's totally hypocritical of me to say, considering I used you. You were right about that, too. I was no different from any of your clients."

It all became clear as day—I had systematically pushed her away, kept her at arm's length, and had expected her to see through it, defy my intentions. I was just being me—cool, suave, pleasure-serving Devin-the-Escort.

Except that *wasn't* me. Not anymore. That guy was an asshole. How had I not seen it? How had I so thoroughly deluded myself into thinking that was the way to be, that I wasn't hurting anyone?

"I was way out of line when I said that," I said.

"But you weren't wrong. We used each other."

"To better ourselves," I said in some desperate attempt to salvage us. "We both benefited from it. You taught me a lot, Andi."

"And you taught me a lot, and I am so grateful to you for that."

But...

"But why do you have to leave?" I sounded like a little kid.

"I'm ready for more," she replied, resolute. "And less, too, I suppose. I'm ready for a more challenging position as both a writing program director and a published textbook author. I want to publish a collection of memoirs next. And I'm ready for a more fulfilling, stable relationship, too. I met someone at the conference back in January."

Talk about kicking someone when he's down...

"Really." I said it like a statement. Because I knew. I'd known that evening at Claudio's. Perhaps I'd known even before then. I'd allowed myself to think it was Andrew because I couldn't bring myself to think it was someone else. Someone new. Someone way better than Andrew. Hell, someone way better than me.

"His name is Sam," she said. "He teaches at Edmund College, and we've been e-mailing and calling each other. In fact, he's the person I went to see during spring break."

And there you have it. The obliteration of my heart is complete.

"We're going to start seeing each other seriously once I move. I think I'm—I really, really care about him a lot. And you know, that's something else that's changed since meeting you. I never got to really know a man before. I was always so preoccupied with the sex thing and whether I was satisfying him and terrified of being rejected. By spending all this time with you, I got to know you. And I got to know and be myself—my real self. I just sometimes wish we could've started it this way and not as a proposition. And yet, in its own way, it's the most honest relationship I've ever been in, I think. And I guess now I want to try that with someone else."

How could I argue with that?

Before I could say anything, she added, "I should've told you sooner, I know. I'm sorry about that. I don't know why I didn't."

Tell her now.

"And the less?" I heard myself ask. "You said you were ready for more and less."

"For as long as I can remember, I wanted to live the life of a single New Yorker. I wanted to be a part of the city, part of a scene—coffee shops, bookstores, galleries, dating, whatever; knowing my way around, riding the subway fearlessly...All those years in New England, I passed myself off as that New Yorker. But I never was. I faked it. I was just a sheltered girl from the Long Island suburbs. This past year, I lived the life I always wanted, and you know what? I was still faking it. I was trying to cover up so much: my body, my sexuality, my insecurity, my fear..."

You're not the only one, I wanted to say. She wouldn't let me interject, however.

"But not anymore. I'm still a suburban at heart; I'm just not a sheltered, frightened girl anymore. Strange, I'm neither a New Yorker nor a New Englander. Or maybe I'm both now. I don't know. But I don't need the city streets and the train and the noise anymore. I don't need the crowds or the skyscrapers or Junior's or Heartland. I don't need to take cover."

I was so in love with her at that moment—the closed off bud I'd met, poked, coaxed out of her shell—had blossomed into a beautiful rose. And yet, she had become someone else's rose.

And I escorted her to him.

Exactly what I'd been hired to do. I'd done my job, the only job I'd ever been good at, splendidly, perfectly.

I sucked in a breath and exhaled forcefully through what felt like a gaping hole in my chest. "Well, sounds like you've made up your mind," was all I could say.

"What about *you*, Dev?"

I looked at her, perplexed. "What about me?"

"Aren't you ready for more? You once told me that I'm more than my body. So are you. *You can do so much more.* Don't you want more…and less?"

I was so done being Devin. So done with being a toy to be played with. Of playing others, and playing myself. I was all faked out.

Yes, Andi. Yes to all of it. But where to start? How?

"Why don't you go all the way with your clients?" she asked. She spoke with such love and tenderness, and my entire life came rushing from deep within the cells of my body to the surface of my skin.

I met her eyes, and knew exactly what to say.

And then my cell phone rang. I didn't need to look at the caller ID to know it was my sister. And I didn't need to speak to her to know what she was going to say. But I did both anyway.

"Yeah," I said sharply.

"It's time," said Joannie. Get over here now."

No. This can't be happening. Not now. Not yet.

"I'll be right there," I said, and ended the call without saying goodbye.

A worried expression came over Andi's face, as if we'd just

been shooting the breeze about baseball rather than breaking my heart. "Is everything OK?" she asked.

"I have to go," I said as I stood, grabbed my coat, and headed for the door, forgetting to pay for my coffee.

"What happened?" she asked, popping up and chasing after me.

I stopped and turned to face her for a second—"It's my father"—and then ran out the door, leaving her behind.

Chapter Twenty-Six

We were all in his room—Mom, Jo, and Ro—and each of us had taken turns saying goodbye, spending a moment alone with him. I'd never been so terrified in all my life to be alone with my father, who lay in bed pale, skeletal, almost ghostly. He'd had so much power over me all my life, had been so menacing, and yet he frightened me way more in this state.

I sat beside the bed, leaning in as close as I could so we could hear each other, and could practically smell the putrid odor of life draining from him, broken breath by broken breath. I touched his hand delicately, as if I could crumble the bones of his fingers with one squeeze. He'd hate me holding his hand.

"Dad, I'm sorry I wasn't a better son," I said, choking on every word. "I disappointed you, but I'm going to do better now. I promise." He didn't answer. I wasn't even sure if he heard me, much less understand. I feebly babbled on. "I'm quitting. And I met a woman. I love her."

His eyelids fluttered. "You're a good son," he murmured. "You're a man I'm proud to stand next to, because you have courage, respect, and brains. And who can tell his father to go to hell when his father is wrong."

"I never told you to go to hell, Dad." *No, I only told you to drop dead.*

Look at this, I'm still arguing with him, even now.

"And I never said you were wrong."

"I was wrong to think you could be like me, and thank God you're no fag, or worse—a goddamn bloodsucking lawyer." *Some things never change.* "But Geezus, David. You've got talent. You have more to give. You—"

He stopped when he heard me sob. "Now don't go crying on me. I'm only saying this because it all suddenly makes sense. Son of a bitch, what a rotten thing to do: give you all the answers right before you croak. Goddammit."

He'd said all this not in one sentence, but between broken breaths and morphine-induced stupors. I had to laugh to cover my tears.

"You'd better quit swearing, Dad, or else they might not let you in."

I swore I saw him smile.

"The hell with 'em."

My father grimaced in pain that he could no longer hide. I sputtered out the words as he squeezed my hand in an effort to relieve some of his pain and avoid crying in weakness.

"I love you, Dad."

I said it. Thank God I said it.

He gasped for air. "I love you too, David. Always have."

I clung to those words with his very last breath.

Chapter Twenty-Seven

Time had passed so slowly in the last seventy-two hours. I spent the next few days helping my mother and sisters prepare for the wake and funeral, staying at my parents' house, which felt like an abandoned dwelling. Even with our activities, the place echoed an uneasy silence.

I'd never called Andi to tell her what happened. Had forgotten to do it until the evening wake service, when I found myself missing her. My throat ached with every "Thank you for coming," I uttered to extended family I hadn't seen in years, who asked me what I was doing with my life and nodded politely as I told them I was in sales, marketing, customer relations, anything to keep the conversation brief and cryptic. Friends of my father's who told me I resembled him—were they saying it out of irony or politeness?

I wished I'd called her. Wished she'd been standing by my side, the way my sisters leaned on their spouses. At least my mother could lean on me.

The morning of the funeral, I'd taken off my Versace suit at the last minute and changed into no-name slacks— my father would've been furious with the Versace suit. Needing some kind of armor, I grabbed a Helmut Lang jacket on my way out. Hell of a time to be eclectic.

The limo arrived at the church, and I'd entered the vestibule awaiting instructions and the other pallbearers.

And then, like a dream come true, she appeared.

She wore a light V-neck sweater the color of forget-me-nots, a long skirt with a flower print to match the sweater, flats, and a denim jacket draped over her shoulders. The outfit was simple, bordering on bohemian, perhaps even underdressed. But there was something uplifting about it. Dad would've liked it.

"What are you doing here?" I asked, dazed.

"I had to drag it out of Christian, the rat-bastard," she said.

I couldn't help but laugh. "How did you know where to come?"

"I looked in the obits under 'Santino' and remembered you telling me that you were from Massapequa."

Andi. Thoughtful, caring Andi. I should have ditched whoever I was with at that publisher's cocktail party—who was it, Allison?—quit my job, and married her the moment I laid eyes on her.

"I'm sorry I never called you back," I said.

She smiled at me, one of understanding, and then hugged me. "You had more important things to do."

I squeezed her and didn't want to let go. She smelled like flowers.

"I'm so sorry for your loss, Dev," she said in my ear, holding me tightly. Only Andi could call me *Dev* and make me feel comfortable. The word *loss* fell on me like a boulder.

Although I'd wanted her to sit with me during the mass, I didn't invite her to—how could I introduce her to my family at such a moment? She sat several rows back, positioned in her seat so that she could see between two heads. We made eye contact a few times, and she affectionately, encouragingly smiled at me, as if to say, "You're doing fine; you can get through this." Every time our eyes met, the rows disappeared and she was right beside me.

When the mass was over, I invited her to my parents' house, opting to drive with her rather than ride in the limo. My mother and sisters didn't seem to mind.

We were silent during most of the drive.

"It was cancer." I finally spoke up, just as we got off Sunrise Highway.

She kept her eyes on the road. "When did it start?" she asked casually.

"A year ago. They told him he had six months."

"Where was it?" she asked.

"It started in his pancreas but spread to his lungs. He was a two-pack-a-day smoker before he quit fifteen years ago."

"Did you know he had cancer?"

I nodded. "He's been bad these last couple of months—in and out of the hospital—that's why I wasn't around much. When I got the call at Junior's, he was at the end. He died two days later."

"Did you get to say goodbye?"

I didn't answer her, except to point out the house. She pulled into the driveway.

I couldn't stop watching her. I watched her as I introduced her to my mother and sisters, who greeted her warmly. I watched her as I spoke to my relatives while she looked at family photographs on the mantel in the living room. I watched her as she helped carry in and cover Pyrex dishes full of casseroles and pasta from the dining room to the kitchen, and throw out paper plates littered with scraps of food, unfinished salads, and half-bitten pieces of bread. I entered the kitchen to find her talking to Joannie, saying, "There's always something else we can do, if only we weren't so busy listening to other people's voices." Joannie looked perplexed by the comment, and clammed up when she saw me. No doubt they'd been talking about me.

My aunt Maria insisted that Andi didn't need to help with the cleanup, yet she continued helping anyway. I watched her smile shyly as she saran-wrapped dishes, and wondered if it was the light coming from the kitchen window that illuminated her skin and shined her honey-roasted chestnut hair. I studied her body— short, curved, and luxurious—as she stretched to reach the high shelves of cabinets, and surrendered to her stunted growth by leaving things on the counters when she couldn't. I wanted everyone to disappear. Everyone but the two of us. I wanted to lift her onto the kitchen counter and wrap her legs around me and move my hands underneath her skirt and up her thighs...

Oh my god—my father died, and I'm thinking about sex?

Perhaps Andi was like this at every family's post-funeral gathering; a people-pleaser who did what she thought women should politely do. No. She'd told me stories about Thanksgiving dinner when she'd convene in the den with the rest of the guys to watch the Cowboys game, quickly dispelling (and resenting) the assumed gender roles and the notion that she was merely interested in Troy Aikman's butt. Besides, I knew her better than that.

But what captured me the most was when she crouched down on her knees, her long skirt covering her now-stocking feet, and knelt beside my almost-six-year-old niece, Meredith, who was sprawled out over a pad of paper and a box of half-spilled Crayolas as if they were classified blueprints. I couldn't hear what they were saying, but I watched Meredith trustingly allow Andi into her aura, pointing to her pictures, while Andi gave her undivided attention. There was Andi, at Meredith's level, seeing the world, the day, and the man through those five-year-old eyes; Meredith had plenty to say, all the more wiser than Joannie, who was already pestering Mom to consider putting the house up for sale while the market was still hot. They had all abandoned this little girl in their efforts to shelter her from the truth. No wonder Meredith forgot that Andi started out a stranger. She must have seen the same assurance in Andi's eyes that I now saw: eyes that flickered in darkness, that found lost objects, that made diamonds look lackluster.

I was overcome with the urge to write. To describe the scene before me. To document the day. Andi had given me that gift as well.

I finally approached them. "Hey, you've got enough for an exhibit!" I said with enthusiasm for Meredith. Andi whisked around, startled, and looked up at me.

"Geez, you scared me!" she said. "How long have you been there?"

"Not long," I replied, grinning with a contentment I hadn't felt since that day Andi and I were in the MoMA, and I told her my real name. I was so in love with her in the present moment, and trying to tell her telepathically.

She arrived knowing no one and left kissing everyone goodbye, wishing them well. My uncle Larry leaned over to me and said, "I don't know where you found her, but she's a real gem." And I had to shake my head and laugh as I recalled that day and pictured myself trying to explain it.

Nighttime had finally arrived, and Andi insisted that I stay with her at her apartment rather than at the house. She must have seen the exhaustion on my face, coupled with dread of spending another night in the cavernous, cancer-ravaged house, although I didn't want to leave my mother alone. My sisters promised to look after her. Thus, I accepted Andi's offer, simultaneously thrilled to finally be alone with her and guilty for my selfishness.

I was quiet in the car, trying to process the last twelve months. Hell, my entire life.

"I know you're probably sick of everyone asking this, but are you OK?" she asked.

"I'm fine," I said. "Thanks for being here today, and letting me stay with you."

"No problem. Can you imagine you going all the way back into the city and getting caught in the traffic?"

"No, I mean it." I reached out and placed my hand on her arm. "You don't know how it felt to see your face today. And I couldn't stay in that house tonight, or go back into the city. You don't know how much it means to me that you even knew to come."

"What do you mean, that I *knew* to come? If it wasn't for Christian—you should have *told* me. How could I not come?"

Again I was filled with remorse and regret, and not just for not calling her. "I don't know why I didn't tell you."

She looked at me compassionately, despite her reprimand. Every little glimpse from her, every glint from those green marbles and thick lashes folded around me and pulled me inside their warmth.

Was this what it felt like for women? Was this how they wanted to be enveloped by men after sex—to be pulled inside and then fully embraced and enveloped with all their love and security? To feel the touch—the actual, physical touch? What does that *feel* like? Is that what they really mean when they say, "go inside me"?

I needed to know.

When we arrived at Andi's apartment and I got ready for bed, I emerged from the bedroom to find her dressed in nothing but a T-shirt. My focus went right to her calves.

"Do you want to sleep on the couch or the bed?" she asked. "The couch is pretty uncomfortable. It kills my back, so I don't know how you would feel about it."

Did I hear her correctly? Did she want me to sleep in the bed with her? I'd spent nights with her before, lying next to her on the couch, feeling her feet brush against my leg, and knowing she was resisting the urge to snuggle close to me. Now I found myself trying to resist my own urges, and trembled at the very idea.

I knew I should've taken the couch, but I couldn't bear the thought of being alone. Maybe that's what she had intuited when she offered the bed. I thanked her and crawled in. And apparently I didn't misinterpret her because she followed me, and when she turned out the light, I inexplicably felt alone and afraid. We both lay there, awkwardly and deliberately apart. I breathed in the scent of her skin, and for a moment felt lightheaded with awe. She smelled so good, like lavender and vanilla.

The phone rang.

Andi let out a sigh indicating *worst fucking timing* and let the phone ring until the machine on her desk in the other room took the call. I heard a man's voice speaking, and could've sworn the word "sweetheart" began the message.

Fuck. It was the guy. I forgot his name.

"I'm sorry about that, Dev," Andi said softly.

The boulder of loss practically crushed my trachea. I couldn't speak, couldn't move, even though I wanted to scream and run.

"It's OK," I finally said. It was so *not* OK. "You could've answered it, you know."

"Not tonight," she replied. I appreciated that. Maybe she was having second thoughts about him. After all, she had invited me here, into her bed. Had spent the entire day with me. She still looked at me in a way that conveyed desire, caring, love.

We lay in the dark, still not touching, waiting for sleep that we both knew would be arriving late that night, if at all.

"Did you miss your father?" I piped up. "After he died, I mean."

"I really don't remember," she said. "I suppose that means I did."

"What if I don't miss him?" I said. "What would that say about me?" I'd finally found the courage to share my deepest fear.

"You'll miss him," she assured me.

And it was then, in the darkness, without warning, that I began to sob uncontrollably, and seconds later I felt Andi's soft touch, like a silk scarf, on my shoulder and then across my back and she leaned in close and whispered, "It's OK." And in that instant I wasn't just crying for the loss of my father, but my lost boyhood, the missing affection and disconnection that echoed in hollowness all these years.

He did love me after all.

She continued to lean in and over me, across my back and around my shoulders, hovering and protecting me like trees do to children in a storm, stroking my hair. How I loved when she stroked my hair.

Calmness started to overcome me like a passing cloud, and I began to feel very warm and full.

I turned to face her, and could make out her features in the dark. Her perfectly rendered features—lines and shadows and points and hues. I met her lips, soft and waiting. And then all my sadness, longing, and lust rushed forth, breaking through the dam I had so carefully constructed for so many years. I kissed her long and hard. I slid my hands under her T-shirt and cupped her breasts, warm and firm, before taking hold of her T-shirt and pulling it over her head. She wrapped her arms around my back and took hold of my own T-shirt, clumsily pulling it off before pushing me down and climbing on top of me. This once-insecure, inhibited woman was *climbing on top of me*, almost naked. She was Aphrodite. She was Diana. She was Venus.

She stretched out to the nightstand next to my side of the bed, pulled open a drawer, and reached for a box of condoms.

Please don't tell me she bought them for the guy. Please don't tell me she's already used them.

I playfully took hold of her and pushed her over before rolling and landing on her, pinning her to the bed and kissing her once again, moving from her neck, along her shoulder, to her breasts, tasting her smooth, sweet skin, feeling her move beneath me.

"What do you want?" she whispered.

I stopped and looked at her. She was so confident, so ready. She was a graduate out in the world, full of idealism and passion and enthusiasm, eager to apply all she'd learned. And I'd helped her get there. But it was more than that. I'd spent ten years paying attention to what women wanted, catering to their pleasures, meeting their needs, figuring that doing so would meet my own. But so few, if any, had ever asked me what *I* wanted. They were desperate to be the one to make me happy, but they never *asked*.

"I want to make love to you," I said softly. *I want to be your first. Your only.*

We made love, and it felt like it was my first time.

We lay together under the soft bedding, our warm bodies intertwined. "Andrea," I slurred in a sleepy whisper.

"Dev," she whispered back in a sigh.

"Am I your first?"

She didn't respond, and I could hear by her breathing that she'd fallen asleep.

Chapter Twenty-Eight

I awoke to find myself alone in bed. That right there should've been the first sign of things to come.

My folded clothes sat on top of the chest of drawers. I haphazardly dressed and went to look for Andi. Not that I had far to go. I spotted her sitting sideways on the loveseat in the living room, leaning against the armrest, wearing nothing but last night's T-shirt (and God, was that a sight), and visibly deep in thought.

"Morning," I said. She jumped and returned to the here and now.

"Hey, Dev," she said, her voice distant, yet casual. As if we hadn't just spent the night having sex following my father's funeral.

Some invisible stun gun had both immobilized us and rendered us speechless. Andi was the first to break out of it, standing up and pulling her T-shirt down in what was probably a reflexive gesture of modesty. "How are you?" she asked.

Oh, please. Please don't let this be awkward.

"OK," I replied.

"How'd you sleep?"

"Fucking great."

"Good," she said. She looked so delectable standing there in nothing but that T-shirt. The sight of her was enough to arouse me. She seemed to be experiencing the same thing as she fixated on my unbuttoned shirt. And yet, we each remained motionless.

"So, I don't really have much here in the form of breakfast," she said. "I could either make you some scrambled eggs or nuke some vegetable lo mein. Or we could go out to the diner, if you want."

I knew at that moment: sex was not going to happen again. The truth of it crushed me.

"I should probably go back home—to my parents' house, I mean," I said.

"Are you sure?"

"I don't want my mom to be all alone so soon after."

I couldn't read her expression. Was she relieved? Disappointed? Horny? Whatever it was, she wasn't acting on it. "OK. I'll go change and drive you there," she said.

"No need. I'll just get a cab."

"A cab will clean you out."

"I'm good for it," I snapped.

My sudden mood swing was contagious. "Honestly Dev, you're better off lighting a fucking match to your wallet. Case closed: I'm driving."

The nickname was starting to grate on me. Sign number two.

"Fine," I muttered. "I'll get ready."

As I turned toward the bathroom, Andi said, "Devin, wait…" *Devin.* Ugh. Forget *Devin.* That's not who made love to you last night. That's not who's in love with you. Just as I stopped to pivot toward her, she practically knocked me over as she rushed me in an embrace. I held on to steady her, and then to inhale her morning scent. I could feel her breasts against my torso, and it only made me more aroused. Could she feel *that*?

She let go and looked at me, her eyes registering temptation, frustration, confusion, indecision.

"Last night…" she started.

No. I don't want to hear it. I don't want to hear that it was a mistake, or a one-time only thing. I put my fingers to her lips to suppress her, but she took them away and continued. "Last night was incredible. I'm so glad it was you. I mean that."

I knew what she was saying. Perhaps she had heard my question last night.

Despite my being glad to know this, I was overcome with fatigue, sadness, longing. "It was *you*, Andi," I said, embracing her again. "You gave me so much more."

"I just, I just wish it didn't happen this way, that's all," she said, with a muffled voice. "Under these circumstances."

"It is what it is," was all I could come up with.

She let go and looked intently at me again, and we then simultaneously drew to each other like magnets and kissed.

Lust charged between us like static electricity. We breathed so hard, so in heat. Her mouth and fingers were practically on fire. I certainly was. And yet, we pulled away from each other as quickly and forcefully as we'd pushed together. Maybe the timing wasn't right. Maybe it was the blinking answering machine reminding us that a third party was in the room. Maybe we were just plain too late.

We barely spoke in the car. When Andi pulled into the driveway of my parents' house, I took in a lungful of dread. I had no idea what I would find when I entered. Or maybe I was more wary of what *wasn't* there. An occupied recliner. A dispensary of pill bottles. A Mets game on the television. I unclasped my seatbelt and faced Andi once more, trying so hard to communicate non-verbally. I think we were both tired of dancing around each other, avoiding the obvious. We were all faked out.

I extended my hand to her cheek in a caress, and she, in turn, extended hers to mine. A single tear slipped down her cheek and slid onto my finger. I smudged it away. Sign number three.

Without saying good-bye, I got out of the car and walked to the house, refusing to look back. I didn't want to see her pull away. What goes around comes around.

Chapter Twenty-Nine

June

"Would you stop being a douchebag for one minute and help us out?" I said to Christian when I asked him to help Andi load her furniture into the rented U-haul while her friends Maggie and Jayce did some last-minute labeling on cardboard cartons.

"You're helping the woman you love move away without even putting up a fight, and you're calling *me* a douchebag?"

I know. Surreal. I was helping the woman I loved return to Massachusetts. And a new job. Not to mention a new lover.

I hadn't spoken to her since she drove me back to my parents' house the morning after the funeral a couple of weeks ago. I'd avoided two of her calls too, until she left a message informing me of her moving day.

Why did I do it? Why did I help her leave? Maybe because I didn't want things to end horridly between us. Maybe I couldn't stand the thought of being angry at her. Maybe deep down I didn't think I deserved her.

Or maybe it was because when all was said and done, Andi and I had always been friends. And I wanted to be her friend right up to the very end.

Didn't mean it wasn't killing me to know in a few short hours she was going to be out of my life.

I didn't say much other than barking commands, taking charge of the whole moving out process like a loading dock foreman. Christian, on the other hand, maintained a sense of levity, especially with Andi's friends as he jokingly tried to recruit them as clients despite the fact that we were both in the process of turning over the business to two of our employees. Andi seemed to be a mix of nerves and stress and impatience, although she too joined in with Christian's joviality every so often.

When everything was packed and cleaned out, Andi thanked Christian and gave him a hug. "Stay cool," he said to her. He then took my hand to shake, and mouthed *Don't let her get away* to me.

I lingered as she exchanged long and tearful goodbyes with Jayce and Maggie.

They drove away, leaving just the two of us, outside, beside the U-Haul. Summer loomed around the corner, as indicated by the sun still bright in the late afternoon, accompanied by a light breeze and fluffy clouds.

We couldn't even look at one another.

"Thank you for everything," she said quietly. I suspected she meant more than my helping her load the U-Haul.

I didn't answer her.

"You know," she began, "we never got a chance to talk about any of this."

"What's there to talk about?" I said. "You made your choice."

It suddenly occurred to me that I was grieving. And I was angry.

"I don't know how you feel about it," she said.

I shook my head and laughed in exasperation. "You don't know how I fucking feel about it…geez, Andi."

"What," she said rather than asked. I recalled having used that same tone on her once.

"I'm in love with you."

Her mouth opened.

"What?"

"You heard me," I said. Although I sure as hell didn't sound like I was in love.

She looked like she was about to hit me.

"*Now* you tell me this?" she said.

"I've been a little distracted lately."

She raised her voice. "You couldn't slip it in somewhere?"

I matched her raise. "When? As my father was going into the ground? Between gag reflexes over my aunt's fucking stale casserole?"

"How about the day I told you at Junior's? How about the night we…" she trailed off.

"I didn't know then," I lied. *You mean you were too much of a coward.*

She didn't buy it.

"You didn't know then?" she repeated. "When did you have this epiphany?"

"I don't know." Devin, the guy who had an answer for everything, went MIA. And a moron had taken his place.

She paused.

"I can't help but notice that you're back to work, so maybe you're not that distracted after all," she said.

Christian's jokes must have led her to the assumption. But I hadn't worked since before my father died. Rather than correct her, I resented her righteous indignation. "Don't you dare make this about my work."

She paused again, as if giving me a chance to change my tune. But I didn't. Like I said, all systems had been set to Moron.

"So, how am I to respond to this confession?" she asked.

"How should I know?"

"What do you want me to say?"

I folded my arms across my chest. "Forget it, Andi. Just get in your car and go." *Go to the guy. Go to Sam.* I'd heard her say his name earlier.

She looked away for a second, drew in a breath, and faced me again.

"You know, for someone who has all the right words to sweep a woman off her feet, you really suck at this."

Wow, did she have me pegged.

"Nice fucking good-bye," I retorted.

"No, I mean it," she said, raising her voice again. "What are you so afraid of, Dev? You know, you've never really been honest with me. You've extolled the virtues of my body and my sexuality, and you complimented me on my kissing and you've written some excellent pieces. But you've never told me what you *think*. What you *feel*. Did you think I wouldn't approve of you either?"

"Would it have made you stay?" I asked.

"Maybe."

And then I lost it. "Oh *bullshit*, Andi! You said yourself that you don't approve of what I do for a living. Hell, you just insinuated it two minutes ago with that smarmy, righteous tone of yours."

"I never said I don't approve—I said I could never accept it if we were together."

"Whatever. Give me a break with splitting the fucking semantic hairs. And don't you preach to me about honesty.

You're the one who kept this little secret from me and dropped it on my balls like a dumbbell. In fact, *you* keep secrets very well."

She hung her head in shame. "I was sorry about that, Devin," she said, her tone softening. "You know that."

"David."

The name put a pause on our fight and took us both off guard.

"What did you say?" she asked.

"My name is *David*," I said.

"I don't know David," said Andi.

Her words were like arrows, and every one of them pierced my heart. Our eyes connected like so many times before, revealing so many truths, and she looked away as if she'd just seen something gruesome, like a mangled body by the side of the road.

"I don't want to say goodbye this way," she said as a tear rolled down her cheek. "I don't want it to end like this."

I finally came to my senses. "I don't want it to end at all."

We looked at each other again, and I took her hand. "Please don't go," I begged, my voice breaking on the first word.

"I have to go, and this has to end," she said, looking at our joined hands. Perhaps she was contemplating the possibility. Or maybe she was thinking of someone else's hand.

"Why?" I asked, feeling so defeated.

"Because it was a lie."

Our entire relationship flashed in front of me like a film on fast-forward, beginning with me extending my hand with my salesman's pitch: "I'm Devin," and leading up to the night of my father's funeral, in her bed, on top of her, inside of her…

"Not all of it," I said.

"Too much of it."

She was right. I couldn't bear to admit it, but she was.

"So, we can start over," I offered.

"As what? Friends? Lovers? What are we now—the escort and his former client? I can't and I don't want to start over. I want to start something new with someone else."

This was what she'd wanted that day outside of Junior's, when she'd asked me to teach her to be a better lover. She'd wanted to start something new with someone else. She'd wanted to be better than someone else. No—she'd wanted to be a better form of herself. And I fulfilled her desire. I was a good escort. I was a good teacher too.

Thing is, she'd made me want the very same things. I'd thought I needed everything in place before I could have and be those things. But I'd gotten it colossally wrong. I'd waited too long to get to know my father, and to tell him that I loved him. To even *try*. I'd thought I was doing Andi a favor. I'd thought she was doing the same thing I was doing—waiting for me to get my shit together. And I'd lost them both at the same time.

"God, don't do this to me, Andi," I begged again. "Please. Not right now."

She caressed my face with her free hand. "I don't want to hurt you," she said.

In a last-ditch effort, I took hold of her and kissed her hard. I was done with words. My words had failed me. So had my actions. This was the only way I knew how to persuade her. I let that kiss speak on my behalf, say everything I had withheld, spill all my secrets, reveal my true self. And judging by the way she was holding and kissing me back, I was certain it was working…

She stopped, then kissed me one last time before letting go.

"I'll always love you, Dev, and I'll always be grateful to you," she said.

"David," I corrected a second time, knowing that I'd lost her for good.

"I don't know David," she repeated, even more painfully than the last time.

"I want you to," I pleaded.

She stood on her toes and spoke in my ear. "Then start *being* David."

And then I realized: As long as Andi saw and knew and believed me as Devin, we would never have a chance. We never did.

I was still holding her hand, to the point that she needed to unclasp it with her other. She then backed up to the U-Haul.

"Will you get back to the city OK?" she asked. I nodded, rubbing my eyes to keep my tears at bay. She got into the car and waved.

"Goodbye," she said.

I raised and lowered my hand in a brash gesture. "Bye."

When she was out of sight, I went to my car parked next to the curb in front of the house with a now-vacant apartment, and sat in it. I didn't start the engine right away. Just sat with both hands on the wheel, looking at the road ahead where Andi had driven away, perhaps waiting to see if the U-Haul would return.

Of course, I knew it wouldn't.

And then, something came over me. Not quite serenity, but more like conviction, a promise.

Then start being David.

"OK," I said. And then I turned the key.

Chapter Thirty

October—Sixteen Months Later

Life can be a series of happy mistakes.

I was still new to the Boston area (and its art scene) when I decided to check out the Senior Art Show at the Boston School of Art.

Keep in mind that I'm a relocated New Yorker. Manhattan, to be exact. I'd gotten used to grids. I'd gotten used to numerical progressions, to cross-street references (57th and 5th, 7th and Lex). I'd gotten used to dichotomies: East and West, Upper and Lower, Uptown and Downtown. So you can imagine what a city like Boston does to a guy's sense of direction. How many times have I gone in circles only to find that my intended destination was right down the block?

And so, after a series of wrong turns and getting caught in a downpour, I conceded that I was lost yet again and stumbled into what turned out to be a belly dancing class to ask for directions. The cymbal-clicking, veil-waving temptresses were actually a group of printmaking students who privately met once a week to "unleash their inner goddesses." And although the dancing was certainly an art form unto itself and undoubtedly worthy of my attention, it was not what I had in mind. So I politely (and soggily) declined their offer to join their group, and instead thanked them, heading out once again.

Quickly dismissing an image of my soaking body flopping and gyrating, surrounded by printmaking belly dancers, I'd hoped I was getting close, until I passed a propped door with a brushed bronzed plaque that read Graduate Gallery. This was still not my final destination, but the low lighting and satisfying purr of the air-conditioner drew me in; and once inside, I almost immediately felt a shift in reality. A sign near the gallery's entrance introduced me to the collection by Jesse Bartlett, and I decided to stay and get acquainted. Together, the paintings displayed a balance of the energy, movement, and warm, earthy colors of the cave paintings of Lascaux partnered with the edge of modern city life and a skilled, albeit young, hand.

Each piece contains its own voice, its own message. A fragment of city life as seen, experienced, and recorded from every angle and position imaginable. Twenty-six-year-old Bartlett brings a unique perspective to his paintings. "City life was unlike anything I'd ever seen before," says the Granby, Vermont native who relocated to Boston for his graduate work in contemporary painting. "It was just raw and I was blown away by it. Blindsided, you know? And everybody just walks around like nothing's happening. And I just stop and stare," he shrugs, "because it's all I can do."

"And then you paint," I respond.

"*Yeah. I paint what I see, and what other people don't see. 'Cause you got to see this, and you got to see it for what it is.*"

"*So, what is 'it'?*"

"*Life,*" he says simply. "*People. The good stuff.*"

Like their subjects, these paintings are innately beautiful—abstract, literal, human, and personal. They are also rough and textured, unbalanced, and sometimes even harsh. Viewing this art feels almost voyeuristic, much like seeing everything about a person in one glance. Process and narration are evident in each piece. Layers of weathered newspapers, flyers, and found objects are washed with color to construct the scaffolding behind a strong drawing hand and confident use of color, shape, and form. The subject and material blend in formal voice, creating a texture and even scent of life. Individually, these pieces are sensual; together, they are compelling.

The images aren't clean, they aren't perfect, and they aren't always refined. But they are real. They are telling. Alive. The show comes together in a world of tone, light, and atmosphere. It gets under your skin until it seeps out of your hair. You feel this art. To view it is to truly experience city life, be it Boston or the Big Apple. And it feels good. Pleasurable.

Jesse Bartlett has something to say, and he is just beginning to learn how to say it. He's the kind of artist you'll want to discuss someday at a cocktail party, bragging that you knew him when. And you'll have every right to brag, because he's worth the experience.

You won't forget it. Neither will I.
And neither, hopefully, will those belly dancers.

I re-read the draft for the umpteenth time before finally sending it to the editor at the *Boston Leisure Weekly*, an indie newspaper with a small but cozy readership. I'd learned about blending genres from Andi. She'd encouraged using anecdotes, incorporating what she called "the personal-expressive," and although it wasn't a typical review, so far the readers (what few I had—I hadn't been writing the column for long) seemed to like it, although I still felt like a novice when I wrote.

Of course, my intended reader, my imagined reader, was Andi. Always. I had no idea whether she'd seen any of them. Whether she'd recognized the byline in fine print. Whether she remembered.

Can you believe it? I'm a writer now.

Well, once in awhile, at least. My main job these days is as a gallery owner-in-training. I'd done very well networking while working for Travis, who, at a dinner party, introduced me to Georgia Paris, owner of Paris Gallery in Boston. "It was love at first sight," Georgia tells people about us. "Platonic, of course. Something tells me that if we slept together, we'd kill each other afterwards." Georgia wanted to sell her gallery, and I practically got down on my knees and proposed to her. We both knew I was the one. Besides, I was done with New York. I knew too many people in New York. Too many women, to be precise. I needed a clean break.

Boston seemed like a good place to start over.

I know what you're thinking: Massachusetts. Andi. You're probably right.

Not that I had plans to stalk her, disrupt her life, keep tabs on her. No, I had come to accept that we didn't work out. I had been complicit in our demise, and I accepted the consequences of it. Maybe that kind of strange comfort, just knowing she's dwelling somewhere in the state, was enough. Like going to some historical place and having a sense of awareness of who'd walked on its hallowed ground before you.

Besides, I liked Boston. And I wanted to stay in the northeast. The art scene seemed to be good for someone like me—someone who knew so much yet had never been on the inside of it all.

So far Georgia Paris was the only person I'd confided to about my previous business, especially since it turned out an acquaintance of hers had been one of my clients. She was OK with it—impressed, actually—and took me under her wing. She was even more impressed by how quickly I got a handle on the business, and how well I interacted with both artists and patrons. "You should've gotten into this twenty years ago," she said. "You would've been stinking rich by now."

Damn straight. I guess better late than never.

I loved every minute of my work—the newness of it, the activity, the challenge, even the difficulties and the mistakes I made. I felt so *free*, having never realized how much mental and emotional energy I exerted servicing my clients night after night. For the most part, I left work at work. Like before, my hours were flexible. And I slowly but surely was building some semblance of a social life. I made friends. I even started dating. Nothing to call my mother about, but it was nice not to try so hard, if that makes sense. Not that I didn't care. But I wasn't in full-out charm mode. Rather I had slowed down, took time to get to know the women I went out with, even if I knew a second date wasn't forthcoming. Granted, I had mastered the art of active listening when I was an escort, but I'd done it more so out of customer service than personal intention even though I'd found myself interested in what my clients had to say, and I'd learned a lot from them over the years. I'd gotten as far as four months with one woman—Corinne Martin—until she broke it off, insisting that her feelings for me ran far deeper than mine for her. I was disappointed. Hurt, even. I cared about her deeply, and found her attractive. The sex was good too. I'd wanted to fall in love with her, was practically praying for it. But it hadn't happened yet. I'd wanted to ask her to give me more time, but clearly she wasn't willing to be strung along, and I respected her for that.

I was quite depressed after that, worried that I wasn't over Andi, or worse—wouldn't ever be over her. Georgia insisted that I was still in the grieving stage, both for my father and Andi (although I never mentioned her by name), not to mention that I was still getting used to being David Santino, gallery manager and soon-to-be owner, rather than Devin the Escort. I needed to cultivate a relationship with myself before I did with a potential love partner. Or so she said. Made sense to me. Maybe I was grieving the loss of Devin, too.

Tonight was a new and local artist, Jesse Bartlett's, debut exhibit. I had worked overtime making sure everything was in order. It was also the first time Georgia completely handed the reins over to me. It's possible I was even more nervous than twenty-something Jesse.

Paris Gallery was a small loft space on the second floor with buffed, honey-colored hardwood floors and well-lit, white walls.

I'd selected the paintings to be showcased, the order of viewing, and I oversaw the hanging and lighting of each one—I thought I knew about lighting until I met Georgia. She was a master, and I was indebted to her for teaching me everything she knew. Jesse had arrived earlier in the day to approve of it. He was impressed. Bewildered, in a way. I think the magnitude of the event got real for him at that moment. For me too.

The opening was a smashing success. New and returning patrons showed up, along with Jesse's friends and family. The champagne and hor d'ourves circulated incessantly, and I made it a point to schmooze and shake hands with every single person who set foot in what would soon be officially *my* gallery. My home.

I happened to be checking in with the bartender at the cash bar when one of the champagne servers approached and asked for ginger ale. In a champagne flute. Special request from a patron.

Holy shit.

Quickly scanning the gallery, I saw *him* first: Medium height, fit, dressed in a casual-yet-cordial sort of way. Short, tapered hair. Blue eyes. Looked like a professor. I'd seen enough of them to know the type. Looked a little like Rob Lowe, actually.

That was as far as my assessment went, until I saw the hand he was holding. I don't know why that had caught my attention, or if I'd even recognized the hand. But my eyes traveled up the arm to the shoulder, until I saw the honey-chestnut hair. Interesting that I didn't check out her legs first.

And then I saw her face.

My insides turned to jelly. I reached to grab hold of something to steady myself, and found nothing. My head went woozy, my brain soggy.

I had imagined this day so many times, especially at night

when I closed my eyes, alone in bed, and waited for sleep. Had even scripted a conversation in my journal. But nothing prepares you for when it really happens. Everything you imagined or planned disappears in an instant, as if it never even existed. You're on your own, in the tall grass.

And then, as quickly as the anxiety attack rushed me, it left me, replaced with a sense of calm I hadn't felt since my trip to Europe last year, when I was sitting in one of Rome's many plazas, taking in the air and the language and the scents and the scenery, and feeling so at home and at peace with myself.

I knew who I was. And I knew who I wanted to be.

And there, in the present moment, I was *excited* to see her.

I took the flute from the bartender and crossed the gallery floor. They were standing in front of the final painting of the exhibit.

She turned around before I had a chance to say, "Excuse me." No way I could contain my elation as we came face to face for the first time in sixteen months.

"This has to be for you," I said, extending the glass to Andi. I may have even winked.

Chapter Thirty-One

She stood in front of me, completely agog.

I decided to reach out to the guy first, and extended my hand. "Hi, I'm David Santino, co-owner of the gallery."

Believe it or not, I was still getting used to introducing myself as David.

"Sam Vanzant," he said, shaking my hand heartily, "and this is my fiancée, Andrea Cutrone."

Fiancée.

My heart dropped to my feet.

I should've expected it.

But she was happy. Even in her current state of shock, she was obviously happy to be with Sam. She was dressed in black boot cut slacks with a button-down poplin shirt and a short, tapered leather jacket and matching pumps. Her hair was short again, and framed her face in layers. She applied her makeup flawlessly, creating the smoky eyes effect.

That, in turn, made me happy. As happy as one could be in such a situation.

She didn't move a muscle. I took her hand into my own and held it for a second longer than I probably should have, not averting eye contact.

"It's nice to see you, Andi."

Sam perked up the second I called her "Andi." He darted between her and me. "You two know each other?"

She opened her mouth, and out came something like a sputtering mess of sound, like every instrument in an orchestra starting on the wrong note and not listening to each other to find their way back.

"I…eyuttuttuttya…eeya…"

Oh my God. That's so freaking cute.

"We had mutual friends at Brooklyn U," I said.

"Really?" Sam replied. "Sweetheart, you didn't tell me you know the owner here."

He didn't sound distrustful or jealous. More like pleasantly surprised. Shit, he was a nice guy. *Come on, man—give me something to make me hate you.*

"Oh, I've only been here for about six or seven months. Georgia Paris is the other owner," I said, pointing to her nearby, talking to Jesse and another couple. She caught me pointing her out and gestured in acknowledgment. OK, so I embellished a little by saying "the other owner." It wasn't official yet. I confess: I wanted to impress Andi. Not for the purpose of trying to win her back, but to show her how far I've come. That, for the most part, I was happy too. Happier than I'd been in a long time. And I was. Even seeing her there with Mr.-Perfect-Face, calling her sweetheart and proudly introducing her as his fiancée, hadn't deterred me.

"I sold my other business, sublet my apartment in the city, moved here, and became a partner. Georgia's teaching me everything she knows so I can take over," I said, unable to take my eyes off Andi. She looked at me, taken aback by the mention of the selling of "my other business."

"What did you do before?" asked Sam.

For a split second, I considered telling him the truth, just to see his reaction. Scratch that—just to see *her* reaction. Making her squirm like I used to—correction: like Devin used to.

"I was in the service industry." I winked at her. Couldn't resist.

She looked as if she was about to topple like a bunch of Jenga blocks.

"Well, fancy meeting us here. Small world," said Sam.

"He knew the dean," Andi blurted to Sam. I shot her a quizzical, yet amused look. Sam seemed equally perplexed. "At Brooklyn U," she attempted to clarify before turning to me. "Didn't you?"

This was getting fun. "You look great," I said.

"So do you," she replied. Her face turned pink, which, selfishly speaking, delighted me even more. "I almost didn't recognize you. David," she tacked on after a beat. She said my name as if trying it out for the first time. Which she was. Did she like it? Did she like *me*?"

"So, what do you think of the exhibit?" I asked.

"Good stuff," said Sam, shooting a panorama of the exhibit with one turn of his head. "We read a great review of it in the *Boston Leisure Weekly* this morning, and it was dead-on accurate."

Dammit. Now I have to like this guy.

"Thanks—I wrote it," I said.

And then, as if recognizing me for the first time, Andi opened her mouth and pointed. *"Oh my God—it was YOU!!!"*

You know that scene in *When Harry Met Sally...*, when Sally blurts out "It just so happens that I have had plenty of good sex," and the entire diner goes silent? That moment pretty much happened. All heads turned to us. Andi, although visibly mortified, maintained her composure and played it cool.

I didn't bat an eyelash. "Yes, Andi. I'm a writer now too. I have an occasional review in the *Boston Leisure*. I'm trying to make it into a regular column, though. Still an amateur, I guess."

"You were always a writer," she said so matter-of-factly. You'd think showing my first exhibit on my own would be the highlight in and of itself. But no. *This.* Validation from Andi. I wanted to kiss her.

"Well, you've got a flair for narrative," said Sam. "Andi and I are both memoirists."

"Yes, and I happen to know that *she* is quite talented," I said, beaming at her. Was I trying to rub it in Sam's face that Andi and I had a history? Or was I simply stating a truth?

She beamed right back, and Sam put his arm around her and pulled her to him, kissing the side of her head in both a proud and affectionate gesture. I envied him. Maybe he could sense the history, feel the chemistry. Maybe he was having a macho moment of *She's mine, asshole.* "You got that right," he said.

A pregnant pause took over, and Sam asked me the way to the men's room, excusing himself after I pointed the direction.

"So..." she started. I could've finished her sentence for her. "You really left the business, huh."

"Yep."

"How come?"

Seriously? You don't know?

"You know, it's funny. I swore the only reason I'd ever stop being an escort was because I'd lost a limb—certainly not because of some moral conscience."

"You had a moral conscience?"

I folded my arms and cocked my eyebrow, as if to say, *Well played.* Her feigned straight face broke into a grin.

"Actually, I stopped enjoying it," I said. "Doing it just got more and more pointless—not for the clients, but for me. There didn't seem to be anything for me to want anymore." *Except you.* I would've said it out loud had she not been engaged to Mr. Likes-My-Review.

"When did you stop?" she asked.

"About a year ago, I think. Shortly after you left." Technically, I'd stopped when my father died. But I was out completely after she'd left. I don't know why I wasn't being more straightforward with her, other than the fact that we were in a public place and her fiancé, Mr. I-Wonder-if-I-Could-Take-Him-in-a-Fight would be back any moment.

"What did you do?" she asked.

"I divested myself from the business, turned it over to Christian—who then turned it over to James and Kyle, our chosen successors—and I had a shitload of cash laying around, so I decided to take a long vacation in Europe. Italy, Spain, France, you name it. I found every big museum and backstreet gallery imaginable. Even got robbed one time, smack in the middle of the day, although I only had a couple of travelers' cards and the equivalent of fifty bucks on me...You know, American Express really is good about getting stolen cards replaced."

Sam returned, which signaled the end of our conversation. I knew that if she walked out that door, I might never see her again. "Here," I said, reaching into my pocket and pulling out a business card. I handed it to her. "I'm almost always here. Give me a call and we'll have lunch sometime."

What on earth had I just done? Had I just asked out this dude's wife-to-be? *In front of him?*

No. I invited my friend to lunch.

But why?

She took the card and read it with the focus and concentration she gave to student papers or scholarly texts. As if she were analyzing every word on it.

"Thanks," she said, sounding ambivalent. I couldn't blame her. Maybe she was questioning my motives as well.

"Well, I've got to tend to my patrons. Thanks so much for coming." I shook Sam's hand again. "It was a pleasure to meet you," I said. I think I meant it too.

"Same here," he replied.

I turned to Andi. "And so nice to see you again." I definitely meant that.

"Welcome to New England," she said. And then *she winked.*

I carried my smile all the way to the other side of the room and introduced myself to a new group of patrons, willing myself not to turn my head and see if Andi and Sam were still there, or if she was watching me. When I finally did, they were gone.

Shortly afterward, Georgia approached me. "Darling, who was that?"

"Who was who?" I asked, knowing damn well about whom she was inquiring.

"The woman who put that goofy grin on your face."

I looked at the spot where Andi had been standing, as if she had made a mark.

"An old friend," I replied.

Georgia knew who it was. And she knew that I knew that she knew. "She's adorable," she remarked.

"Engaged," I shot back.

Georgia looked at me more earnestly than I've ever seen her. "Mark my words, darling. You'll be together someday. Don't worry about the how and when. It's what you do with yourself in the meantime that counts."

No way I could allow myself to cling to such a notion. "Time to lay off the champagne, my love," I said. She gave me a wet, platonic peck on the lips.

"You just wait," she insisted.

Chapter Thirty-Two

I honestly didn't think she'd call. But I was thrilled when she did, two weeks after the Jesse Bartlett exhibit.

We sat at a table in a Peruvian coffeehouse down the road from the gallery. I appreciated her coming all the way to Boston from Northampton to meet me. We mirrored each other, attired in faded T-shirts, blue jeans, and leather jackets, and laughed amiably at the sight, as if a moment hadn't passed between us. That alone was a delicious feeling of normalcy.

The diamond and sapphire ring on her left finger practically screamed for my attention. Funny how I'd not noticed it two weeks ago.

"When did you get engaged?" I asked.

"End of May," she replied.

"Hm," I said, perhaps as a tease. "Seems like a good guy."

"He is."

I could see it on her face, and even in the way she sat. She was in love with him. She was content. She had every intention of marrying him. And no question he was in love with her. How could he not be? Maybe that's why I'd given her my card and invited her to meet me. Maybe I wanted to know for sure. And maybe I wanted to see if I was truly OK with it.

I was.

Maybe she'd wanted to find out the same thing. Did she see that I was OK?

A slice of chocolate cake sat between us, and we took turns slicing our forks into it.

"I think it's great that you're writing," said Andi.

"I kept a journal the entire time I was in Europe. I wrote a lot about my father and growing up, and about you too."

Her eyes misted over.

"And then, one day all I wanted to do was paint. There I was in Positano, completely lost in the sunset, dying for a set of oils. And then, it came to me—and I swear it was in my father's voice: 'You're an artist, David.' And that was it. I came home."

It felt so good to talk to her like this. For all the sharing we'd done, I'd never been so forthcoming, so truthful.

"Then how come you're not painting now?" she asked. "I mean, you're a gallery owner instead."

"Because for me, the true love isn't in making the art; it's being surrounded by it. I once had a client who had a brother who worked in a bookstore. She said he could have easily been the next Vonnegut or Ellison, but he absolutely loved being around the books. That's what felt like home to him."

She gave me a look of validation.

I continued. "And that's what the gallery feels like to me. For me, art is born out of my witness. I guess it's the same with you and memoir."

She nodded. "Precisely. I suppose that's why I've always loved rhetoric—it's always in response to something else."

This time I nodded. "I can write about it, talk about it, see it. Might as well show it and sell it, too, because I also do that very well."

"You sure do." She paused for a beat. "So…I guess you left New York because of Devin?"

I rolled my eyeballs around. "A city of eight million people— you'd be surprised how often I would run into my fucking clients."

She chuckled. "Why Boston?"

"Good art scene. Good city. Good opportunities. I met Georgia, one thing led to another, and the rest is history."

She processed this as she took long and slow bites of cake.

"Do you ever miss being an escort?" she finally asked.

I shook my head. "Surprisingly not. Do you ever miss being in New York?"

"Surprisingly not."

We sat and stared and smiled at each other. And I couldn't help but let myself hope…

"Do you ever miss *me*, Andi?" I heard myself ask.

She stared at the near-empty cake plate, as if fascinated with it, yet wistful, and didn't respond. I had to know what she was thinking.

"Why did you call me?" I pressed.

"I'm not sure," she said.

"I'm glad you did."

This time she paused for a beat before asking, "Do you ever miss *me*?"

I blushed and grinned again and took the final bite of cake.

"So when's the wedding?" I asked.

She seemed thrown by the question, but quickly recovered. "Next October," she replied. "A year from now."

"Hm," I said. "Not June, when school's out?"

"We both wanted an autumn wedding."

Her next pause lasted for several beats, as if she needed a moment to brace herself, or get up the nerve.

"Are you seeing anyone?" she asked.

"Not right now," I answered casually. "I mean, I've been dating, but nothing's stuck so far. I'd like to, though. Get into a serious relationship, I mean."

To my surprise, my next thought wasn't *With you.*

I glanced at my watch. "I need to get back to the gallery."

We left the coffeehouse and walked down the street, stopping at the corner. The sun brightly blazed over Boston, against an azure canvas of sky. Andi and I turned to face each other, our auras touching, and she practically stood on her toes to look up at me, helplessly towering over her.

"I'm glad you called," I said one more time. At that moment, I was overcome by the urge to hold her. I took her into an embrace, and she let me. She smelled like coffee.

"Oh, Dev," she said, the words caught. "I do miss you." I could hear the hurt in her voice, the conflict, and my heart ached for her, in more ways than one.

"I miss you too," I said as I stroked her hair.

Everything came rushing up inside me at that moment—and Georgia's prophecy the night of the exhibit clanged like bells in my brain: *Mark my words. You'll be together someday.*

Somehow every fiber of my being knew it. I just didn't know when.

And surprisingly, I didn't need to know. *It's what you do with yourself in the meantime that counts.*

I resolved to make the most of that meantime.

I kissed Andi gingerly on her forehead. She looked at me, and I could see her glassy eyes through the lenses of her shades.

"See you, David," she said simply. Perhaps she'd made a resolution of her own.

"See you," I said.

I watched her as she turned to walk to the T, and heard myself call out to her: "Hey Andi!" just before she turned the corner and out of sight. She spun around as I jaunted and quickly caught up to her. I invaded her space once more and peered at her.

"I have to ask: how's the sex with Sam?"

A grin not unlike the proverbial Cheshire cat spilled across her face. "Fucking fabulous," she said.

I beamed like a proud teacher.

"That's cute," I replied.

We each turned the corner and walked away, in opposite directions.

I wasn't going to wait, I decided. I was going to *live.*

Acknowledgments

Faking It was conceived in 1999, written in 2004-05, independently published in print in 2009 and e-book in 2010, re-released by a then-new publisher in 2011, translated into German in 2014 and French in 2015, and to date has sold, in all formats and languages, over a quarter of a million copies around the world.

This will never stop blowing my mind.

I wrote *Faked Out* in early 2014, and I was surprised even then by some of what Devin had to say. I wish it hadn't taken me so long to bring this beloved story from his point-of-view into the world, but I'm glad it's finally here.

Special thanks to:

Erika Simon for reading and responding to an early draft, and Sarah Girrell for being a cheerleader then and now.

Kelly Sutphin, who never lets me forget who's older.

Heather Grace Stewart, for being my accountability partner as well as my friend. Larry is watching and smiling.

The many book clubs and passionate readers who asked to hear Devin's side of the story.

Chris Noth, whom I met briefly in 2000 and who has no idea his smile was the inspiration for Devin's.

Judy Blume, who inspired me first as a girl, then as a reader, and today as a woman and a writer.

Peter Elbow, who, after reading *Faking It*, coined the term "romance rhetoric." It perfectly encapsulates my books.

Aaron Sorkin and the late Nora Ephron, whose talent and inspiration also encapsulate my books.

Lake Union Publishing for their continued support of the *Faking It* series, and Missouri Breaks Press for picking up the baton and running with it.

My dear friends and family, who have accompanied me on this publishing journey.

Jovana Shirley, who formatted the e-book version.

David Otey, who gave voice to Devin in the audiobook version.

Spatz, who is a terrible editor but a fabulous cat.

And always, my darling husband, Craig Lancaster, who is my favorite writer and cover designer, my best friend, and my partner in every way. I can't imagine taking this road trip with anyone else.

Photo by Casey Page

About the Author

Elisa Lorello is a Long Island native, the youngest of seven children. She earned her bachelor's and master's degrees at the University of Massachusetts Dartmouth and taught rhetoric and writing at the college level for more than ten years. In 2012, she became a full-time novelist.

Elisa is the author of eight novels, including the bestselling *Faking It*, a memoir, and a book about writing. She has been featured in *Montana Quarterly* and *Rachael Ray Every Day* magazines, and Jane Friedman's blog series 5 On. She also was a guest speaker at the Triangle Association of Freelancers 2012 and 2014 Write Now! conferences. In May 2016, she presented a lesson for the Women's Fiction Writers Association spring workshop. She continues to speak and write about her publishing experience and teach the craft of writing and revision.

She lives with her husband, bestselling author Craig Lancaster.

On Facebook: Elisa Lorello, Author
On Twitter: @elisalorello
Subscribe to elisalorello.com and receive exclusive updates, offers, and gifts!

Don't Miss the Other Books in the *Faking It* Series

FAKING IT

*Elisa Lorello's
debut novel,
a worldwide bestseller*

ORDINARY WORLD

*The compelling sequel,
continuing Andi and
David's story*

SHE HAS YOUR EYES

*The introduction of
Wylie Baker
into the series*

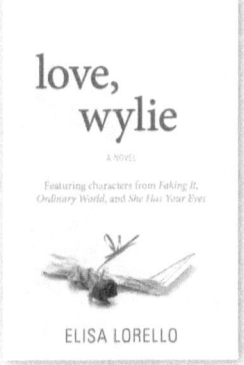

LOVE, WYLIE

*A young adult story
of first love and
trying to find a place*